Rocco and the Price of Lies `

Adrian Magson has written eighteen crime and spy thriller series built around Harry Tate, ex-soldier and MI5 office, and Gavin & Palmer (investigative reporter Riley Gavin & ex- Military Policeman Frank Palmer). He also has countless short stories and articles in national and international magazines to his name plus a non-fiction work: *Write On! – the Writer's Help Book*. Adrian lives in the Forest of Dean, and rumours that he is building a nuclear bunker are unfounded. It is in fact, a bird table.

Rocco and the Price of Lies

Adrian Magson

CANELO

First published in the United Kingdom in 2019 by The Dome Press

This edition published in the United Kingdom in 2021 by

Canelo
Unit 9, 5th Floor
Cargo Works, 1–2 Hatfields
London, SE1 9PG
United Kingdom

Copyright © Adrian Magson 2019

A CIP catalogue record for this book is available from the British Library.

Print ISBN 978 1 80032 710 8
Ebook ISBN 978 1 80032 247 9

Look for more great books at www.canelo.co

Printed and bound in Great Britain by Clays Ltd, Elcograf S.p.A.

1

To my big brother Barry, for old times' sake

Chapter One

1964 – Picardie, France

The first letter was delivered in a yellow Citroën 2CV _fourgonnette_.

Drifting along a curving street of elegant houses, tall trees and sculpted gardens in Le Vésinet, an outer suburb to the west of Paris, the van wore the familiar colour of the PTT, the French postal service. It received no more than a glance from the area's residents, those few who were up and about – they valued their leisurely lifestyle as much as they did their privacy. PTT yellow was commonplace and safe, as much a part of everyday life as fresh baguettes, Johnny Hallyday and, when called for, enthusiastic renditions of _La Marseillaise_.

Only one old man, on a morning stroll with a tiny rat-like terrier, looked faintly surprised at the van's appearance. He stopped to check his pocket watch, the driver noted. He would find it read seven a.m. Earlier than normal for the mail. But this delivery wasn't in any way normal.

He gave the old man a casual lift of his hand. The other responded automatically before dragging the dog away from a lamppost in mid-performance, causing it to hop inelegantly with one rear leg stuck out at right angles. The driver watched in his mirror as the old man continued on his way, no doubt bound for a bowl of coffee and a nice warm brioche.

The driver's name was Georges Peretz. Despite his friendly wave, he didn't know the old man, whose name was Baptiste Dupannet, from a hole in the hedge. But postal workers were known to interact with their customers and he'd been instructed to act the part; it would allow him to pass by and be quickly forgotten. Peretz, who'd lived his life careful never to stand out, was unremarkable to a degree that made him almost invisible.

It was what made him so useful to his employer.

He slowed after a hundred metres, studying the name plates on the gates of the houses. The one he wanted was *Les Jonquilles* and, if the directions he'd been given were correct, it should be just up ahead.

Neither the van nor Peretz belonged to the PTT. And had Baptiste Dupannet been a little more alert, he might have noticed that the mustard-coloured vehicle bore none of the official insignia normally emblazoned on the side panels or doors. It was a deliberate omission. Postal workers in the Paris area were not noted for their casual acceptance of anyone trying to take over their jobs. Any official PTT member might question another delivery van encroaching on their patch, and that was to be avoided at all costs. But the yellow would be enough for the general public, like Baptiste Dupannet and his rat-like dog.

Peretz pulled into the kerb a few metres beyond a driveway marked by an impressive set of sturdy metal gates, currently open. A mailbox was set into the wall to one side, with an ornate metal bell-pull to alert the occupants of a delivery. Pulling a leather mailbag strap over one shoulder, another piece of misdirection for idle onlookers, he climbed out and approached the mailbox. The open gates suggested that a visitor was expected. There was little time to delay.

He extracted a plain white envelope from the bag and dropped it into the slot, casting a quick glance through the railings. The gravel drive ran between twin sweeps of immaculate lawn and colourful flower beds. He couldn't see any of the flowers after which the house was named, but that was because it was late in the season.

The drive ran up to the front of a mansion. It was elegant and imposing, impressively broad, with double sets of tall French windows opening on to a stepped patio flanked by two sand-coloured griffins. The traditional mansard roof was topped with black filigree ironwork, giving it a faintly menacing air. Peretz couldn't help a touch of nervousness, sensing eyes watching him with suspicion from behind the darkened windows. If he were fortunate enough to live in this gilded place, he decided, he'd be just as wary of everyone and anyone who came near.

He gave a firm tug on the bell-pull, hearing the rattle of the connecting wire behind the wall followed by a distant tinkle from the house. Then he returned to the van and drove away. It was a close call; just around the curve in the road he saw an official-looking black limousine approach, then indicate to turn into the open gates.

–

Peretz was several kilometres away and merging into the traffic heading towards the city before he finally felt fate wasn't about to clamp a heavy hand on his shoulder. Anything to do with government officials made him nervous. Like his peers, he believed that such people were always watchful and skilled at spotting those with ill intent. Blending in was a skill he'd cultivated many years ago which came as naturally to him as it did game birds in deep cover, but even game birds got caught. He had two further deliveries to make, neither of them in the immediate area, and the sooner he was away from each one, and had reported the jobs completed successfully, the sooner he could relax.

He spotted a café up ahead, on the edge of a small industrial area. It looked quiet enough and he slid into a car park at the rear, tucking the van between a beer truck and a weather-beaten garage with rusted sheet-metal sides. He'd seen no signs of police vehicles in the area, but there was no point in tempting providence by leaving the van out in the open.

The café was quiet save for four men in work clothes hunched over rolls and large cups of coffee, and a delivery driver in a grey uniform exchanging paperwork with the owner. The air smelled of stale beer, tobacco, fresh coffee and sweat-stained clothes, an aroma familiar to Peretz from his regular haunts. He caught the eye of the owner, ordered a coffee and made a signal with one hand for the use of the telephone. The owner pointed to a short hallway at the rear of the room and moved towards the coffee machine, scooping up a cup on the way.

Peretz found the phone on the wall above a shelf holding a clutch of directories. He dialled a number and waited. It rang three times before being picked up.

'It's done.' His instinct was to say more, that he'd completed the delivery before the man left for the office as instructed and had done so without incident. But it wouldn't be well received. The man he was calling had little time for unnecessary words. All he needed to know was that his orders had been followed to the letter. No more, no less.

'Good. Call me only when you've completed the next two, not before. Space them out, as I instructed.' A click ended the call.

Peretz replaced the phone, feeling a shiver of relief down his back. It was ridiculous at his age, feeling like a kid in front of an angry headmaster. But he knew others in the man's employ felt the same. The soft voice had carried no hint of threat, but it was there all the same, lurking beneath the surface like a hungry pike. They were paid well, but employees who did not measure up were never forgiven and quickly removed.

He dropped the phone back on its rest and returned to the bar, where he drank his coffee, paid up and left. By the time he got back in the van the owner would have trouble remembering anything about him.

In the van, he opened the flap of the mailbag, revealing two more white envelopes just like the first. He had twenty-four hours in which to deliver them. He knew nothing of the contents, but he was familiar enough with the man he'd just spoken with to know that the recipient of this first letter was probably finding his morning omelette curdling in his stomach like a round of cheap Camembert.

Chapter Two

On the south-eastern outskirts of Paris, in the district of Ivry-sur-Seine, Yuri Serban sat back in his chair and stared through the window towards the centre of Paris, which shimmered in the heat a few kilometres away.

Serban was not averse to taking risks. In his trade, which mostly entailed making money in any way he could manage, whether through manipulation of circumstances, argument or outright force, they came with the territory. Profit was profit and if it meant taking from others – and it usually did – so be it. However, this latest endeavour was a departure. He had taken a while to be convinced that it would work, but the lack of manpower required and the apparent absence of direct risk had seemed attractive, as had the potential returns. Most importantly, the scheme avoided stepping on the toes of the more powerful criminal groups closer to the centre of the city. And this had been sufficient to clinch his co-operation.

He enjoyed the irony of the situation: that the targets for the scheme proposed were not in any position to go running to the law, something he knew the other gangs would quickly pick up on once they heard. Even more of a reason to get in, make a profit and move on before they came calling, looking to take over. Serban was no coward, but he knew his limits. He wasn't equipped for a fight with bigger organisations, preferring to stay out here in Ivry-sur-Seine where he could run his businesses and his lines of girls and clubs, away from the furious undercurrents that had dragged other groups into open conflict, burning business and freedom of movement in a vicious downward spiral.

He reached forward and picked up the telephone, dialling a number in the city.

'My driver has made the first drop.' His voice was soft but echoed deep from his large chest. A former boxer and wrestler, he still carried an impressive amount of muscle, something that had done him no harm in establishing his local crime operation.

'Excellent. We should hear something very soon.' The voice on the other end was cultured, the tone confident and pitched to convince and reassure. Yet there was an undercurrent of something else, too, which appealed to Serban: was it relief? Gratitude for a service rendered?

'I sincerely hope so,' Serban murmured, adding for good measure, 'for everyone's sake.' This last came with an emphasis which the other man couldn't fail to notice.

'Of course, I understand,' he agreed quickly. 'I'm certain it will.'

Serban smiled. He wasn't convinced by the reply but neither was he unduly concerned. He'd learned long ago that all guarantees were subject to change. In his view trust was strictly a one-way street. And the man on the other end of the line was someone he wouldn't trust if his life depended on it. However, he was useful in a number of ways and, in Serban's business, that counted for a lot. This endeavour – he liked the word endeavour, which sounded almost noble – had yet to show signs of reaping any reward, but it had cost little more to set up

7

than Peretz's daily wage and the provision of a suitable vehicle. Most endeavours cost a great deal more and they too brought varying degrees of success.

'And if it doesn't?'

'Pardon me?'

'What if your scheme doesn't work?'

There was a brief pause as the reminder of whose idea it had been sank in. 'I'm sure it will. In any case, that's why I prepared the other two to fill any... shortfall. You have the details, don't you?'

'I have.' Serban reached into a drawer and took out three photographs and a sheet of paper. The paper held three names and addresses. The photos were of paintings: two nudes and a clothed portrait. He studied the latter carefully. It was of a young woman with an inviting expression. He liked this one best. He had young women in his employ who would be naked at the click of his fingers, but this one was different. He wasn't an art lover as such, but he could appreciate beauty like any other man. Maybe he'd buy some paintings of his own some day. An investment for the future. Good ones, though. Proper paintings, not copies like these.

'Your man is delivering them soon, as arranged?'

Serban took a moment before replying. His patience was wearing thin at the other man's superior attitude, as if he were the master and Serban the slave. One day he might enjoy the pleasure of putting him in his place. 'He will deliver them soon,' he confirmed. 'There's no rush.'

'As you see fit.' There was a pause. 'I believe I did caution you that this scheme might not work every time. However, there are plenty more opportunities like these out there. All we need to do is exploit them.'

'If you say so.'

'Well, I haven't let you down in the past, have I?'

Serban put the telephone down without answering. It was a trick he'd learned some time ago, and it worked well with those in a more vulnerable position than himself. The sudden cut in the connection acted like a physical turning and walking away from a conversation, leaving the other wondering what had gone wrong, what they might have said.

He tossed the photos back in the drawer, on top of three letters. He wasn't supposed to have seen these, which had been in sealed envelopes, but he'd taken the precaution of opening them and having copies made. Being used as a mail service to deliver sealed letters was akin to playing with unstable explosives: if you didn't know what you were handling, it could blow up in your face.

And Serban hated surprises.

Chapter Three

Back in the mansion in Le Vésinet, Jean-Pascal Bourdelet, Secretary of State for Finance, was just completing a phone call to his secretary. He suspected at times that Cécile Boyesse actually slept in a cupboard at the Louvre Palace, where the Ministry of Economy and Finance was located, as she was always there, early and late, running the office and his busy appointments diary like a well-oiled machine. He thanked her courteously and replaced the phone, reflecting on how long the day's first meeting would take. No doubt there would be the usual round of deflections and power-plays that were endemic to every department of government, with certain members of staff looking for openings and signs of weakness in others to exploit for their own advancement.

Today, however, he was in good spirits and inclined to put up with the in-fighting. The weather looked far too pleasant to be stuck indoors and he longed for the chance to stay out of the city for the day. However, as secretary of state he had to attend to business; there was no chance of avoiding it.

He heard the jangle of the post bell and walked out of the front door and down the drive. His housekeeper would normally have dealt with this, but she was off this morning for a doctor's appointment. He sniffed appreciatively at the aroma from the flowers in the borders, and relished the crunch of gravel beneath the soles of his shoes, so much more gratifying than on everyday paving, and the sound so much richer.

He glanced towards the front gates as he heard the tinny clatter of an engine moving away. No doubt the post van. But when he opened the box on the inside of the stonework, instead of the regular banded clutch of letters he received every day, a single white envelope was lying there.

No stamp, he noted.

He took the envelope out and slit it open with his thumb. He scanned the contents, the first few words enough to bring a thud of incredulity and dread. He read it again to make sure he hadn't misunderstood, his hand shaking as the full meaning began to hit home.

Bourdelet stepped quickly through the open gates to check the street. There was nobody there save, in the distance, the retreating back of an elderly man dragging a tiny dog. They were too far away to have delivered this, he realised, and remembered the sound of the departing vehicle. Just then another engine sounded, this one smoother, the familiar mellow hum of his official car. Its tone dropped as it slowed and he quickly jammed the envelope and note in his pocket before hurrying back to the house, pursued by the crunch of tyres on gravel as Lopez, his driver, drove through the gates.

Bourdelet gave a vague backward wave of acknowledgement, then walked inside and scooped up the phone. Lopez would wait until he was ready. Cécile answered with her usual briskness.

'You'll have to postpone the meeting,' he muttered without preamble. 'Something's come up – I'll be in later. Can't be helped.' He felt idiotic at making such a lame statement and picked at his lips, which had gone unaccountably dry.

'Is anything wrong, sir?' Cecile queried.

'Nothing. I feel a little unwell, that's all. A small ulcer, I think.'

He dropped the handset back on its cradle and wondered what the reaction would be at the office. No doubt rumours about his health would erupt the moment Cécile made it known, followed by the inevitable game of musical chairs that always began when a position threatened to be vacated. It was standard among civil servants, but it would in no way compare with the fallout if the contents of the letter in his pocket ever became known.

He shook himself. It was far easier to justify and excuse his actions, than contemplate the details going public. The revelation would be catastrophic. He would be scorned in some quarters, humiliated in others, and it would bring pure contempt from the public. Worst of all would be the response of the prime minister, who had the moral tone of a Catholic convert allied to a powerful sense of self-protection. With the contents of this letter, he could say goodbye to his political career and to elevation to the Council of Ministers. Once out, always out, was the firm credo in government circles. He'd be cast aside and into the wilderness, with whatever meagre pension he might manage to keep hold of and with the cold rush of derisive laughter following him every step of the way.

And that didn't compare, he thought, taking out the letter to read again, with what else he would be saying goodbye to if it ever became known that government funds were involved, as was pointed out – correctly – in this note. He swore profusely at the wretched decision to use a little-known *caisse noire* or departmental slush fund to indulge himself in a moment of weakness. What on earth had taken hold of him? He should have known it would become known sooner or later. Was it some kind of bitter attempt at rewarding himself when those around him – especially the prime minister – seemed to treat him with disdain?

Still, he told himself, grasping for a straw – any straw – it was serious, but at least he wasn't guilty of any unusual sexual misdemeanours, unlike a couple of colleagues he could mention, one of whom was close to the very top of government, a political as well as a personal favour appointee, who was rumoured to have a liking for very young teenage girls. In that comparison, perhaps, lay his one hope of salvation. *Mea culpa*, he thought wryly, but not as much as others.

He checked the letter again, hoping for some indication of its origins. But it was unsigned, with a line advising him that payment instructions would follow. He retreated to his study at the rear of the house. It overlooked an expanse of garden, complete with a small lake and dotted with trees and borders. Here he made his most important decisions, whether on matters of state or, more recently, personal matters: granting his wife a divorce because of the growing toxicity of their marriage. At least letting his wife go had been less costly than he'd anticipated, largely because an investigator he'd hired had discovered that she had already replaced him with a younger, sleeker and more athletic model. Young enough to be her son, for God's sake, he thought. Still, it could have been worse. Now he could at least consider his options regarding this bombshell free of the restraints of an unsympathetic and, at worst, unhelpful wife.

He looked up and found himself standing beneath the very reason for his discomfort. The irony didn't escape him, but he gave it only a passing glance, as if not acknowledging its presence might allow him to deny its existence for just a little longer.

The painting was large, dominating the wall as much by its size as the presence of the subject. She was a beautiful young brunette with an enigmatic smile and an inviting look about her, dressed in the classical style. He'd loved it the moment he'd set eyes on it, and although it had cost a small fortune, he'd deemed it worth every *centime*. Coming in here every day and being alone with Madame Récamier, as she was known, invariably soothed him after a hard day's work.

He stared instead at the wall opposite. But reality soon came rushing in. He could deny the contents of the letter, of course, until the proverbial cows came home. He could even take the painting down and hide it. Unfortunately, that wasn't going to help. He'd been hoisted by his own brand of hubris, because there were people who knew of the painting's place in his home, just as they did his not-so-guarded hints as to its considerable cost. The pleasure for him had been seeing the awestruck expressions on their faces at the information, and even a hint of respect for his financial situation and artistic appreciation.

No, a denial wouldn't do. The only alternative was to follow the instructions in the letter and pay up. It would be costly, even painful, on a personal level. But he could see no way round it; he'd have to take the hit, as he'd once heard an American diplomat say.

He took another tour of the room, his thoughts ranging around the alternatives and on what else might follow. What if the matter didn't end there? Blackmailers, once they had their hooks into a target, were known to come back for more. The very fact of a victim having paid up in the first place confirmed that they had something to hide. More demands would follow, he knew it in his bones. His position guaranteed it. His wealth, such as it was, was mainly inherited, a fact gleefully documented in the press more than once by his political enemies. But that particular well wasn't so deep that it couldn't be emptied, no more than his capacity to withstand the public humiliation if the blackmailer made good the threat outlined in the letter. He felt sick as the full import of what he'd brought upon himself began to hit home. The humiliation would be complete and lasting; the thought of everyone knowing he was a thief and a liar – a fraud, no less – was like a dagger to the gut. The downfall would be swift and his enemies would relish seeing him end his days in prison, a figure of contempt. By the third tour of the study, he'd come to a firm decision. He couldn't count on the PM to defend him if and when the news came out, and the idea that he might be able to use some personal leverage to slip out from under the axe was a pipe dream. The fact that others had managed to do so for greater indiscretions was no guarantee. For one, the PM and he had never quite made that kind of connection. Forced together by circumstance and convenience, he knew above all else that his position was at best tolerated, at worst, on eggshell-thin ground.

He rummaged in a lower desk drawer and picked out a wooden box, transferring it to his briefcase. Walking outside, where he was greeted by Lopez standing by the open rear door of the car, he reflected that he didn't need the briefcase, but carrying his badge of office was as instinctive as breathing. Without it he would feel naked.

He climbed into the car and closed the dividing glass partition to indicate his need for quiet. Conversation, right now, was the last thing he wanted.

On reaching the office, he walked upstairs, relishing the smell and atmosphere of the building, and feeling that in getting this far in his chosen profession, he had achieved something concrete in his life.

He walked past Cécile, already busy at her desk, and nodded briefly, telling her that he needed a few minutes and not to come in. She acknowledged this with a faint frown and watched as he closed the door behind him.

Once inside, he turned the key in the lock before taking his seat. He took the box from his briefcase and opened it, laying it on his desk. Inside was a moulded tray. Nestling against the felt cushion was something that both frightened him and filled him with awe. It was a steel-grey revolver.

He lifted the heavy weapon out and set it to one side, then took out the letter and envelope. He placed these on the open box, which he pushed to the front of his desk. He had no idea who the author was, but there was some bitter salvation in that, from it, any investigators would be able to find a lead.

He removed his jacket, his eyes on the gun. There was no need to check if it was loaded because he knew it was. Nor was he inclined to take a final look out of his window; the view had never been much good: a stretch of dull grey wall in permanent shadow from the building next door, uninspiring and soulless. And right now, anything more attractive would have been an unwanted distraction.

He took a deep breath and thought through what he was about to do. There would be no payment of the blackmail sum for what he'd done, at least he could deny them that. And, if living under the conditions that faced him was impossible to contemplate, he might at least in the alternative achieve some small level of belated integrity. Whatever revelations or humiliation might be heaped on his name afterwards, there was nothing he could do to change it. Nor, he reflected, would there be too much sorrow from his passing, especially from his ex-wife or his daughter Karine, both estranged beyond return.

With a final thought for the one person who had always been loyal to him, now sitting in the office on the other side of the door, he picked up the gun and pulled his jacket over his head. After a moment of hesitation, maybe even a fleeting sense of regret, he put the tip of the gun barrel beneath his chin and pulled the trigger.

Chapter Four

'So, what is this place?' Inspector Lucas Rocco stepped up alongside the solid figure of Detective René Desmoulins, who was squinting through the late afternoon heat haze across a stubble-covered field towards a building in a slight depression at a crossroads some five hundred metres away. The structure was decrepit, sagging, with holes in the roof and shutters hanging off the walls like an old man's inside-out pockets. Surrounded by rusted and broken barbed wire hung with faded notices warning people to keep out, it seemed to be a long way from anywhere, and Rocco wondered what had driven the original owner to settle at such a remote spot.

Checking the map for directions before leaving the office in Amiens, Rocco had noted that the minor routes which joined at the crossroads were no longer accessible, having been replaced by a single diversionary road and closed off several years ago. The move had been the death knell for the already isolated building, as if fate had been determined to make sure that it eventually sank into decay and ruin.

'It was a café once, a long time ago,' said Desmoulins. He was young and fair-haired, with a nascent moustache that struggled to achieve a full growth, much to the amusement of his colleagues in the Amiens *commissariat*. 'Then the authorities discovered an old map showing a huge World War One ammunition dump in the back garden. They didn't have the money to move the ammunition, so they declared the place out of bounds. The owner couldn't get compensation and went bust.' He shook his head. 'Nobody goes near it any more.'

'Except for two out-of-town bank robbers looking for a place to hide.' Rocco had scanned the incident report from earlier in the day. Two men had entered the Rue Massena branch of the Crédit Agricole in Lille late yesterday afternoon, just before the weekly armoured van collected the cash from the tills and safe. The amount taken was unknown but thought to be considerable, due to recent livestock sales and harvest revenues from farms in the area. One of the two robbers had been armed with a shotgun and, whether by accident or deliberately, had blown a hole in the ceiling on the way in, bringing down a large quantity of plaster and lathes. Two members of staff had been slightly injured by the debris and, in the confusion, the robbers had made their escape in what had been described by onlookers as a new white Mercedes.

Rocco borrowed a pair of binoculars from the detective and studied the building. 'And they definitely headed this way?'

'They were tracked because of the car,' Desmoulins said. 'Not many Mercs in this part of the world, and both men were covered in plaster dust from the ceiling.' He grinned. 'You could say they stood out a bit.'

'Not your top-of-the-heap robbers, then.' Using a white Mercedes was hardly brilliant planning, especially in a rural area not known for fancy forms of transport. And drawing attention to themselves by using a gun to scare people was stupid. It might and sometimes did work in big cities like Paris, Rocco conceded, where confusion and fear allowed robbers to disappear among the streets and back runs before any alarm could be raised; but out here they might as well have tied a skull and crossbones to the car aerial and played loud pirate music on their way out of town. 'How come you're here?' he asked. 'I thought this was a Lille case.'

'It is.' Desmoulins gestured towards two uniformed officers standing nearby, armed with MAS-49/56 rifles. They were staring at Rocco as if he was a being from another planet. No doubt they had heard of his exploits in the area since arriving from Paris, but seeing him in the flesh was evidently hard to take in. 'These two were here keeping a watch with a Detective Aubrey, but his wife went into labour an hour ago and Commissaire Massin sent me to fill in until more men got here.'

'From Lille.'

'Yes. There's been a breakdown in communication, apparently. I think they mean a balls-up.'

Rocco was about to question whether the robbers had managed to slip away unseen in the meantime when he noticed movement at one corner of the building. He focussed quickly on a face pressed against the crumbling wattle and daub wall. It disappeared again in seconds, leaving behind a puff of smoke from a cigarette. But the glimpse he'd caught of the person's features was enough to leave him with a feeling of surprise.

'Fontenal?' he said softly. 'What the hell—'

'You know him?' Desmoulins had also seen the man appear and duck back.

'I wish I didn't.' Rocco explained that 'Bam-Bam' Fontenal, nicknamed after his liking for letting off guns, was a career criminal operating around the outer reaches of the Paris area, who only occasionally ventured into the city proper. He'd spent years in and out of prison, but so far had avoided lengthy sentences because his crimes, in spite of the guns, had never netted him more than a handful of cash or cheap jewellery. He had never actually killed anyone. Rocco had arrested him more than once for low-level robberies in the Clichy district, putting him away twice for a couple of years. It seemed Fontenal hadn't benefitted from the experience.

'He's a long way from his normal base, then,' Desmoulins commented.

'Because he's an idiot. He gets carried away with his own sense of ambition and tries to act like Bonnie and Clyde.' Rocco handed back the binoculars and took out his service weapon. 'Let's get this settled, shall we?'

'Our orders are to wait, Inspector,' one of the Lille uniforms put in. 'More help will be arriving soon, they said.'

Rocco looked at the officer. He was young, tough-looking and seemed capable and confident. He didn't look like the sort of young cop accustomed to waiting for things to happen. 'What's your name?'

'Officer Pouillot, sir.' He gestured towards his colleague. 'This is Officer Maté.'

'Well, Officers Pouillot and Maté, right now there's nobody else here, so this makes it your responsibility and your arrest. Detective Desmoulins and I are here merely as observers.' What Rocco didn't say was that he knew Fontenal well enough to figure that the crook would probably come out without a fight if they made the correct approach. 'Waiting will only increase the risk that those two morons will do something stupid. You really want to wait for someone else to come along and grab the glory?'

'Not a chance,' Maté said quickly, and nudged Pouillot. 'Come on, he's right – let's do it.'

Rocco didn't wait for further discussion and said, 'Spread well out and walk slowly. Watch for my signals. Give them time to see us but don't shoot unless they do. I'd rather take them alive.'

The two men nodded and moved away, checking their weapons and separating themselves by a good twenty paces.

Desmoulins looked at Rocco with raised eyebrows. 'You know this man that well?'

'Well enough. I've put him away a couple of times.'

'How do you know he won't shoot or make a run for it?'

'If he was going to run, he'd have done so already.' Fontenal was too tied to his own base near Paris to stay away for long; he might have chosen this place to get out of sight for a while, but it would have been for one night only. After that he'd have felt the strong pull of the *banlieue* – the suburb he called home. 'Something must have kept him from leaving. Car trouble, perhaps.'

'With a new Mercedes?'

'It happens. Anyway, I doubt it's his and he probably got so excited he forgot to fill it up before he came out this way. He's not used to long trips.'

'Or something else intervened.' The words seemed to come out before Desmoulins could stop them.

'What do you mean?'

Desmoulins took a deep breath. 'Don't quote me on this, Lucas, but when the café was closed down the owner went bust. He also discovered his wife was cheating on him with one of his customers. The story is he took a shotgun to the pair of them, planning to shoot himself afterwards. But he'd run out of cartridges so he tied a rope to a beam in the bar and jumped off the counter.'

'So?'

'The place is haunted. Everyone says so. They won't go near it.'

'Nothing to do with there being a massive amount of old, highly unstable explosive in the back garden that would blow off peoples' socks ten kilometres away?'

'Maybe. Who knows?'

Rocco stared at him. 'You believe that ghost stuff?'

Desmoulins shrugged and rubbed his moustache with the back of his hand. 'Not really, but a couple of years back they got a priest to go in and do a… what do they call it?'

'An exorcism. It's mumbo-jumbo. Did it work?'

'No. In fact the priest refused to go back in there. Said it contained forces beyond his control.'

Rocco shook his head. Cops were usually too cynical for talk of ghosts, but there were a few who might have claimed that anything that couldn't be written up on a charge sheet must be from darker realms. 'So apart from Fontenal and his pal we're up against the spirits of a dead café owner and two adulterers, and an unknown quantity of old explosive. I wonder if Bam-Bam knows that. It's about time something gave him a good fright.'

He set off across the field and waved the two uniformed men to advance, while Desmoulins jogged out to his right, drawing his own pistol. The ground was firm, and a covering of long, dry grass scratched at the cuffs of his trousers, chafing his ankles. High overhead a skylark sang, unaware of the human drama being played out below, while the rumble of a tractor engine drifted over the fields.

When they were a hundred metres away from the building, Rocco stopped and signalled to Pouillot for him to fire a single shot over the roof.

The man nodded, aimed and fired. The shot was loud and flat, drowning out the tractor and silencing the skylark. The men instinctively looked up for signs of feathers. Echoes of the shot drifted away over the café and were quickly absorbed by the landscape.

The reaction from the café was instantaneous. A section of shutter still clinging to the building's rotting exterior was thrown back and a face appeared in the dark space behind. Another appeared alongside it, followed by the glistening barrel of a shotgun.

'Don't be an idiot, Bam-Bam,' Rocco called out, and lifted his service weapon above his head so that the men inside could see it. He didn't want to use it, but there were always instances where it was the only option. 'You couldn't hit a stationary train if you were standing on the platform. Give it up before you get hurt.'

A momentary silence was followed by a voice, shouting, '*Rocco?* Is that you? What the hell! So, this is where they sent you!' The man swore fluently, cursing his bad luck.

'Yes, it's me. And that means you're on my turf – again. And the men with rifles are military sharpshooters trained to shoot the buttons off shirt fronts. Think about it.'

He saw Maté beginning to bring up his rifle as if to prove it, and waved a hand to stop him. Fontenal may have been hopeless with a gun, but if he got nervous and let loose at this distance, even he might, for once in his life, hit someone.

The two faces disappeared and there was silence. Ten seconds went by, then twenty. Just as the counter in

Rocco's head reached thirty, and he was about to send the men off to the sides of the building with orders to place a couple of intimidating shots through the windows, the shotgun appeared again. This time it dropped from the window to the ground with a clatter.

'Is that it?'

'Yes. That's it – my word of honour.'

'Right. You know what to do,' Rocco called, and signalled for the officers to spread out further and wait. Hopefully Bam-Bam had prevailed on his colleague to come out quietly and not to try something idiotic like shooting from concealment.

A puff of cigarette smoke at the corner of the building was followed by the familiar beanpole figure of Bam-Bam, a hand-rolled yellow *mégot* hanging off his lower lip. Behind him came another man, a stranger to Rocco, shorter and rounder and wearing the same air of defeat. Both men had their hands on top of their heads, a sure-fire indication that they'd been through this before and knew the drill.

'What's the game, Bam-Bam?' said Rocco, as they drew close and Pouillot and Maté moved forward to cuff them and check them for other weapons. 'This isn't your usual kind of stunt, coming out this far from civilisation. I'm surprised you haven't got a nose bleed.'

Bam-Bam scowled and winced at the tightness of the cuffs. 'We thought we'd chance our luck out this way for a change. It was the Merc let us down, otherwise we'd have been home and clear, enjoying a few drinks by now.'

Rocco nodded at Desmoulins, and the young detective walked across to the Merc to check it out.

'Nice car. Bit above your usual level, though. What did you do, win the *Loto*?'

'I acquired it, if you must know,' Bam-Bam muttered haughtily, 'from a mate.'

'Of course you did.' Rocco's scepticism was unconcealed. 'And this "mate" was a kind garage owner who gave you the pick of his fleet. Nice to have mates like that.' He knew that when they came to verify the details the car would be logged as having been stolen sometime within the past few days in the Paris area.

Bam-Bam said nothing. He watched as Desmoulins climbed into the car, bending to the ignition.

'It's a load of German rubbish, anyway.' Bam-Bam's voice was heavy with resentment. 'It worked fine when we picked it up, but when we came to leave here last night, nothing. The battery was dead. You'll probably have to tow it out of here.'

As the words left his lips the Mercedes burst into life, ticking over with the smooth hum of a quality piece of engineering. Desmoulins gave a wry grin and a thumbs-up. When he got out of the car, he was dragging two large bags with him, no doubt the proceeds of Bam-Bam's clumsy bank heist.

Fontenal looked incredulous and spat on the ground. 'I don't believe it! It wasn't working last night, I swear.'

'Never mind,' said Rocco. 'You must have upset the spirits of the dead.'

'Eh?'

'Don't worry, you'll have plenty of time to think about it. How's Edith?' Edith, Bam-Bam's common-law wife of many years was as pleasant and cheery as her man was inept. It could have only been love that had kept her by his side in spite of his numerous prison terms regularly disrupting their life.

26

'She's fine, thanks for asking. She'd be happier if you let us go, though.'

Rocco shook his head. 'Nice try.' He indicated to the two officers to take them to their patrol car up the field.

As Bam-Bam went by, he leaned towards Rocco, his stale tobacco breath strong enough to choke a horse. He said, 'If this is your new patch, Rocco, I feel sorry for you. Why'd you bother coming out here? It's a dump.'

–

An hour later, checking in at Amiens while the two robbers were taken back to Lille, Rocco found an envelope on his desk. The room was deserted save for a duty officer in one corner, busy on the phone. The envelope contained a letter of instruction from Commissaire François Massin, Rocco's boss. It was ordering him to present himself at the café *tabac* in the village of Douligny-la-Rose the following morning, where he would meet a man from the Ministry of the Interior. The man's name was Marcel Dreycourt and Rocco was to comply with whatever might be requested of him.

'Another Ministry job?' Rocco muttered. 'I thought they'd had their litre of blood from me after the last business.'

'Problem, Inspector?'

Rocco turned and saw Deputy Commissaire Perronnet standing in the doorway. Stiff as a board and immaculate as always, Perronnet believed implicitly in the rulebook as laid down by the Ministry of the Interior, and made sure everyone knew it.

'No,' said Rocco, and folded the letter into his pocket. Arguing with Perronnet would be like fencing fog. He would go to the meeting as ordered and speak to Massin afterwards to see if he could be excused whatever it was they wanted him to do. Having only recently completed an assignment directed by the Interior Ministry, which had involved babysitting a foreign government minister taking refuge in France after a coup in his home country, he'd been foolish enough to think that might be the last he'd hear from them for a while.

To his surprise, Perronnet said softly, so that the duty officer could not hear, 'We all know you have reservations about the Ministry's occasional calls to unusual assignments, Rocco. I sometimes share your puzzlement, especially with an ever-increasing case load in our normal policing matters. But there are some things we cannot choose not to do. Besides, this could be one of your last cases here and I think you might find this one particularly interesting. I'm sure you'll carry it out to the best of your abilities. Good evening.'

Rocco watched him go, and wondered at Perronnet's words. He'd been referring to the recent job offer which had dropped in Rocco's lap, although Rocco himself was trying hard to put off thinking about it for as long as possible. Going back to Paris to work offered both attractions and disadvantages. Evidently others had not forgotten and were keen to remind him.

–

By the time he arrived home in the village of Poissons-les-Marais, most of the day's light had leached away, bringing a soft dusk and a welcome breeze. He locked his car and walked up the path to his rented house, then stood by the front door for a moment, enjoying the quiet hum of the countryside, so very different to the bustle and noise of his old patch in Clichy, Paris. There, the very idea of a quiet evening was a joke. Even retreating to one of the parks, where an impression of space might be found, rarely brought escape from traffic noise and voices raised in laughter or anger, often both.

He'd been in Picardie just over a year, and now he was being offered the chance to leave and head back to the city, his old beat. A chance of advancement, a move up the ladder and an opportunity to get back to the kind of policing he knew best: fighting gang crime.

Before he could dwell further on the problem, a small figure appeared at the gate and bustled up the path. It was his elderly neighbour, Mme Denis. Motherly by nature and inquisitive by inclination, she had immediately welcomed the tall outsider to the village and looked after his wellbeing with a regular supply of eggs, vegetables and good advice, in return for whatever inside information he could share about his latest investigation. On occasion she'd even traded local gossip culled from her network of friends in the area, although none of it turned out to be the kind that would draw Rocco's professional attention.

This evening, however, she didn't seem inclined to pass the time of day. Instead she thrust a small basket containing half a dozen eggs into his arms and said briskly, 'I don't know what the hens are going to do,' she muttered, before turning away. 'But at least they're lucky enough not to realise when they're being kept in the dark, unlike the rest of us. Enjoy your eggs.'

With that she turned and disappeared into the gloom without a backward glance, leaving Rocco thoroughly confused.

Chapter Five

Despite its elegant name, Douligny-la-Rose was too small to qualify as a town, yet too sprawled for a village. Neither were there any roses in sight, thought Rocco, as he entered the community limits. Deserted and deathly quiet, it lay still as a lizard in the morning sun, a rambling array of houses and bungalows connected by a single street with a high centre curving down to dust-filled gutters. Apart from a few faded flyers on trees and telegraph poles advertising tag wrestling bouts and a visiting circus that had passed through a year ago, there was little colour to be seen, as if the locals had decided on a sepia life.

In other words, Rocco estimated, the place was bigger than Poissons but nowhere near as lively. The thought reminded him that he'd seen no sign of Mme Denis this morning. Usually up and doing with the skylark, the old lady's shutters had still been closed when he'd left home. It was unlike her, but then so was last night's abrupt behaviour. He made a mental note to check on her as soon as he could, wondering what he could have done to upset her. Maybe she was having problems with her back, which had been troubling her recently.

He looked across a nearby garden, spotting the tip of the gothic cathedral of Amiens just visible on the horizon between two houses and the rooftops. It was only about fifteen kilometres away, but might as well have been a hundred, for all the aspirations Douligny's citizens seemed to harbour. Ancient and fort-like walled farmhouses, with double wooden doors wide enough to admit a horse and cart, were dotted around in a haphazard fashion. They were interspersed with with more recent buildings – meaning those less than two hundred years old – all huddled together. It seemed a community held together with reluctance, born of necessity. Only the stone church seemed above it all, standing on a slight mound at the end of a narrow track, a dark presence looming over the community.

Rocco parked his car in the shade of a large beech tree. The sight of the vehicle would undoubtedly arouse some interest, but then the black Citroën Traction was as hard to ignore as its driver. Rocco, too tall and sombrely-clothed to pass unnoticed in this rural area, had long given up trying to blend in. It hadn't been so difficult in Paris, but out here he was taller than the average man and dressed in a way which guaranteed he would be noticed. He'd also resisted the suggestion by his superiors that he change the Citroën for something a little more innocuous and up-to-date. His counter was that it was reliable, solid and comfortable, so why bother?

Up ahead he could see where the street opened out into the inevitable village square, with the tall roof of the town hall, topped by a *tricoleur* hanging limply against the flagpole, untroubled by a hint of breeze.

He walked along the rutted pavement, passing a handful of houses with polished steps and shuttered windows, each wooden fascia closed to the street save for a hand-sized diamond cut-out in the top centre. Had Rocco been able to see inside, he knew he would have found a series of small front rooms, neat and little-used, darkened by the shutters to keep out any unwelcome heat. Most of the households would possess impressively sturdy furniture handed down by their forebears, would see no reason to spend money on new items.

Rocco stopped at the corner of the square and looked around. It was more of a lopsided triangle, formed by the main through-route and two short stretches of paved road no longer than a hundred metres on either side. A small war memorial stood at the top against the iron railings of the town hall, with fading ribbons hanging from the stonework. The handful of shops around the square comprised a co-op, a bakery, a garage with a single fuel pump and a *crêperie* which appeared to be closed. The only sign of life was a dog sprawled in the sun outside the co-op, a hind leg kicking as it dream-chased a cat.

Immediately to his left was a café with three small tables and a number of chairs arranged haphazardly along the narrow pavement outside. They seemed perilously close to the kerb, with a line of wooden posts on flat bases in the gutter, although whether in an effort to safeguard the customers or claim more territory wasn't immediately obvious.

Only one customer was in evidence, a man in a smart suit sitting by the front door. He was studying a newspaper. Before him was a large, white cup and saucer and a box of sugar cubes, and he couldn't have looked any more out of place in this sleepy village setting if he'd been stark naked and wearing a chef's hat.

This had to be Dreycourt. Ministry of Interior suits had a look all of their own. Like peas in a pod only greyer.

Without looking up the man raised one hand and beckoned Rocco to join him. With the other he reached to one side and hammered on the café door. As Rocco went over, a shambling figure in a loose shirt and creased trousers stepped outside and flicked a stained tea towel at a couple of wasps buzzing around the awning. He nodded at Rocco then looked at his suited client.

'Two coffees and a jug of milk,' the man said, folding the paper and pushing it to one side. 'Strong, preferably. The coffee, I mean.' He squinted up at Rocco and made a gesture for him to take a seat. 'I've been advised by my doctor to take milk with mine. Bit late in life to start worrying, but what can you do? Your work file suggests you have a liking for coffee. I take it that hasn't changed?'

'Not entirely.' Rocco sat with his back to the wall. 'Do they actually employ someone to do that – note our likes and dislikes, I mean? It's a touch intrusive, isn't it?'

'I agree,' said the man, 'but that's the Ministry for you. They see it as one of their strengths, having a finger on every pulse. They've got a file on me, too, God rot them, but that's one of the penalties of government work. Marcel Dreycourt.' He smiled dryly and held out a hand. His grip was firm but didn't linger. Not a professional hand-shaker, thought Rocco, the kind who uses a greeting as an opportunity to show superiority or dominance. He had a direct expression, too, with no hint of guile, and the clean-shaven look of a man who took pride in his appearance without being obsessive. 'Between you and me,' Dreycourt continued, 'I think it's something they've copied from the *Bundespolizei*. I'm sure you know of the German passion for detail, even when it seems unnecessary.'

Rocco nodded but said nothing. If he'd learned one thing in his two careers as a soldier and policeman, you got more information by employing silence than speech.

And right now, he wanted to know what this smartly-suited and booted man from the Interior Ministry wanted of him.

Dreycourt must have learned the same lesson, or maybe he was instinctively discreet when out in public. He smiled briefly, nodding towards the café door as an indication to wait for the owner to return with their coffees. Moments later, the large man appeared and placed the cups and a small jug of milk before them, then swatted at the wasps again before disappearing inside.

'I'd like to clear up one small misconception you might have about me,' Dreycourt said, stirring sugar into his coffee. 'That I'm a Ministry employee. I'm not.'

'Really?' Rocco could do without the mystery; it was far too early and he had too much to do, too many case files to review to waste time sitting here. 'So why the official letter?'

'Because that was my instruction. I'm sorry – I couldn't avoid it. I'm employed by the government in an advisory position, but that doesn't mean I can ignore direct requests.' Dreycourt sipped his coffee and pulled a face, although not at the taste. 'I was on the payroll once, one of the worker drones, but they dispensed with my field of speciality as it was seen as too… special, I think one of them put it.' He grinned sourly. 'You know civil servants: getting rid of something when they don't understand it is as natural as breathing.' He broke off and looked down into his cup with an expression of surprise. 'This is amazingly good coffee. I wasn't sure with the first cup, but this confirms it. I might come here again. It's always good to get out of the city when I can.'

'What was your original job?' Rocco tasted his coffee; Dreycourt was right – it was excellent. Maybe he'd give the man another few minutes before heading back to the office.

'Was and still is: combatting art fraud, specifically forgery. I track down forgers passing off works of art as genuine.'

'And it's a full-time thing?'

'It is when it leads to suicide, Inspector. Or murder.'

Chapter Six

'Come again?'

'You'd be surprised at how many people with money to spare have a powerful desire to show off how cultured they are to their friends – even, and especially, if culture isn't their strong point.' Dreycourt settled back, as if making himself comfortable for what he was about to say. 'That they are living a lie is less important to them than their need to impress. Doesn't matter how successful they are in their professional life, they seek the approval of others. I suppose it's a part of the human condition, a desire to validate one's place in society.'

Rocco, like many cops, wasn't given much to psychology. He dealt with criminal acts which were usually prompted by greed, emotion or ambition. Desperation or fear played a part in others but, in his experience, they were less common. 'Where does suicide and murder come in?'

'I'll come to that. Due to the market demand, there are a number of forgers who cater to the needs of these egotistical self-styled art lovers. You want a Monet or a Matisse to hang on the wall? No problem. A Constable or a Raphael to grace your staircase or study? Whatever you say. Given the correct amount of hard, untraceable cash and a guarantee of silence about the picture's provenance, they can provide whatever you require.'

'I'll bear that in mind for any important birthdays.' Rocco had come across a few forgers before, but only those producing fake French franc notes in a backstreet lock-up with a stolen printing press. 'Are these forgers any good at what they do?'

Dreycourt nodded. 'Indeed. Some are masters in their own right, others are workaday technicians with as much art in their souls as a gravedigger. Like anything else, you get what you pay for... Or rather you get what you want your friends and colleagues to *think* you've paid for it.'

'Because everybody knows the real one is actually in the Louvre?' Rocco suggested, and wondered if Dreycourt was going to get to the point.

'That's the subtlety of the whole thing. It's all about perception and probability. We're not talking about your average businessman or local commune staff member here. This is a market for those with more than average wealth.'

'Undeclared?'

'More often than not, certainly. The friends are led to believe the owner actually has the kind of wealth required to buy a genuine work of art. His friends aren't entirely sure, but they're prepared to believe that what they see on the wall is actually the real deal and that the Louvre or wherever has a fake but is too embarrassed to admit it.' He shrugged. 'It's a form of confidence trick, but it works for some.'

'And how does this concern me?'

'I need your help.' Dreycourt shifted in his seat. 'I used to have two colleagues but, since the department was done away with, I now work alone. I sometimes have to rely on hiring associates or freelance investigators to assist me. That's easy enough in Paris and other big centres like London or Geneva, but there are none available right now

– at least, none I can rely on. I was given your name by the Ministry, and with their agreement and that of your Commissaire Massin, I've been allowed to rope you in, if you'll excuse the term. The reason we're meeting out here is because this particular investigation has some sensitive aspects.' He hesitated. 'Massin mentioned that you'd undertaken one-off assignments for the Ministry before, but I get the impression this one comes as a surprise.'

'You could say that. What do you expect of me? What I know about art a miniaturist would have no trouble putting on the back of a postage stamp.'

Dreycourt smiled and took a slim envelope out of his pocket. He slid it across the table. It contained three photographs and a slip of paper. Rocco unfolded the paper first. It contained a name and an address in the village of Passepont, just a few kilometres away from where they were sitting. Not far, either, from Rocco's home village of Poissons-les-Marais.

'Sébastien Cezard?' Rocco read out. 'Should I know him?'

'Probably not. He keeps a low profile most of the time. Like a lot of his kind.'

'You don't like him?'

'I don't like forgers.'

'Is he one?'

'Yes. One of the best in the business. Very few people know he exists. His main strength is he's very skilled and always careful about how much he exposes of himself. He works through an agent and most of his "clients" never get to meet him except on his terms.'

'Such as?'

'If the money involved is unusually high or, as some-times happens, he's being hired to do a genuine commission, such as a personal portrait.'

Rocco could appreciate what Dreycourt was driving at. The kind of criminals who relied on deception, such as conmen and fraudsters, were only successful if they remained elusive to the people they'd preyed on. A conman who remained in one place and played the scene too long was always in danger of one of his 'marks' coming across him by accident and deciding to wreak vengeance for having been taken to the cleaners. He'd dealt with scenarios like that before, and it didn't always end well for the angry victim, in spite of what had been done to them in the first place.

Rocco turned over the three photographs. The first showed a large, friendly-looking individual with a generous smile, heavy spectacles, a small black cigar in the corner of his mouth and glass of milky liquid in his hand. He was facing a woman with her back to the camera, and Rocco guessed the photo had been taken without Cezard's knowledge.

The other two photographs were identical, a framed painting of a young woman with a cool, enigmatic smile, dressed in loose-fitting clothes. She was seated on a chair, her shoulders bare, her hair dark and lustrous. He had no idea how old the painting might be but guessed it was somewhere in the 18th or 19th century.

'The painting is known as "Portrait of Madame Récamier",' said Dreycourt. 'Painted by Gérard in 1805. The photo on your left is of the genuine article which sits in the Carnavalet Museum in Paris. The other is of a fake which I firmly believe was painted by Sébastien Cezard.' He produced two more photos, of a similar figure but less attractive. 'These are by a lesser known artist, one fake, the other genuine. I'm showing them to you as an example. Again, Cezard painted the fake – or the copy, I should say.'

'Is there a difference?'

'If the copy is sold as an original with a signature, yes. It's fraud. A forgery. If it's a copy of a nice picture because someone likes it… well, that's a different thing altogether. No signature, no pretending it's real, no crime.' He patted the new photo. 'Until recently this painting was owned by an Italian industrialist who died of a heart attack after being caught by his wife dallying with a young woman of not-so-impeccable character.' He gave a dry sniff. 'I was called in to verify it, and the wife wasn't amused when I broke the news. She'd put it up for sale when her husband died and was hoping to make a good amount of money on the deal. The auctioneer had his doubts about it, which was how it came to my attention.'

Rocco couldn't tell the difference between the pairs of pictures, and said so. They were little more than postcard size, which didn't help, but he couldn't tell them apart. 'They're an exact copy.'

'That's the general idea,' said Dreycourt. 'They look like the real thing, even to experts.'

'Like you?'

Dreycourt pulled a face. 'I have some expertise, but art is an extremely broad area. I often need to consult experts in specific subjects to be certain. In the case of this picture I was certain it was a copy but to make sure I consulted with a professor who'd made a lengthy study of Gérard and the Récamier painting in particular. He confirmed a characteristic of the paint strokes used which betrayed its true origins.'

'So how is it Cezard isn't locked up?'

'Because the man's wife had assumed it was genuine and was too embarrassed to make an official complaint when she found out it wasn't.' He shrugged. 'It happens a lot, especially if someone claims they bought it in good faith, which is more often than not a transparent lie. In this case the lady was adamant: no complaint and no publicity. I knew it had to be Cezard's work, but with no charges against him and no testimony, I was powerless to push it any further.'

'Have you spoken to Cezard?'

'Of course. He denied ever meeting the client, producing the painting or even possessing the skills to do so. But I've been studying him long enough to know he's perfectly capable. He's charming, as open as the day is long and entirely believable.'

'Perhaps he's innocent.'

'Possibly, although I don't think so. I'm hoping that after you've met him you might be able to convince me otherwise.'

Rocco looked at him. 'Say that again?'

'I want you to get to know him. Rattle his tree a little, see what your instincts tell you.'

'What, just pop in for a chat on the off-chance? You do know that most criminals have a built-in radar for trouble. The moment a detective shows up on their doorstep, they tend to sense that it's more than just a traffic offence or a minor land dispute. And one excuse I can't use is being interested in art. He'd spot that lie in a moment.'

'Oh, I'm sure you'll think of some plausible reason to drop by. The fact is, Lucas, Cezard doesn't deal solely in selling his forgeries to rich clients; I believe he's involved in blackmailing them afterwards.'

'With what?'

'With their lies. They've lied to their friends and colleagues, pretending to own an important work of art when they don't, in some instances gaining respect, status and even position they don't deserve. I know of two men who, on the back of their lies about their supposed wealth, were given sizeable bank loans at special rates. One might argue the banks were at fault, but it's still fraud and gaining financial guarantees under false pretences.'

'That makes them vulnerable.'

'Exactly. In my experience friends and colleagues finding out they've been taken for fools are not very forgiving. Business partners even less so. Of the few stories I've come across, most of those who've bought into this fraud appear to have paid up to keep their petty egos safe. But now Cezard's gone too far and chosen the wrong target. Two days ago, a blackmail attempt drove a prominent individual to take his own life.'

'Who?'

When Dreycourt hesitated, chewing his lip, Rocco wondered if he was being cautious until he was certain Rocco was on board with the investigation. He sat back and waited, staring at the art expert until he gave way.

'Secretary of State for Finance Jean-Pascal Bourdelet,' he said, and explained about the letter found on Bourdelet's desk.

Ouch, thought Rocco. That would be enough to boot it up from a mild case of self-deception to something worthy of investigation. Even so, proving that it was the blackmail attempt that had driven the man to take his own life was no simple matter, and he said so.

Dreycourt nodded. 'Maybe so. However, there's a growing body of opinion that blackmail leading to death

42

should be a criminal offence in its own right. That's why the Ministry have handed the investigation to me... and, by association, you. This is not a normal situation and I think it could be the start of something worse.'

'What do you mean?'

'I suspect this isn't the first case of its kind, and that Cezard or whoever might be helping him has tapped into a new source of making money. I believe he might be going back over his past clients and reminding them of their deception to see what he can get out of them. Some will brush him off and suffer the embarrassment; others won't be so resistant. It's possible Bourdelet's death wasn't the first, and I doubt it will be the last.'

Chapter Seven

'I'm disappointed. I'm sure you know why.' Serban launched into the attack the moment the other man picked up the telephone. He'd just heard the news about Bourdelet's suicide from a police contact. Going on the offensive was another trick he'd learned worked well with those outside his own 'trade'. As outsiders they were unaccustomed to blunt approaches and the abandonment of social etiquette. It confused and wrong-footed them, giving him time to press home the advantage and remind them of his superior position.

'I'm sorry, Yuri. It was unforeseen, I assure you.' The tone was calm, but the words came out in a rush. 'Nobody expected him to... do what he did.'

'What? Blow his head off? Or am I being too brutal for you, *maître*?'

'Please, don't mention my na—'

'Please nothing.' Serban was on a roll. He leant forward as if his words were a physical assault. His use of the other man's title had been deliberate, to unsettle him and knock his confidence. 'I have no reason to think anybody is listening to my calls, so spare me the theatrics. Or have you been misbehaving and attracted the attention of the police without telling me?'

'No, of course not!'

'Let us hope not. Otherwise your name might just slip from my tongue in a moment of weakness.'

'There's really no need for threats, Yuri.' He sounded angry and resentful, but wisely kept his temper. 'We'll proceed with the other two targets as planned.'

'I'm not talking about them; I mean with Bourdelet. The suicide of a government minister will hardly go unnoticed, will it? Is there anything that could rebound on us?'

'No. The letter's source is untraceable. As long as your man made no mistakes in delivering it, we shouldn't have any problems.'

Serban felt a dig of anger at the implied criticism. 'My employees do not make mistakes,' he said heavily. 'Remember, you said there was no risk. I'll ask you now, what is likely to be the procedure?'

'Well, there will undoubtedly be an internal investigation, in view of Bourdelet's position, based on the contents of the letter. I understand he didn't speak to anyone after receiving it, but it was on the desk after he... killed himself.'

'Why would he have left it there?' Serban muttered. 'That's crazy – it will implicate him in theft at the very least.'

'His memory, certainly.' The man on the other end sounded unconcerned. 'Who knows what a desperate man will do when looking over the edge of a precipice? Perhaps he was past caring... or imagined it might regain him a scrap of honour, tainted though it will be. Either way, it will have been gathered up as evidence and the office sealed pending an enquiry.'

Serban said angrily, 'And that shouldn't concern me?'

'No. They won't want the contents of the letter to come out, believe me. The misuse of government funds in the finance ministry at this level is a scandal they can do without. The government machine will take over and suppress all but the most basic details: namely that Bourdelet took his life while under intense stress or some such medical condition. He won't be the first official to have done it, nor the last. It will soon blow over. However...' He paused.

'Yes?'

'They might decide to investigate the painting itself.'

'Why would they do that?' Serban felt a ripple of unease. While he himself was remote from any connection with the painting, the fact that the man on the other end was connected was reason enough for caution. Their past association was hardly secret.

'To find out where it came from.'

'He bought a copy of a known painting; who cares who produced it? I would have thought the misuse of government funds was far more important.'

'Unfortunately, that's not how the police think, you should know that. The painting is a forgery, and has brought about a death. As such they will follow it up because that's what they're conditioned to do.' A snort came down the line. 'They're like dogs chewing at a bone; they lack imagination.'

Serban felt concern at the open contempt in the other's voice. He was well aware that the man had no love of the police, but this went a step further. He distrusted people who voiced their feelings too loudly, because inevitably they would come out, and might impact on anyone seen to be connected with them. Something, he decided, to be stored away for the future.

46

'Where will it lead?'

'Nowhere. They'll go round in circles.' The reply sounded confident, even dismissive, which worried Serban even more. People who overestimated their own cleverness invariably made mistakes.

'Who will head the investigation?' It was an open question. Even if he knew the names of the officers concerned, there was little he could do about it. But he didn't believe in leaving matters to chance. It was a trait that had kept him out of the clutches of the law so far and he intended keeping it that way. Whoever they were they were unlikely to be ordinary cops, not when it involved the death of a senior ministry official. No doubt some high-flier from internal security would be handed the job, someone unknown to him and therefore untouchable. Even so, it would be good to know the name if he could get it, in case some form of leverage became possible.

'There's one man I know of who might become involved, a specialist in art fraud and forgery. His name's Dreycourt. Marcel Dreycourt. He's retained by the Ministry of the Interior.'

'Can he be bought?' It was Serban's default position: find a man's weakness and exploit it to the full. Government servants were not highly paid, a fact he was prepared to exploit.

'I doubt it. From what I've heard he has money and is not interested in more. His job will be to identify the source of the painting.'

'And will he do that?'

'He might. But I doubt it. There are few forgers working at the highest level, but pinning it on one specific person is almost impossible unless the artist confesses. I know this particular painter and he won't say a word. Even

47

if he is identified, there's no law against producing copies of paintings for admirers. Galleries do it all the time. Once they hit a brick wall, they'll hand the investigation over to another department, and when they also get nowhere, they'll close the case down.'

Chapter Eight

The second delivery made by the yellow Citroën van was to a quiet avenue on a hill to the north of the resort of Mers-les-Bains. Overlooking the English Channel, and one of three 'sister towns' along with close neighbours Le Tréport and Eu, Mers-les-Bains boasted a seafront façade of 19th-century art-nouveau villas, high chalk cliffs, a long pebble beach and small casinos where wealthy Parisians could gamble their money in a pleasing atmosphere and healthy sea air.

Not that any of this interested Peretz. The casino might have proved a draw in different circumstances but, as he'd learned long ago, gambling meant running the risk of getting both legs broken if someone didn't like the way you were winning. The stakes and pots were higher than in licensed casinos, but there was always someone who wanted a cut and had to be paid off if you valued your health. Bad bets and sore losers were a lousy combination no matter how civilised the venue.

All he was aiming to do today was get in and out again as quickly as possible, even more so once he'd seen the name of the recipient. In fact, having this letter in the mailbag alongside him had been about as comforting as sitting next to an unexploded hand grenade. Even if he had harboured ideas of spending a couple of hours in the resort before heading off, the name and title had killed them stone dead.

He found the address he wanted amid a row of newly-developed brick-and-rendered villas with sculpted gardens, stepped entrances and *au sous-sol* garages beneath the gardens, with double doors opening on to the road.

Peretz checked the street for observers, but saw none. Pulling an official-looking cap low over his face, he took the letter from the bag, hopped out of the van and stepped across the pavement. Slotting the letter into the mailbox atop the retaining wall, he returned quickly to the van and drove away, heading back towards the centre of town and the road east.

–

As he drove away from the house, a man appeared at the front window. Wrapped in a dressing gown and carrying his first cup of coffee of the day, he watched the van leave. It was too low down to see the registration plate, but he noted the familiar PTT colour and decided to finish his coffee before venturing down the steps to the mailbox. Was there anything these days that couldn't wait? Retirement brought several benefits, one of which was that nothing was urgent any more, save for the desire to keep on living at the level of comfort his police pension had earned over many years of loyal and diligent service.

He finished his drink while deciding what to do that morning. A stroll down to the seafront would be pleasant, although with the tourist season in full swing it might be better to go sooner than later to avoid the crowds. Perhaps he'd call in to a *salon de thé* where they served excellent pastries.

But first he had a situation to deal with. It involved his housekeeper, Anne-Marie Guillard, with whom he'd enjoyed until recently a pleasant physical relationship without strings... or so he'd thought.

He'd ended the affair when she'd begun to involve herself just a little too much in the fine details of his life, including going through some documentation he preferred to keep away from prying eyes. She had insisted on coming round this morning to collect a few of her belongings. He wasn't looking forward to it. He suspected that the passionate character which had first attracted him probably fuelled a less forgiving nature when roused in another way. Even so, a part of him was already regretting ending their arrangement, though he was certain he would soon find a replacement. The town was a popular retirement community with many widows and he'd sensed more than one of them sending him silent messages over the past few weeks.

As he turned to the front door, pulling his dressing gown around him, he saw another vehicle come to a stop at a house across the road. Another yellow van. He watched as the driver climbed out and delivered a selection of envelopes to one house, then walked across the road to his mailbox with a folded magazine and fed it into the slot.

Something about this double delivery stirred his gut: a sting of suspicion that had served him well throughout his career. He waited for the van to leave before walking down the steps and opening the mailbox. Inside was the magazine, a familiar monthly subscription on all things ornithological, and a plain white envelope. He flipped the envelope over.

No stamp. Just his name typed across the front: Jean-Marie Gambon, Director General, *Sûreté Nationale*, followed by his address.

The title seemed to mock him, but he didn't know why. All he knew was that something about this wasn't good news. He was no longer the director general of the national police force, which could have been a mistake easily made, but the disquiet he'd felt moments earlier was building to a pounding in his chest, causing his heart to flutter wildly.

He hurried back up the steps and into the house. Dropping the magazine onto a side table, he ripped the white envelope open and pulled out a single-page letter. There was no address or signature, simply a flow of text which made his breath stick in his throat.

Chapter Nine

Rocco was deep in thought as he entered the office in Amiens following his meeting with Dreycourt. Receiving instructions of an unusual nature from the Interior Ministry was nothing new; the reach exerted by its staff was wide, and they were not beyond using official muscle to get results or manpower wherever they felt the need. But this latest move was from a self-described 'consultant', albeit a former member of staff. To take it further without double-checking with his superiors first might be a mistake.

He headed for his desk, planning to check for any urgent issues, then go up and see Massin. The *commissaire* ran a tight ship and, although he had clearly passed on the Ministry letter, undoubtedly with Perronnet's knowledge, running past him the substance of the talk with Dreycourt wouldn't be a bad idea.

As he entered the rambling main office, usually a smoke-tinted place of ringing telephones, slamming drawers and coarse jokes, he was met by subdued looks from uniformed and plain-clothed officers alike. One man, an older detective named Émile Anselin, was giving him a knowing smile as if enjoying a secret joke. As he caught Rocco's eye, he turned away with a brief bark of laughter that carried a hint of derision, and made a comment that Rocco couldn't quite hear.

Rocco ignored him. Anselin was a recent transfer-in, nearing retirement and assigned to the Amiens office to coast down to his final day of service. He wasn't required to contribute much, thanks to an agreement between the Ministry and the independent police union, SIPN, and was fast becoming more of an obstruction than a help, content to amble around the place getting in everyone's way. But it wasn't Anselin's attitude that surprised him. The usual laughter and banter that accompanied the drudgery of work – at least, when the senior officers were not in evidence – and countered the darker aspects of the job was absent. There was a subdued atmosphere in the office, and a quick shifting of eyes away from him as he moved between the desks to his own small patch of police territory.

As he dropped his side-arm into his drawer and locked it, Detective René Desmoulins approached. Desmoulins was the polar opposite of Anselin: keen, hard-working and genial, he had proven himself to be a good right-hand man for Rocco, as he'd shown in the café siege.

'Got a moment?' he said softly, and gave a faint nod towards the rear door leading to the yard outside. Without saying more, he led the way across the room and out of the door leading towards the workplace of the stand-in pathologist, Dr Bernard Rizzotti.

Rocco followed, wondering what was going on. There was definitely something in the atmosphere today; even Desmoulins was acting strangely.

He soon found out. As the door closed behind them, he tapped Desmoulins on the shoulder and said, 'What the hell's going on in there, René? They're all acting as if their favourite pet just died.'

Desmoulins turned, nodded and cast a quick look around before saying, 'Anselin says you're bailing out and moving back to Paris.'

'Anselin talks too much.'

'So, it's true.' Desmoulins looked surprised.

Rocco ignored the question. 'What else is he saying?'

'He claims he saw the transfer order in the admin office. It's all over the station that you're up for promotion to a new unit and can't wait to kick the mud off your shoes for a cushy number and a bigger desk.' He held his hands up. 'That's not me saying it; I'm just telling you what's going round the building. You know what the rumour mill's like: anything to brighten up a dull day. It's your business, I know, but... you're not denying it.'

Rocco didn't know what to say. He felt a measure of annoyance towards Anselin for spreading rumours, but also towards whoever had allowed the information to come out in the first place. However, he owed Desmoulins an explanation at least. The younger man had proven himself loyal and trustworthy, and was not the kind to be looking to benefit from a colleague's potential departure. The rest of the building could wait until he was good and ready to make a decision.

'I've been offered a new posting, it's true,' he admitted. 'But that's as far as it's gone. It's a new unit being formed in Paris to fight organised gang crimes – but that's all I know. I only heard last week and haven't even agreed to talk to anyone about it yet. Why are people getting their pants in a twist?'

'I don't know.' Desmoulins looked embarrassed. 'I guess it's the same whenever anyone moves on. A bit of envy, someone getting a promotion when they're not; a sense that everything's going to change. People don't like that, do they? Change, I mean. Anyway, I thought you liked it here.'

'I do. But change happens all the time,' Rocco countered darkly. 'Promotions, transfers, retirements – even death in service. Nothing stays the same for long, especially in this job. Even idiots like Anselin get moved around.'

He checked his watch. He had to talk to Massin. Not just about Dreycourt but about the new job offer. He'd thought of little else since hearing about it through Massin himself a week ago, but hadn't yet decided what to do. And that worried him. Rocco always tried to make decisions quickly and firmly. Chewing over something endlessly implied that he had doubts.

The truth was, he was still getting over the mental and physical bruises incurred while dealing with the assassin, Nightingale, who had been sent after him by Lakhdar Farek, one of Paris's leading gang lords. Ideally, he should have been relishing the opportunity to get to grips with more of Farek's kind, backed by the better facilities and budgets promised in the new anti-gang unit known as the Research and Intervention Brigade (BRI). But the prospect wasn't thrilling him for some reason and he could only think that the pressures of the past couple of weeks had something to do with it.

'You don't know what to do, is that it?' said Desmoulins.

'Not yet. But I'll let you know as soon as I do. That's a promise. And this stays between us, understand? Doesn't matter what anyone's saying.'

'Of course.' Desmoulins shuffled his feet and flushed. 'It wouldn't be the same, you know. And I bet I'm not the only one to say that.'

Rocco clapped the young detective gratefully on the shoulder and walked back into the building. He was going to have to make up his mind one way or another. Putting it off would only make him look lame and indecisive. He'd go up there and tell them that his decision was made. They might not like it, apart from Massin, of course, who might be glad to see the back of him, but better to come out with it and be done.

He rang Massin's secretary, and after a few moments she told him to come up.

Massin was with his deputy, Commissaire Perronnet, and Captain Eric Canet, who gave Rocco a smile. All three officers looked as if they were waiting for examination results rather than a report by a subordinate.

Massin didn't waste time with preliminaries. 'I'm sorry, Rocco, but I appear to have conspired to put you once more under the eye of the Interior Ministry. I'm hoping you agree to take on this case as you have the experience.'

Rocco felt the wind taken out of his sales. What the hell was Massin talking about? Was this his obtuse way of giving Rocco a shove out of the door?

'I don't understand.'

'The authorisation letter to assist Dreycourt.' Massin's forehead creased in a faint scowl. 'Don't tell me you're not interested. I've agreed you'll be assigned to it until further notice. It means putting off your decision about the new job a little longer but, in light of the importance of the deceased person, I think it's something we can't avoid. The Ministry agrees and is understandably taking a very close interest.'

Rocco finally understood. So, they weren't waiting for his decision about the new job after all. Not yet, at least. 'The deceased. You mean Secretary of State Bourdelet?'

'Dreycourt told you?'

'Yes. He didn't want to but I beat him up until he talked.'

Massin didn't even blink. 'Now why don't I find that impossible to believe?'

Chapter Ten

Rocco drove to Poissons after making a quick phone call to Claude Lamotte, the local *garde champêtre,*and arranging to pick him up. Rocco and Claude had worked together several times now, and he trusted the man implicitly. As a rural guard, which involved him in countryside matters, including policing poaching and fishing licences, Claude did not fall under the direct rule of the *gendarmerie*, but that hadn't stopped him helping out whenever he was needed. He was a conduit for information on most people and most business in the area, and was Rocco's most logical way of getting to meet the alleged master-forger, Sébastien Cezard.

Claude was waiting outside his house on the opposite side of Poissons from Rocco's. Heavy-set and dressed in his standard brown and green work clothing, there was no visible sign that he was any kind of policeman save, perhaps, for an official badge concealed somewhere: he could have been any one of the farm workers from the village. Even the shotgun held under one arm was common enough in most parts of France not to set him apart, which was how he liked it.

'This all sounds mysterious,' he said, approaching Rocco's side of the Citroën. 'What's going on?'

'Sébastien Cezard,' said Rocco. 'Do you know him?'

Claude nodded. 'I've met him a couple of times. I wouldn't say we're friends, but he seems nice enough. Why, what's he done?'

'I don't know that he's done anything yet. I'm just filling in some background. Anything you have on him might be useful.'

Claude puffed out his cheeks. 'Well, he's some kind of artist, I gather – a painter. He lives in Passepont. He's never been in any trouble to my knowledge. I'm not sure how successful he is. He never seems to be scraping for a living, so I suppose he does all right. As far as I know he doesn't go out much, and prefers to stay at home in his château and paint.'

'His what?' Rocco looked at him. There were a few châteaux scattered around this part of the country, although not many were in habitable order. Down in the Loire region and further south, where they were becoming tourist sights, it was a different case, but this corner of Picardie seemed to have allowed such places to slide into disrepair. 'A real one?'

'Real enough, although I hear it's pretty much a ruin for the most part. One wing has been rescued, which is where he and his daughter live, and there's a studio of sorts in the old coach house. Other than that, I don't know much about it or them.' He glanced at Rocco from beneath heavy eyebrows. 'Is this a new case?'

'I'm not sure. I've been asked by a man at the Ministry to take a look at him. It's an ongoing case they're investigating. I need a reason to go and see him, though. Do you want to come along?'

Claude smiled. 'You mean you want me to provide an official excuse?'

'Is that a problem?'

'Not at all.' He gave it some serious thought. 'Ah, I know: there's been some out-of-season hunting on his land in the past, and only the other day somebody reported hearing gunshots over that way. I think it's about time we had a chat about that.'

'And were there any? Gunshots, I mean.'

'Not that I know of. But I doubt he'll know either way. Anyway, it's reason enough to allow me to have a talk with him. How you handle your part is up to you, of course. You can drive me if you like.'

'Why not? If you're good I'll let you play with the car radio.' He waited for Claude to climb aboard, bringing with him a smell of damp earth and gun oil. He laid his shotgun on the back seat before reaching for the car radio in search of a music channel.

'I don't think you'll need the gun,' said Rocco. 'We're going to talk to the man, not blow his head off.'

Claude frowned. 'It's my badge of office, that is. I'd feel naked without it. And everybody expects a *garde champêtre* to have a gun. Don't worry, it's not loaded. Anyway, I hear these artistic types can be a bit excitable. I like to be prepared.'

'In that case, if he looks like beating us senseless with a loaded paintbrush, I'll step aside and let you handle it.'

–

Cezard's château lay on the outskirts of the village of Passepont in a sleepy fold in the countryside. The village itself consisted of a church, a café and maybe twenty houses. A blink would have had a driver passing through without noticing its presence. The château, however, was not so easily overlooked, standing on a piece of elevated ground and surrounded by a high stone wall, green with moss and creeping ivy. A gateway flanked by a pair of impressive stone pillars looked sturdy enough to have withstood a tank had one happened along, Rocco thought, although back in its heyday the worst it would have had to face was a marauding crowd of peasants with pitchforks looking for rumoured *aristos*.

Rocco drove up the cobbled drive to the main building and parked where it broadened out close to the front doors. Whatever Cezard did besides painting, gardening was clearly not high on his list of priorities. The grounds at the front still showed signs of terracing, with stone steps leading to each level, but sprouted generous clumps of couch grass, dandelions and nettles, while the sides bore a variety of bushes and trees with low-hanging branches heavy with untamed foliage.

The two men climbed out and studied the building. The front and one side rose to three floors of solid stone blocks, but one wing had long crumpled. Most of the original roof had gone, but had been replaced by newer modern tiles which gave the building a comic, lopsided appearance, like an old lady in a skewed top hat. Heavy shutters opened either side of the large front windows on the ground floor, but no higher, the glass in the first-floor windows staring back at them, dark and mysterious.

'Bit creepy,' said Claude. 'But attractive in a tumble-down kind of way.'

'I think barely standing is the style you're looking for,' Rocco commented, and turned to look at a sporty soft-top Renault parked at the side of the house. A soft powder blue, it had several dents along the front wing and a scrape down the side. Pretty much like a lot of cars in Paris, he thought.

'That's his daughter's,' Claude said, following his look. 'According to the locals she drives like a maniac.' He turned and climbed the steps and knocked on the front door with the flat of his hand. The *slap-slap* echoed back at them. Moments later they heard footsteps on tiles and the door opened to reveal a smiling young woman. She wore a blue skirt and yellow blouse with flat shoes, and had a silk scarf tied loosely around her neck.

'Gentlemen,' she said softly, brushing back a shock of brown hair. 'What can I do for you?'

'Good morning, *mademoiselle*,' said Claude, flicking a hand towards his forehead in a casual salute. '*Garde champêtre* Claude Lamotte, out of Poissons. May we speak to *Monsieur* Cezard, please?'

The young woman lifted an eyebrow, and stared at Claude's weather-beaten corduroy trousers and heavy cotton shirt. 'Aren't you supposed to wear a uniform, Officer Lamotte?' She glanced at Rocco with a twinkle of amusement. 'And who's the big silent type – your driver?'

Claude scowled in faint disapproval, although by the gleam in her eyes, it was clear she was teasing. 'I prefer to wear my own clothes, as a matter of fact. And this is Inspector Lucas Rocco, also out of Poissons, but based at the *commissariat* in Amiens.'

The young woman fixed Rocco with a pair of dark brown eyes. 'An inspector, no less? And so smartly dressed. My, we are honoured. What have we done to merit such important visitors? Do I need to call my lawyer?' Before either of them could answer, she laughed and stepped aside, sweeping an arm invitingly towards the interior. 'Come in, the pair of you. I'm just teasing. My name is Eliane, by the way. My father's in the back room. If you follow me, I'll introduce you.'

With that she turned and walked across the tiled entrance hall and along a passageway towards the rear of the building. She moved with a swing of her hips and glanced back once. Rocco wasn't sure if it was to see if they were following or to check on the effect she was having. Either way, he kept his eyes firmly ahead, wondering at a mix of music in the air, part something contemporary and, behind it, a classical piece Rocco recognised but couldn't have named if his feet had been on fire.

'Sorry about the clash of music styles,' Eliane called back. 'Pa likes his highbrow stuff while he's working but I prefer something a bit lighter at this time of day.' She waved vaguely towards a number of large canvases of rural scenes on the walls on either side. 'He painted all these. He has a thing about bare walls: he can't stand them. It's a bit of an obsession in my opinion, but he says it's to do with creating an artistic and relaxing ambiance for his work.'

'You don't share that view?'

'Not entirely. I mean, I like them well enough but my mother wasn't very artistic and she must have passed it on to me. I prefer people.' She stopped and turned, smiling. 'They're a lot more fun.'

Rocco stopped and studied a scene that might have been of the marshes around Poissons. Filled with reed beds, trees and the glint of faint sunlight off dark water, it was beautifully executed but not what Rocco would have chosen. Maybe Cezard had been in a dark mood when he'd created it, but it seemed a little too full of menace to be relaxing, if that's what he'd been aiming at. On the other hand, from Rocco's close encounters with the local marshland it was an accurate representation, showing the contrast of natural beauty while hinting at unseen dangers lurking beneath. A quick glance showed other works on similar themes, and he saw Claude nodding his head in recognition.

'*Eh bien*. Not bad,' he said approvingly, jutting out his lower lip.

They both turned as Eliane opened a door at the end of the passage and stood aside to usher them in.

A man was standing by the window, puffing on a cheroot and staring out at a stretch of grass and a pond full of dark water and a mass of waterlilies. He was holding a half-glass of yellow liquid in his other hand; Rocco guessed pastis. The classical music they'd heard was coming from a record player on a sideboard. The man turned as Claude and Rocco stepped inside, followed by Eliane, who walked over to him and kissed him on the cheek.

'Sorry to intrude, Pa,' she said softly, 'but these two policemen want to speak with you. They're Officer Claude Lamotte and Inspector Lucas Rocco.' She turned and gave Rocco a dazzling smile. 'I think I got that right, didn't I?' She turned back to Cezard and said, 'I thought I'd better let them in before they called for reinforcements and bashed the doors down.' She turned and clapped her hands together. 'Now, I was just about to make tea. Everyone want some? Good. I won't be long.' With a swish of her skirt, she disappeared through the door and hurried back down the corridor, leaving a heavy silence in the room and the three men looking at each other awkwardly.

Sébastien Cezard merely smiled and shook his head. He put the glass down and lifted the head of the record player. Silence took over the room. 'You'll have to forgive

Eliane. She has a habit of disregarding convention and her humour is sometimes questionable, as is her taste in music.' He shook hands with both men and invited them to sit on a sofa to one side of a large fireplace, before taking an ancient armchair on the opposite side himself. 'What can I do for you, gentlemen?'

Heavily built, with an expansive belly and a curly grey beard, Cezard seemed to fill the room with his presence, even when sitting down. His hands, shirt front and trousers were spotted with paint of various colours, and a smear of dark blue crossed one cheek like a scar. The cheroot was now shuffled into one corner of his mouth and he reached up to adjust a pair of thick-framed spectacles perched on a broad, flat nose that might have been broken with a shovel.

'I'm just along for the ride,' Rocco explained easily. 'We're on our way to Amiens, but I believe Officer Lamotte wanted to ask if you had heard any shooting close to your land recently.' He nodded at Claude to continue.

'That's right,' said Claude. 'We had a report of gunfire a couple of days ago and I was wondering if you were aware of anyone hunting in the area?'

'Gunfire? Around here?' Cezard shook his head. 'I'm sorry, Officer Lamotte, but I can't help you. I don't own a gun and I haven't heard any shooting. In the hunting season one gets the feeling we're living in a war zone, as you probably know, but right now? Nothing. Although I have to confess that when I'm working, I tend to be oblivious to anything short of a bomb falling on the roof. Ask Eliane – she might have heard something.'

Just then Eliane appeared with a tray of cups, saucers and a teapot, and placed it on a low table between the three men. 'Here you are,' she said cheerfully. 'Already poured. Add sugar, lemon or milk according to taste. Personally, I prefer the English way, with milk.'

'I was just telling these officers,' said Cezard, 'what I'm like when I'm working.'

Eliane rolled her eyes. 'My God, he's like the walking dead. Put a paintbrush in his hand and he goes deaf, dumb and… well, not blind, of course, but as good as. Trying to have a decent conversation with him when he's in full flood is virtually impossible.' She softened her words by bending over and kissing him on the head, then turned to the door. 'Excuse me, I have a few errands to run and some marking to finish.'

'Eliane's an emergency supply teacher,' Sébastien explained, when she had gone. 'She fills in for schools who are short-staffed. They want her to go full-time but she likes it the way things are.' He sipped his tea then studied Rocco. 'I get the impression you're not local, Inspector… may I call you Lucas?'

'Of course.'

'Thank you. I'm Sébastien. You must be the detective from Paris I've heard talk about.'

Rocco nodded. 'That's correct.' He explained briefly about being transferred as part of a policing initiative, then steered the conversation back to the painter. 'What kind of work do you do – apart from the pieces in the hallway, I mean?'

'That's pretty much it, actually. I do what I have to, like most working artists.'

'You've been to the *marais* at Poissons,' said Claude. 'Spot on with the detail I have to say.'

Sébastien smiled in gratitude. 'Thank you, Claude. They're part of a commission for a gallery in Paris. They wanted several scenes from the local area, so I spent a few days down there sketching out some ideas. Eliane will be taking them into the city any day now while I get on with some other work.'

'Do you always work to commission?' Rocco queried. 'I thought artists chose their own work.'

'Ha – I wish.' Sébastien replied. 'Truth is, I'd rather dabble in a variety of styles and see what comes out, but commissioned work is what puts food on the table.'

'Portraits?'

'Some, although not many people these days have the patience to sit still for long enough. They'd rather give me a photo and come back when it's completed. There's a favoured pet once in a while, but that's about it. The pastoral scenes are the biggest sellers.'

'So, no special jobs?'

Cezard blinked. 'I'm not sure what you mean.'

'I thought people liked paintings in… what do they call it – in the style of someone famous?'

'Ah. I see. Well, that's one line of work, I grant you.' He winced as if in distaste at the idea of producing copies. 'Cheap impressions of Monet's 'Sunrise' or 'La Plage de Trouville' go down well in certain quarters. I even know a couple of artists who knock them out on a regular basis for clients in England. They're pleasant enough to look at, I suppose, but they'll always be copies, nothing more.' He turned towards a sideboard, alongside which were three canvases stacked on the floor. He lifted one out so they could see it. It was of a young woman sewing against a backdrop of roses. 'Take this, for example: it's a copy of a Berthe Morisot painting I was asked to produce for a client in Paris. Unfortunately, he died before I could finish it.'

'A copy?' said Claude. 'Looks like a pretty damned good copy, if I may say so.'

Cezard smiled. 'Thank you. But no signature, you see, and there's some detail included in it to differentiate it from the original.' He smiled. 'That way I can't be accused of supplying a fake.' He put the painting back against the wall. 'Who knows – I might be able to find another client for it someday. The thing is, in this business, you're only as good as your last job, and abstract expressionism is much more fashionable these days.'

'Expressionism?' Rocco asked.

'You know – the jazzy shapes and colours brigade. And now Warhol has decided that coke bottles and Hollywood film stars can be art.'

'You don't approve.'

'Actually, I think he's very clever, even inventive. And the young seem to like his work. But like it or not, it won't last, in my view. How long can you look at a picture of a soup can on your wall?' He waved a hand. 'That makes me sound like a resentful old goat, doesn't it? You're probably right.' He gave a last puff of his cheroot before tossing the butt into the open grate, where it bounced off a log, spraying sparks into the shadows. With that he stood up, waving away the smoke, and looked at Claude. 'I'm sorry I can't help you, Claude. I haven't been hunting I can promise you that; it's never been of interest, chasing harmless animals for sport. I know that puts me at odds with most of the male population, but I'm too long in the tooth and Eliane's an animal lover. She would string me from a tree if I even suggested it.' He gave a disarming smile. 'If that's all, I'm afraid I really must get on.'

Rocco and Claude took the hint and followed him down the hallway to the door. There was no sign of Eliane, and they said their goodbyes and thanked Sébastien for his hospitality. As he drove out of the gate, Rocco looked across at Claude. 'What do you think?'

Claude shrugged. 'He came across as genuine enough. His daughter, too.'

Rocco nodded. 'That's what I thought.' At the same time, he found his cop's instinct clicking in. He had to ask the question he'd asked about many people he'd met in the line of duty: too good not to be true or a brilliant actor? Only time would tell.

His radio crackled into life and he pulled over to take the call. It was the operator in Amiens. Marcel Dreycourt had called asking for another meeting at the same place as before, same time tomorrow. More bad news, apparently.

–

'What did they really want, Pa?' Eliane had returned an hour after Rocco and Lamotte had gone, and had walked straight through the house to her father in his studio. She found him staring out of the window, drumming on a side table with a long paintbrush. To her, it was a sign that he was worried about something.

'Sorry?' He looked round, his expression vague and distracted.

'Rocco and Lamotte. You know who I mean. Why were they here?'

'Ah. Well, you heard them. Someone's been shooting in the area. Most probably a poacher after a cheap meal.' He dropped the brush and began to tidy up a bench covered in tubes of paint, knives, brushes, rags and bottles of spirit. It did nothing to restore any kind of order to the chaos, and he eventually sighed and gave up.

'You really think an inspector concerns himself with poachers?' She placed a hand on his arm. 'I've heard things about Rocco. They say he deals with serious crimes, like the shootings near the British cemetery outside Poissons last year, and the dead man found at that sanitarium three months ago.' She paused, then said softly, almost apologetically, 'Pa, you haven't got yourself into any trouble, have you?'

'I've no idea what you mean, *chérie*. I expect Rocco was just helping out. After all, he can't be chasing serious criminals all the time, can he? Don't worry about it.'

She stared at him, frowning at the tightness of his expression and the fact that he suddenly wouldn't meet her eyes. They had few secrets between them, father and daughter, but she knew that the death of her mother five years ago had left an indelible mark on his soul, and he'd retreated into himself in a way that concerned her. It wasn't merely grief for a lost one, she was certain, but a weakness that had entered his body after losing the love of his life. He drank more than he used to, she knew that, although rarely to excess, but she'd suspected for some time now that he was keeping things from her. And she had a feeling that she knew the cause.

'You're not working with that horrible man again, are you?' she asked, and pulled at his arm, forcing him to turn and look at her.

He gave a weak smile and touched her face with a paint-spattered hand, the fingers trembling. 'God, *ma petite*, you sound just like your mother when she caught me sneaking a glass of cognac to help me sleep.' A shadow crossed his face at the memory, and her heart went out to him. But she persisted. He was hiding something, she was certain of it.

'Don't change the subject. Are you?'

He shook his head, but it wasn't a denial. 'My dear, that horrible man, as you call him, has helped us keep a roof over our heads these past couple of years. Without Laurent's help we'd have been reduced to God knows what kind of existence. You know me: I'm not a salesman. I don't have the skill to talk to people when it comes to selling my paintings and getting new commissions, and neither do I have the contacts.' He sighed. 'There isn't the same appreciation for art these days, you know that. It's all about quantity and cheap printed copies for the masses.'

'You did all right before he came along, didn't you?'

'Call it good fortune. I was lucky to get my work into a couple of active galleries and it gave me a base to work from. But that was years ago. The world has changed since then and got a lot harder.'

'So you are working with him.' Even to Eliane's ears it sounded like an accusation, and she felt guilty when he winced at the barb in her voice.

He patted her arm. 'In a limited way, I promise. He's found some more clients for me, that's all, so we should be fine for a while yet. That's good, though, isn't it?'

Eliane couldn't even nod agreement; her heart wasn't in it. She felt a tinge of guilt. She knew that he was doing his best for the two of them, as he had done all along when they were three. She wondered how long this 'good thing' could last.

'As a matter of fact,' he added brightly, 'Laurent's coming to see me tomorrow. Promise me you'll be on your best behaviour?'

She gave him a serious look, tinged with displeasure. 'I'll do better than that, Pa – I'll be out all day. Then I won't have to stand his oily presence.'

Sébastien winced. 'Seriously, Eliane – he's harmless. And he's been a great help to me, you should acknowledge that.'

She touched his face with her fingertips. 'So you keep saying. But I still don't like him and I don't like the way he treats you. He acts as if he owns you.' She shuddered. 'And he gives me the creeps.'

Chapter Eleven

The third letter presented Georges Peretz with a different kind of delivery problem from the previous two. The directions to the drop, near the town of Abbeville, described it as a large house on an isolated single-track road outside the main conurbation. Isolated was bad news to a city man like Peretz, accustomed to using busy streets by way of cover to avoid being noticed. By itself it was no different from risks he took all the time for his employer. As a trusted man in the organisation he regularly carried messages and packages – and none of the recipients were what would be called upright members of the community. Had they been, they wouldn't have been receiving drops from Yuri Serban. The messages were invariably in code and the packages were undoubtedly money or drugs, or sometimes heavy and metallic and smelling of gun oil. But Peretz never made the mistake of looking inside. As long as he took normal precautions in his work and wasn't intercepted by the police, it was easy money. But working outside his normal stomping ground, he couldn't rid himself of a lingering concern that his movements might have been observed and recorded, if not by cops then by nosy neighbours with too much time on their hands.

That he also now knew a little more about the background of the envelopes' recipients was an additional concern. A senior politician followed by a former top cop, and now a top judge... that was straying into a very dangerous kind of territory. Especially as Serban had told him the politician, Bourdelet, had topped himself only hours after Peretz had delivered the first letter. It hadn't been in the news yet, but he knew Serban had sources of information inside the police and elsewhere.

He was already beginning to wonder if maybe a new line of employment might not be a good idea.

For now, though, there was another, potentially trickier problem: Serban had warned him that the local Abbeville crime group was resentful of anyone trespassing on its turf. Tentative approaches by Serban to gain permission for his man to enter had been rebuffed unless full disclosure of the reasons for doing so were made. Serban had refused. If the local group knew what they were doing, there was nothing to prevent them taking over the situation themselves. Unfortunately, the group would now be on the lookout for strangers bearing gifts.

Peretz was trying not to be too concerned, as he'd never been here before and, as far as he was aware, had never met any members of the local criminal community. But that didn't prevent the feeling that he was being watched the closer he came to the town. He had found no way around the town to reach the drop, and had to pass through its quieter outer limits. That meant lighter traffic and the danger of being unable to remain invisible.

He pulled on the official-looking cap and drove at a steady pace, passing through a small area of commercial businesses, warehouses and distribution depots, then a sprawl of housing. Eventually he left this behind and found himself on a country road bordered by a lake on one side and woodland on the other. He checked the directions written on a pad. So far so good. Up ahead he saw a sign and signalled to turn left.

He was now on a narrow track curving round the lake itself, with signs showing names which he presumed were single properties backing on to the water. This was rich man's territory and he began to feel out of his depth at the sense of isolation.

He slowed as he rounded a bend in the track and saw a large house up ahead. It was set back from the road with a spread of lush gardens to the front and bordered either side by a screen of trees. Privacy was clearly what the owner wanted here, and he checked the name as he drove by. *L'Abri.* The Shelter. He wondered what the owner might be sheltering from, and whether it had any connection with the letter he carried. Who knew what these kinds of people did or had done to merit the attentions of a man like Serban? Rather them than me, he thought.

Three more properties followed, each set in their own fenced-off space and all backing down to the lake. He didn't look at them as he passed, but kept his head down. When he saw the road ending at a wooden barrier over-grown with grass, he turned the car round and drove back.

He arrived back outside the first house and stopped. The structure was impressive and looked newly-built, wide rather than deep and with an imposing pair of what resembled giant portholes looking out from the tiled roof over a curved wrought-iron balcony across the centre. A double garage stood to one side with a sizeable shed next to it, and he could just make out what might have been a small boathouse sitting on the edge of the water to the rear of the property.

He climbed out and took the letter from the bag, pulling the cap down low over his eyes. If anyone was watching, he didn't want to be identified later, either by crook or cop. A mailbox stood outside the front gate on a sturdy post, and he wasted no time placing the envelope inside and walking back to the van. This was the last one for the time being and for no reason that he could fathom he felt a flush of relief.

The feeling lasted all of thirty seconds. As he drove back along the track towards the road, he felt as if he'd been punched in the chest. A police car was coming towards him at speed, dragging a cloud of dust in its wake.

This was the very thing Peretz had been worried about: that the kind of people he was delivering to, with their fancy houses in discreet locations, had access to security at the other end of a telephone. Someone must have become suspicious about his van and called it in.

He looked for a way out, a gateway he'd missed or a farm track where he could lose himself before they could pull him up. If the cops were here because they suspected he was up to no good, he'd be in trouble. Even being held for questioning could lead to phone calls being made, and if they hit on the right – or wrong – person, being flagged up as an associate of one Yuri Serban would guarantee the letter being subjected to scrutiny. End of game.

Then good sense prevailed and he forced himself to remain calm. Whatever the car was doing here, it was moving very fast, bouncing over the uneven surface and clearly in a hurry. If it was going to stop him, it would have been slowing down by now and signalling him to stop.

He told himself that the cops inside couldn't possibly know what he was here for. How could they? If they stopped him and asked, he'd simply say he'd lost his way on the route into town to meet up with a former pal from military service.

It drew nearer, still making no effort to slow down, and he pulled over to give it room. As it flashed past in a shower of dust and kicked-up gravel, the passenger waved a brief acknowledgement. Peretz returned the gesture and pulled back onto the track, watching its progress in the rear-view mirror. It careered up to the first house, its nose dipping as it showed a flash of brake lights, then continued around the bend and out of sight.

Peretz breathed easier then stamped hard on the accelerator. Seconds later he was back on the main road and heading east as fast as the van would go, determined not to stop until he reached his own kind of civilisation. Then he'd call Serban and let him know it was done.

-

It wasn't until much later in the day that the owner of the house by the lake returned home. Judge Jules Petissier parked his treasured British Jaguar S-type 3.4 in the garage and locked the doors, then walked back down the drive to the mailbox, enjoying the cool afternoon air coming off the lake. It brought with it a rich, loamy smell of water he'd always loved, and a sense of serenity and a return to nature, always reminding him of his childhood days near Avignon.

Tall and slim, with iron-grey hair and an athletic profile belying his age, he possessed a prominent nose and a powerful gaze, two features that had served to bring him a certain fearsome notoriety among those who appeared before him, whether criminal or legal.

After a brutal few days in the Court of Assizes in Paris, where he sometimes spent the night after late sittings,

Petissier was relieved to be home. Away from the smell of failure and desperation, of lost causes, lengthy legal arguments which inevitably went in circles, and of the overpowering and conflicting forces of the state and the criminal classes that he was forced to endure. It was good to be able to spend time appreciating what he had amassed over the years through his diligence and planning.

He reached the mailbox and took out a bundle of letters held together by a rubber band. A single white envelope remained. He took it out and turned it over, tucking the bundle beneath his arm. Unstamped, he noted, so hand-delivered. Unusual.

Seconds later, Petissier dropped the envelope and uttered a cry of alarm which echoed across the garden and vanished among the trees. He felt a sharp stab of pain beneath his silk shirt and clutched his free arm against his body, forcing himself to inhale as a wave of nausea swept through him.

When he was once more in control, and certain he wasn't about to suffer a seizure, he looked around to see if he was being watched. Impossible to tell out here, with the woods and the fields stretching away into the distance. Someone could be quite easily hidden and watching him from among the trees. The deliverer of the letter, perhaps?

He turned and walked up to the house as casually as he could, determined to show no obvious concern. Once inside he went to a cabinet and poured himself a drink. He drank deeply, feeling the pleasant burn of fine Cognac all the way down. He poured another and drank that, too, savouring the flavour in an attempt to divert his attention away from the contents of the letter. But for once the alcohol did nothing to calm his nerves.

This was a disaster, he decided. It had been stupid and risky in the first place, and he should have known that one day it would come back to haunt him. Stupid for giving way to greed and ego, risky for placing himself in a position of vulnerability to people with the morality of the gutter. Head swimming from the effects of shock and the double shot of Cognac, he paced back and forth, trying to think of a way forward. Perhaps there was someone he could call to track down the sender of the letter and deal with them. It wouldn't be any kind of official help, of course. One look from a policeman at the content of the letter would probably have him incarcerated within twenty-four hours.

It was useless. Names and possibilities came up, but they were discarded just as quickly as he thought of them, and he realised eventually that there was nobody he could confide in. With this realisation came the bitter regret at not having done something about this situation before.

Unfortunately, the letter's demands indicated that it was already far too late.

Chapter Twelve

Save for an absence of sunshine, Douligny-la-Rose looked as sleepy as it had on Rocco's first visit and Dreycourt was once more the café's only customer. The art expert saw Rocco and waved a greeting, then banged on the café door. The owner appeared instantly, and Rocco wondered if the man had been waiting just inside for the summons, a rural genie popping out of a lamp to perform magic.

'Sorry about dragging you back out here at such short notice, Lucas,' said Dreycourt. 'But you'll soon understand why.'

--

'More information about Bourdelet?' Rocco replied, taking a seat.

'I wish it was. Unfortunately, there have been two more "events" like it. Let's have coffee first. I need to get my thoughts in order.'

Rocco was happy to do so, although impatient to hear more. Did he mean two more blackmail threats or two more deaths? At this rate a single investigator wasn't going to be sufficient to work the cases fast enough.

The café owner appeared with their coffees and, after using a cloth to dust off the surface with a cavalier flourish, set the tray down and retreated indoors. Both men tasted their drinks, before settling back.

'I'll come back to Bourdelet in a minute,' said Drey-court. 'The latest victims received similar letters threatening exposure. Both, if the claims are to be believed, had purchased paintings and both men are – or were – in positions of great delicacy, if exposed.'

Whoever the new victims were, Rocco thought, the threat of their ownership of copy paintings being made public had to mean more than mere embarrassment. 'Who were they?'

'Ah, now you're officially on the case, there's no problem in disclosing everything.' Dreycourt looked relieved at the idea. 'The second case was Jean-Marie Gambon. Gambon recently retired from his position as Director General of the *Sûreté Nationale*, to settle in Mers-les-Bains on the coast. He was divorced. Gambon's letter referred to the purchase of two paintings, one of which he'd sold, allegedly to pay off some debts and to fund his retirement.' Dreycourt's expression didn't change as he added, 'The letter reminds Gambon that he knowingly sold it to a private buyer in the United States as an original. That claim is so far unsubstantiated and I'm having someone in our consulate general staff in New York look into it. It will take time and it's possible the buyer won't be happy to admit he's been fooled.'

Rocco nodded. *Caveat emptor*. Buyer beware. Maybe the American buyer hadn't been any more bothered by the authenticity of the painting than Gambon himself. Brothers in arts.

'And the other?'

'The third victim was Jules Petissier, a senior judge in the Assize Court. He lives in Abbeville.'

Another high-profile name, thought Rocco. Whoever was doing this wasn't exactly aiming at the bottom of the tree. High-profile usually indicated a measure of wealth and the kind of reputation the owner wouldn't want sullied by accusations of illegal dealings.

Dreycourt had spoken but he'd missed the words.

'Sorry?'

'I was wondering if you might have come across either of these men in the course of your duties.'

'Because one was a judge and the other the head of the *Sûreté*?' Rocco shook his head. It was a reasonable assumption. 'I don't fly high enough for that. What happened to them?'

'Petissier received the letter and folded immediately. In his job you have to be cleaner than clean. Any whiff of a misdemeanour is enough not only to get you dismissed, but in all likelihood to provoke any cases you've adjudicated to be appealed and reinvestigated. A messy and protracted business that would have followed him to the grave. According to the letter, he'd intervened in at least four cases which saw serious criminals walk free, allegedly to his financial benefit. That's not been confirmed yet and is probably unprovable.'

'But Petissier must have believed it was.'

'Yes.'

'Were the cases named?'

'They were. But three of the defendants have since died and the remaining man is in a care home, so I don't see them taking us much further.'

Rocco didn't say anything. Many people forgot that the perpetrators of crimes and witnesses to misdeeds were as vulnerable as everyone else to age, disease and death. But there was always something left behind if you knew where to look, and had some luck on your side.

'Petissier must have seen no other way out,' Dreycourt continued. 'He wrote a letter of resignation and slit his wrists. His gardener found him and they managed to get him to hospital, but he'd lost a lot of blood. He's currently in a coma and it's doubtful he'll survive.'

'And the other man?'

'Gambon tried to bluster his way out. I met him once and I'm not surprised – he's a combative man who doesn't like being bested. Unfortunately for him the letter he received was seen by his housekeeper, with whom he'd recently ended a long and close liaison.'

'Ouch.'

'Quite. The letter referred to loans he'd taken out from questionable sources in order to buy the two paintings.'

'Questionable?'

'Criminals. That matter alone is enough to have him hauled in and investigated. Even knowingly selling a forged painting as a genuine work of art would be enough for him to have been looking at prison time.'

That wouldn't have been fun, thought Rocco. Prison wasn't fun for anyone, but any former cop going to prison faced a greater raft of dangers. Settling scores didn't always have to be against a specific person; in the absence of a cop who'd put you away for your crimes, any other cop would do, especially a dirty one.

'The housekeeper must have known about the paintings because she immediately passed the letter to a local newspaper and confirmed the facts, along with dates and details. They didn't publish the claims but approached the Ministry for a comment. It was the end of the road for Gambon and his reputation. After submitting to initial questioning to verify if the allegations were true, he hanged himself in a copse near his home.' He shrugged philosophically. 'And here was me thinking all cops swallowed their guns when they'd had enough.'

Rocco ignored the dark humour. 'I need to speak with Gambon's lady friend and Petissier's family, if he has one. Bourdelet's secretary and his housekeeper, too. And I'd like to see all three blackmail letters.'

'Petissier's wife died last year. There are no children.' Dreycourt took a thick envelope from his inside pocket and passed it across the table. 'You can read these at your leisure. They're exact copies, nothing has been redacted but they are sensitive so keep them to yourself. I also took the liberty of getting photos taken of the paintings at each house. That way you'll know what you're dealing with.'

Rocco was impressed. It showed Dreycourt to be more than just an art expert; he had an eye for the requirements of an investigator going cold into a case.

There were two photos, both of nudes. He flipped over the first one, which was a study of a young woman lying invitingly on a couch, her blonde hair pinned on top of her head. In neat script were the words: "Mademoiselle O'Murphy" by Francois Boucher – 1751 – currently in the Wallraf-Richartz-Museum, Cologne. Gambon.

The second photo showed another blonde, this one playing with her hair and titled 'The Toilette of Esther' by Théodore Chassériau, dated 1841. Petissier. Like Bourdelet's fake, the genuine article was also residing in Paris, but in the Louvre.

'A touch of sentimentality there, I believe,' Dreycourt commented. 'According to records Petissier's late wife was named Esther, although I'm assured she looked nothing like that painting.'

Rocco said, 'I'm no expert but these look amazing.'

'They do. It's an irony that never ceases to amaze me: like forgers of bank notes, you'd think they would be capable of making a perfectly respectable living doing it properly.'

'It wouldn't be the same, though, would it? Respectable doesn't always appeal.' He held up the photos and letters. 'Thanks for these. I need to get this thing up and running.'

'I'm glad you see it that way.' Dreycourt gave a wry grin. 'It probably won't surprise you if I say nobody else was exactly eager to throw their hat into the ring. Bourdelet's involvement was bad enough, but add in these other two and the whole mess is a potential career killer if the investigating officer doesn't get it right.'

'Thanks for the vote of confidence.' Rocco knew what he meant, though. With Bourdelet alone, toes and reputations were likely to be trampled on in the search for answers, and anyone thrown into investigating the case was likely to pick up some black marks along the way. Not that it troubled him too much; he'd been picking up black marks for most of his career. To Rocco, doing the job right was the main thing, not pandering to other people's expectations or their instincts for self-preservation.

'What will you be looking for?' Dreycourt asked.

'Whoever wrote the letters will be high on the list. Secondly, where the paintings came from. Join those dots together and we might get somewhere.'

Dreycourt smiled. 'Joining dots – I like that. Pointillism. Georges Seurat holds the credit for that.' He waved a hand. 'Sorry – I'm sure you know that. Are you reserving judgement on Cezard?'

'Until I have reason not to.'

'Fair point. Just don't let his genial manner fool you, that's all.'

Privately, Rocco didn't hold out much hope of the letters proving too helpful. They would be devoid of clues, he was certain of that, with nothing to tie them to the originator. The mere fact of them having been sent showed that the author wasn't concerned about their discovery. In fact, that very openness may have had a secondary intention, to bring about their recipients' downfall if the demands for money failed. He suggested as much to Dreycourt.

'Revenge? That's a new one.'

'It's worth considering. Judges, politicians and cops collect enemies like rosettes at a dog show.' Rocco was speaking from experience. The threat of payback went with the job, although most came to nothing: just hot air covering the individual's sense of failure. But all it would take was for a sense of grievance to gain traction in an aggrieved individual's mind, to ferment and blossom over the years, and eventually it could spill over into action. 'Tell me what happened with Bourdelet.'

'It was simple, unexpected and quick. He went into his office, telling his secretary not to come in, then locked the door, placed a jacket over his head and blew his brains out with a service revolver. The letter was on his desk.' He sniffed. 'It got a little… contaminated, as you'll see from the copy, but it's perfectly readable.'

'Has this gone public?' Rocco was well aware of the procedure surrounding bad news and government officials. Diving for cover was instinctive; just how deep usually depended on the power and level of the official involved and the potential repercussions for those around him. For a secretary of state, he guessed it would have been considerable.

Dreycourt looked nonplussed. 'Not yet. But there are indications that details might have been leaked. They've had calls from a couple of reporters.'

'No suicide note?'

'Not as such, but the letter was as good as. It threatened to make public the fact that the esteemed secretary of state had purchased a forgery of a famous work of art, namely the Gérard painting, to hang on his wall at home. The threat was simple: if he didn't make a "substantial" donation, the details of which would follow, the matter would go public. The letter was dated the day before and must have been delivered before he left for the office.'

'Why would buying a forgery be worthy of blackmail? It's his money, he can do what he likes with it.'

'If only that were true. Unfortunately, it wasn't – his money, I mean. The letter went on to suggest that he'd used government funds to acquire it. It's already been confirmed that Bourdelet had access to a little-known finance ministry "special purposes" account. I'm advised that records of the account show that a cheque for cash was drawn at a bank near his office.'

Rocco grunted. Special purposes. A *caisse noire*, in other words – a slush fund. Where else would you find secret money but in large corporate bodies and government departments, where paying for information, for campaign support, for buying off opponents and a hundred other things made back-channel persuasion an essential method of doing business?

'By substantial, what are we talking about?'

'It didn't say precisely. But it suggested that as secretary of state for finance, it would be left to Bourdelet to judge how much his position and reputation were worth.'

'Unusual, for a blackmail letter.' It had placed the burden solely on Bourdelet to decide what to do. Unfortunately, he had chosen what some might see as his only – maybe even the honourable – way out. 'Would the alternative have been that bad for him?'

'For a man in his position, the damage would have been colossal. He'd have lost everything and the government would have been – and undoubtedly will be – enormously embarrassed, with accusations by the opposition of fraud, corruption and impropriety in public office. The media and public would have demanded his head on a plate and he'd have been finished professionally, socially and financially. The unauthorised use of government funds, no matter how secretive they might be, still earns a term in prison.'

'Could that have been the real aim?'

'Possibly. It's hard to say until we dig deeper. With a clever lawyer, the way the law stands, if there was no specific demand it might be hard to make a case if the blackmailer were ever caught. He or she might simply claim they were going to demand that the victim pay back the money to the government to put right a wrong. I think there could be some weight of public opinion behind that.'

'If the accusation is true. What about the painting?'

'I was called in to verify it yesterday afternoon. It's good – very good, in fact. But a fake. I checked with a colleague and she says there's absolutely no doubt. According to Bourdelet's ex-wife, he bought the painting a year ago, which ties in with the secret account withdrawal, and never stopped talking about it. As far as she was concerned it was an ego trip and he should have done what most middle-aged men do which is to acquire a sports car or a young mistress.' He gave a wry smile. 'There's not a lot of love lost there, as you can imagine.'

'Do you have a suspect in mind?'

Dreycourt shrugged and pursed his lips. 'I've tried to find proof that it's not, but I'm inclined to think it must be Cezard.'

Chapter Thirteen

'Why?' Rocco decided to hold off telling him that he'd been to see the artist. If something other than expertise was driving Dreycourt, he'd prefer to know about it sooner rather than later. It wouldn't be the first time that an expert had reached a decision on the strength of suspicion fuelled by emotion.

'Because as an artist he's capable and skilled enough. More so, in fact, than anyone else I can think of – and I've looked hard at all the names I know.'

'But is he capable of blackmail?'

Dreycourt looked conflicted and gave a puff of resignation. 'I don't know. But it could be anyone… Someone helping him, for example. What do you think?'

Rocco hadn't had much experience in the field of blackmail and extortion, but he was guessing that this level of crime was rare, and therefore the list of potential names would be limited.

'Blackmail is a very personal crime and relies on specific knowledge. It's not a case of picking a name from a telephone directory; it takes personal acquaintance with the target's background, their vulnerabilities and the degree to which they can pay up. You won't get all of that by reading the newspapers, not even for a public figure such as a politician.'

Dreycourt looked doubtful. 'I understand what you say, Lucas. But surely Cezard is high on the list of suspects, isn't he?'

'Not on my list, he isn't. I wouldn't have even known about him if you hadn't told me. Are you sure none of the others could be involved?'

'I'd stake my reputation on it. If you want names, I can supply them, but I think you'd be wasting your time.'

Rocco nodded. 'Would they admit to it?'

'Probably not willingly, if they thought a charge of forgery was involved. But most artists like to know who buys their work. Whoever is doing this would have known who bought the painting, which would have given him some indication of the buyer's wealth and maybe even their vulnerabilities.'

'Even to the extent of knowing about a government slush fund?'

Dreycourt tilted his head to one side. It was a reluctant concession. But he wasn't done yet. 'It's an open secret that the prime minister and Bourdelet didn't get on, and no first minister wants to get embroiled in a scandal. Any accusations stick, whether several steps removed or simply untrue.'

'Yet they do get embroiled, from time to time.'

'True enough. But I still think Cezard holds the key to this.'

Rocco sat back. If Dreycourt's suggestion was correct, it stood out as a straightforward case of extortion between a forger and a foolhardy politician. Do as I say, said the threat, or the exposure will ruin you. Providing the blackmailer covered his or her tracks, it would be a difficult nut to crack.

'You don't seem convinced,' said Dreycourt.

'It's a blackmail attempt, certainly,' Rocco agreed, 'but without a specific monetary sum or the name of the person involved, I can't see it going anywhere. And I doubt whoever it is will put their hands up now.'

Dreycourt looked glum. 'True. But Bourdelet's reputation is still ruined, professionally and privately.'

'That could be what the blackmailer really wanted.'

'It would still be good to find out who is behind it.'

'How? I doubt the internal security section will allow me anywhere near the situation.' In Rocco's experience, anything involving a government minister, even a junior one, usually had a blackout imposed on the basis of national security. Any investigation would be carried out by senior officers from the Interior Ministry.

Dreycourt took a letter from his pocket and passed it across. 'That's your letter of authority, countersigned by the deputy minister of the interior and the senior investigator for the finance ministry. It will get you through most doors pretty much – although I'd caution you against trying to climb too high with it.'

Rocco looked at him. 'Or what?'

'You'll find yourself running out of breathable air.' His expression was bland, but along with the words, the meaning was clear. Rocco proceeded at his own risk.

Rocco grunted at the warning; his investigation was going to be limited. He checked the letter. The signatures meant nothing but the names and titles were familiar and impressive.

'Why didn't they get one of their own people to deal with it in-house? That way they'd have full control.'

Dreycourt shrugged. 'I can't say. It's probably hand-washing. Bring in an outsider to look into Bourdelet's activities, and they can avoid any accusations of bias or cover-up.'

'Or of a failed investigation if anything goes wrong?'

'Or that. I can make any access arrangements depending on how you plan to proceed, but how much leeway you'll actually get is questionable.'

'That doesn't sound promising.'

'It's a sensitive issue. Bourdelet's office has been locked and sealed until you get there, so you've got a clear run with that but probably no further.'

Rocco thought it over. As with any investigation, he would need a free hand to ask questions. Lots of them. Some would be delicate, even painful, depending on the interviewees. But if they really wanted answers to why Bourdelet had killed himself, the deeper the probing the more it could lead to embarrassment for the government. That alone would shackle any attempts to speak to people above a certain level.

'I'll need to see his home, the same with the other two victims.'

Dreycourt nodded. 'That's fine. What else?'

'Bourdelet's office and staff. They would have been the closest to him.'

Dreycourt looked doubtful. 'That's the bit that might not be so easy. Government premises and staff are strictly off-limits. The internal security section are the only ones allowed to question civil servants and senior members when it comes to events inside the ministry. Sorry, but that's protocol, I'm afraid. I'll see what I can do as far as his secretary is concerned, but that might be as far as you can go.'

'Fine.' Rocco had guessed that would be the answer, but he could at least take what was offered. 'I'll start with his home.'

'No problem. There's a police guard on the property and Bourdelet's housekeeper will be there for an interview. I understand she wasn't on duty on the morning of his death, so she might not prove very helpful.'

'Was there anyone else working for him, a gardener or driver, for instance?'

'He had a driver supplied by the ministry, name of Lopez. As to a gardener, I'm not sure. The housekeeper will be able to tell you. I'm not sure how much use any of this will be, though. I get the feeling Bourdelet was a lot more guarded about his private life than most people imagined, especially with colleagues.'

Rocco nodded. It was no surprise. Most people who involved themselves in criminal acts were by nature careful about who they allowed inside their circle of confidants. A moment of unguarded conversation and a slip of the tongue could have career-changing results. That left the driver. Other than his secretary, Lopez would have been the last person to have spoken to him. And a regular and trusted driver would be the one person a man such as Bourdelet might have confided in, intentionally or otherwise. Stuck in busy Paris traffic, it would be natural to exchange a few words. Given a regular routine, the few words would soon turn into a level of familiarity experienced nowhere else among Bourdelet's office colleagues and acquaintances.

'I realise this has all come in a rush, Lucas,' said Drey-court. 'But I must impress on you the urgency involved here. Three high-placed individuals – victims – and I think it's unlikely they will be the only ones. I'm being pressed to get this dealt with as a matter of urgency and close down any further attacks.'

Rocco wasn't about to be hustled into making decisions purely for the sake of political expediency, and his instinct was to push back. 'I realise that, Marcel. But you wouldn't rush to verify a work of art, and my side of this investigation will take as long as it takes. All I will promise you and those above you is that I'll move as quickly as I can.'

Dreycourt gave a wry smile. 'It's true what I've heard about you, isn't it? You really don't give much of a toss for authority. I like that.' He reached out and shook Rocco's hand. 'I'll try to get some bodies on the ground to do some of the background leg work for you but it won't amount to much. The ministry wants this kept as quiet as possible to avoid a public scandal, so too big a team would be open to risk. Call me if you have any specific jobs you can't do yourself. We'll talk again soon.'

–

Rocco left Dreycourt contemplating another coffee and walked back to his car. Before heading back to Amiens, he took out the three letters and gave them a quick read while he still had a chance of doing so in peace.

They were typewritten, the words neutral, with no discernible style that would point towards the identity of the author. Simple demands to be simply met. Or else.

Bourdelet's response he knew about. The letter was smudged and dotted with dark marks which he guessed were blood. Gambon's letter mentioned the former police chief's knowing sale of an alleged forged but unnamed Matisse to an unnamed American buyer as an original, and his purchase of a Boucher, both paintings funded by loans from two named sources. Rocco hadn't heard of either men, but presumably airing the names had been enough for Gambon to have decided that he'd reached the end of the road.

Petissier's letter was as Dreycourt described, pointing a finger at the judge's close connections with criminals who had all walked free of serious charges, and of his subsequent receipt of substantial sums of money which had gone to fund his lifestyle and, it claimed, the purchase of the fake Théodore Chassériau painting. The names were vaguely familiar to Rocco but there were none that he'd been involved with. They were serious enough to have caused ripples in the justice system had the accusations been proved.

Three high-profile men in three different locations, three different lives. Instinct born of experience told him that accepting what he was told at face value would be unwise. Somewhere in each of their backgrounds there must be something to point to whoever had driven the three men to take such desperate measures. All he had to do was find it. He'd originally assumed Bourdelet, as a secretary of state, might prove a difficult one to investigate. Now he had a judge at the Assize Court and a former head of the national police force to look into: one dead, the other nearly so. Looking into the backgrounds of all three, if he wasn't careful, would be like walking blindfold through a minefield in clogs.

–

He started the car. It was getting late in the afternoon but he needed to get moving on this before the cases got any older. He had a sense that time was of the essence here, especially with such high flyers. If there was any evidence of criminal activity, it would have to be found and seized before any associates had a chance to cover their tracks. And the only way he could do that with multiple suspects was to get help.

As he left the village and followed the narrow road out towards Amiens, a car drove out from a field gateway and followed at a distance.

A black Peugeot, Rocco noted. Too clean to be local, standing out like a *sabot* dancer in a performance of *Swan Lake*. Two figures were visible through the windscreen. They couldn't have painted their official standing any more clearly if they'd tried.

Rocco put his foot down, raising a trail of dust as his wheels clipped the soft verge, the ground underneath dried out by the summer sun. The black car kept up with him but made no attempt to close the gap. He slowed again, then speeded up with the same reaction.

He sighed and wondered why the Interior Ministry, or whichever agency of the state these two were from, was so openly keeping an eye on him, and whether Dreycourt was aware of it. No doubt someone high up had been propelled by an innate sense of paranoia to set them on his tail, watching in case he turned up something nasty in the official woodshed.

Chapter Fourteen

'More help?' Commissaire Massin looked surprised, and shook his head. It was a sure sign that this wasn't going to be an easy discussion. 'But you've only just begun this assignment for the Ministry. Isn't it rather early to judge?'

Rocco kept his expression blank and counted to five. He was accustomed to Massin's instinctive reaction against using extra resources, but this was urgent and he wasn't going to take a refusal at the first request. He related the news from Dreycourt about the latest two blackmail victims. 'Their names haven't been released yet. I need to investigate their backgrounds to find out as much as I can about them.'

Massin blinked hard. 'Two more? What is this – an epidemic?'

Rocco breathed easier. 'I hope not.' Evidently Massin hadn't yet heard about Petissier and Gambon. The authorities had indeed kept a tight lid on it. Maybe that was why the two men in the Peugeot had followed him from Douligny-la-Rose and his meeting with Dreycourt.

Massin shrugged. 'You know how busy we are already, now that you've been assigned to this investigation. I don't think it calls for more assistance just yet, though.'

'It will do.'

'What do you mean?'

'Because of the people involved. Like Bourdelet, they're high-level. I was wondering if you knew either of them. The first is Jean-Marie Gambon, former Director—'

'Yes, I know who that is.' Massin frowned. '*Gambon?* Are you sure?'

'Dreycourt is. Now I've got to fill in some blanks.'

'I can't believe it. The short answer to your question is I knew of Gambon by reputation only. He would have been present at some of the conferences I attended, but so were many other top police officers and directors. But I don't recall ever having spoken to him.' He shook his head. 'It's appalling that such an eminent figure should be caught up in this. But you said two more. Who is the other?'

'Jules Petissier, a senior judge in the Assize Court.'

This time Massin looked stunned, and turned pale. He shifted in his seat and said nothing. The silence went on for a long time, broken only by a clock ticking on the shelf behind him.

'Sir?' Rocco gave him a gentle nudge.

'I knew him. Petissier.' The answer came almost reluctantly, as if an admission he really didn't want to make, and the name rolled off his tongue with something akin to distaste. 'It was some time ago, however, near the end of the war in Indochina. I doubt I could tell you anything that would help. I wasn't privy to his private life and I haven't seen him since then, although I've been aware of his rise through the ranks of the judicial system. He's had a charmed professional life.'

At the final sentence, Rocco felt a hum in the atmosphere between them. The set of Massin's face told him that the *commissaire* was not telling him everything. He was about to speak when Massin pushed his chair back and jumped to his feet. 'Come with me,' he said. 'And don't ask questions.' He led the way out of his office, down the stairs and out through the front entrance, stiff-arming the door open and catching the guard on the steps by surprise. The man snapped off a belated salute but Massin barely lifted his chin in response. The two men were a hundred metres along the street and passing a small memorial garden with a commemorative stone to the fallen of both wars, when Massin indicated a bench set back against a screen of heavy bushes. There was nobody else around. He took a seat and motioned for Rocco to join him.

'If I'm correct,' he said stiffly, 'your investigation into Petissier's background will be thorough.' It wasn't a question.

'If I'm allowed the freedom to do it, yes.'

Massin grunted. 'I wouldn't expect anything less – of you, at least. Because of that I need to tell you something that might come out during your investigation. Petissier being the kind of man he is, I'm certain he will have kept records of everything that might have proven useful to him during his professional life.'

Rocco waited. Silence was the best response, and the obvious one: what the hell was Massin about to tell him?

'Following my... breakdown in Indochina,' he began, 'I was repatriated to France within a few days. I'm sure I don't need to explain why. It would be evident to you, more than most, that a senior officer in such circumstance is a curse on morale. I was hospitalised for many weeks, undergoing treatment and tests. In effect I was kept isolated from any connection with the military establishment. When I was released from there, I underwent several interviews about what had occurred. They were described as fact-finding interviews and conducted by a man who said he was an acting deputy advocate general on attachment, assigned to me by the military as a courtesy to my rank. A final appearance was before a military tribunal. It was the tribunal which decided my fate based on those interviews.'

'Do you have to tell me this?' said Rocco. He could see the pain etched on Massin's face as he relived the events following his return from Indochina. Even shell-shocked as he must have been, he could not have been unaware of the reactions of the people around him. For a senior officer to be brought back from a conflict under the shadow of what would have been viewed by many as cowardice, it would not have been pleasant, and some would have made their feelings only too clear.

'If I don't tell you,' Massin replied, 'I will have missed the only opportunity to do so. I can't do that.'

Rocco nodded. 'I understand.'

'I won't go into all the details, but the report placed before the tribunal was lacking in accuracy and, frankly, with the benefit of hindsight, a travesty of any kind of justice. But it was under the auspices of the military establishment and their main responsibility was to safe-guard the integrity and honour of the army. However, as I discovered later, the man responsible for interviewing me had never conducted a military interview before. He was not even of the army, but brought in from outside.' He grunted. 'I think it was a question of the military wanting to keep their distance in case of infection. I can only imagine more junior ranks must have suffered greater indignities with even less compassion. The result for me could not have been worse. I came to the conclusion that the acting DAG was concerned solely with using the situation as a stepping-stone on a career path to the top. And having a senior officer – especially a former Brigade C.O. like me to work on – must have been a godsend to him. I was a casualty of another man's ambition. He treated my inability to explain my actions with such casual indifference, even disdain, that by the time I came before the tribunal I had no defence to offer. Mentally I was in no fit state to answer his questions or the charges I faced, a fact which came out subsequently, although by then it was too late. His report consisted of two pages and a summary, which I confess I didn't fully understand at the time. But his verbal report was a lot longer, very damning and brutal in the extreme. I wasn't cashiered, but my military career was effectively over the moment he began speaking.' He stared down at the ground. 'It was pure theatre, much like many of his cases since then. He tore me, my service and any future hopes to shreds and I was in no condition to resist.'

'You couldn't appeal?'

'No. There was no process for doing so at that time. I was charged with two counts: offences against my honour and duty as an officer, and a dereliction of military discipline. It was explained to me that it would be preferable for the honour of the army if I were to take my leave and apply for alternative employment elsewhere.' He looked away, his face ashen. 'Due to the intervention of a friend from my days in the officer academy of St-Cyr, I was offered a middle-ranking post in the police. I was lucky to have even that, so I took it. As for the DAG, he had made an impression, gaining friends in high places in the process, and was marked for higher office in the judicial system. The rest is history.' He looked at Rocco. 'You may be wondering why I'm telling you all this.'

'I think I can guess,' Rocco said.

'I'm sure you can. It's not a confession intended as some kind of salve to my conscience, I assure you. The deputy advocate general who interviewed me and tore my career to shreds was Jules Petissier.' He got to his feet and walked away a few paces, then came back. 'What do you need from me, Rocco?'

'One man, that's all,' said Rocco.

'Desmoulins?'

'Yes.'

Massin stood very still, his eyes on the floor. Then he said, 'I have a proposal. These three men are all at a high level in the establishment. Getting to details of their connections and history won't be easy. In fact, I suspect it will prove impossible unless one can get at the others on the same level.'

Rocco was forced to agree. Desmoulins wouldn't be able to do that. Nor would he, without finding a mountain of hurdles against him all the way. He wasn't going to give up simply because it looked difficult, but wondered what Massin was thinking.

'What do you suggest?'

'I'll do it.'

Rocco nearly did a double take, but tried to keep his expression blank. Even so, Massin must have seen something in his eyes.

'I know what you're thinking: what can an officer like me possibly know of investigation techniques? I have to agree with you… but for one major difference. I know these people and their kind – especially Petissier. I know the way they think and the circles in which they move.

None of that will be open to you by going through official records because you'll be denied access. I'll be able to get to people that you won't.'

Rocco said nothing. He was trying to find an argument to counter Massin's proposal, but couldn't fault it. The *commissaire* was absolutely right; if you wanted information about a criminal gang, you didn't look through official records, you went to their friends, neighbours and colleagues and you did so covertly, using contacts who were above suspicion.

'You can still have Desmoulins,' Massin continued, 'but I suggest for leg-work only. You might not accept it but I think your investigation will be shorter than you expect. I never said this, but make no mistake, they will try to close you down as soon as they can. These three individuals are all too high profile to allow their misdeeds to come out into the public arena. Any one of them, if they became known, would provide a scandal the current administration doesn't need. Governments have crumbled at far less, and this one is currently very fragile.'

'Fine.'

'One other thing, Rocco. My involvement stays absolutely between us – understand?' He gave the ghost of a smile. 'I wouldn't want anyone around here thinking I wanted a change of profession.'

Chapter Fifteen

'You want what?' Detective René Desmoulins stared at Rocco in surprise. 'But I thought this whole Bourdelet thing was... well, a delicate situation, him being who he is. Sorry – was.'

'Are you saying you can't do discreet?'

'No, of course not... I mean, of course I can. But it's why they brought you in, isn't it? Need to know basis only.' He tapped the side of his nose. 'Top secret and all that.'

'You've been reading too many comics. But I suppose it's true enough. In any case, this is an important issue time-wise, and I can't handle it all myself. Nor can I farm it out to other stations. The Ministry is in a hurry as usual but they want discretion – and they're keeping an eye on me.'

'Seriously?'

'A black Peugeot 404, driver and passenger. And they're being very obvious about it. While they're watching me, they're unlikely to spot you. Are you in?'

Desmoulins was nodding eagerly before he'd even finished. 'Yes, of course. What do you want me to do?'

'Door-to-door stuff and finding any background information you can dig up from the three locations: neighbours, gossips, anything. You know what it's like, very few people live in a vacuum. They might have talked to someone they trusted.' Rocco dropped a slim folder on the desk. 'In here are the names and details of the three victims. There's a judge, a politician and a former senior cop, so don't go charging in with both feet.' He gave a wry smile. 'You can leave me to do that. We'll do Bourdelet first. I'll deal with the house and you can canvas the area. Somebody must have delivered the letter and it would help if we could find out who. I'll need to check we're not in conflict with any local investigations first but, as soon as I confirm we're clear, I'll leave you to it. Somebody might have noticed something, a person or car, maybe a motorbike.'

'Understood. What if we find nothing?'

'Then we look again. There has to be something. None of these letters dropped out of thin air. If we find the source for one it will lead to the others.'

'What makes you say that?'

'The letters are the common ground so far. That and the fact that each victim bought copies of paintings, probably from the same source. The writer must have been acquainted with all three men, or at least knew their backgrounds well enough to blackmail them about their weak spots. Finding out who won't be easy.' What Rocco didn't tell Desmoulins was that there was already a potential suspect, namely Cezard, but he didn't want to colour the younger man's judgement. It was better if Desmoulins went into this investigation with open eyes and a fresh approach. That way he might see something Dreycourt and Rocco could miss.

'Got it.' Desmoulins hesitated, scanning the names and addresses. 'Paris, Abbeville and Mers-les-Bains. That's going to take me out of the area. Can I do that?'

'Up to a point. Take it as read that you'll be out of your immediate jurisdiction some of the time, so don't tread on any toes and don't tell anyone what you're doing. I'm the visible face on this, you're in the background. Just keep it that way and stay in touch. Hand over anything urgent already on your desk to Massin and he'll farm it out. I've already cleared it with him.'

Desmoulins smiled. 'Fab.'

'Fab?'

Desmoulins' cheeks flushed. 'Sorry – it's a British expression. I picked it up from a friend. It's short for fab—'

'Yes, I worked that out, thank you.' Rocco nodded at the door. 'Don't let me hold you up. Go.'

Desmoulins went.

Rocco sat at his desk and chewed over what he had to do. A plan of action would be good, as he had a lot of ground to cover and not much time to do it. He would inevitably be forced to go over some of the same ground as Desmoulins, not because he didn't trust the young detective, but because he was going to approach the investigation in a different way. Hopefully when they came to compare notes they would overlap and that would point to a way forward. Gaining a common intersection for all three men would be hoping for too much, but you never knew. A senior member of the government, a judge and a senior cop: on the surface, it was quite possible they had met, even knew each other well. Social circles at the top of the tree invariably brought people together from different backgrounds. Their lives might have touched somewhere along the way, if only like billiard balls glancing off each other on a green baize table.

He still felt discomfited by what Massin had revealed to him. It had been uncommonly open of the man to bare his soul in the way he had, and Rocco felt a level of admiration for him in spite of their past clashes. Even more he sympathised with the loss of his career, and all because of a moment of weakness in an unbearable situation. Being dragged through a careless and uncaring grilling the way he had been was unprofessional and brutal enough, but the subsequent trashing of his character was as much the fault of the tribunal as it was Petissier's. How Massin hadn't harboured a deep abiding grudge against the man all these years was a mystery, and Rocco wasn't certain that he himself would have been so understanding.

He was relieved he hadn't had to work too hard to sell the idea of bringing Desmoulins into the investigation. It would be good training for the young detective. Massin's limited agreement was, Rocco understood, conscious of the Ministry and wanting to avoid reflections on himself if it didn't work out. Not that Massin was the only one with that outlook. It was an instinct for self-preservation common among most senior officers. Promotion was hard-won and the ground easily lost in a growing and flexing agency where competition was tough and there was always someone else on the career ladder looking for a chance to find a slot for their talents.

He pushed away from his desk and took a tour around the office, hoping for some inspiration. Without real-ising it, he ended up outside Doctor Bernard Rizzotti's office at the rear of the building. The stand-in pathologist was behind his desk, studying some papers, and Rocco knocked once and walked in.

'Ah, here comes trouble,' Rizzotti murmured, lifting his spectacles off his face and scrubbing at his hair. 'What have we got now? Don't tell, more dead bodies. I thought things had been a bit quiet lately.'

'No, nothing like that.' Rocco sat down. 'I need some inspiration.'

'Is that all? How about a drink? I have some fresh formaldehyde around here somewhere. Mix it with a healthy shot of fruit juice and it might do the trick. You could have some trouble standing up afterwards, but that's your risk.' He put the papers down. 'Is this connected with your new high-profile assignment in Paris? Bourdelet, isn't it?'

'News gets around fast.'

Rizzotti gestured at the phone. 'Fraternal and professional interest: the grapevine's been vibrating like a harp string, although from what I hear, there seems little doubt about what happened. He walked into his office, locked the door and shot himself while of unsound mind. Is that correct?'

'I'm not sure about the state of his mind, Doc. But it seems that way, from first reports.'

'No other way out, perhaps.'

'That's one of my questions. Is it possible for someone to be pressured into killing themselves?'

Rizzotti shrugged. 'I'm no psychologist, Lucas, but I've known of a few suicides driven by desperation or fear or loss. So yes, I suppose it's possible. They were mostly ordinary people, with what might be described as ordinary lives. I imagine a senior figure like Bourdelet might have seen an impending fall as more drastic than most, professionally speaking.' He gave a weak smile. 'It's not as if there are many jobs like that going around. If he had little else to hold on to, like a family, then he might have decided to let go very easily. But to judge that I'd have to have known him on a personal level.'

Rocco thought about it. Rizzotti was right, everyone had their own limits, their personal sense of what was too much to bear. Reputation and self-esteem were high up on the list for most people, and maybe Bourdelet had seen his imminent fall all too clearly, making his decision the only one possible.

'How about disgrace?'

'It would be more than enough for some, certainly; others might decide to fight it out, even disappear for a while until things blew over.' He gave a knowing smile. 'In my experience politicians are usually adept at weathering that kind of thing before emerging in a new guise once the dust has settled. I wish you good luck with this one, Lucas. You're going to need it.'

Chapter Sixteen

Rocco drove home with his head in a spin. He was followed part of the way by the Ministry car, before it peeled off and disappeared a couple of kilometres from the village. Getting bored already, Rocco thought.

He'd spent a couple of hours thinking over his plans, reviewing the three blackmail victims and what their possible connections might be. In the end he'd come up with nothing but speculation. The problem was he didn't know enough about any of them beyond their professional lives, and could only hope that Massin would be able to fill the huge gaps in his knowledge. Now his eyes felt gritty and he had a bad taste at the back of his throat. If he was going to attack this case, he was going to need a good night's sleep.

The first item on the agenda was a visit to Bourdelet's house. In his experience the place where everything began was likely to throw up some clues, and maybe he could find out more than there appeared to be on the surface. A chat with Bourdelet's housekeeper might help and, if he was allowed access, his driver and secretary.

He stopped at the village café in Poissons to buy some soft drinks. He would have preferred a decent bottle of wine, something light and refreshing such as a Muscadet, but that wouldn't help keep a clear head for the following day.

'Not going dry on us, are you?' said Georges Maillard, the owner, placing two dumpy bottles of orange on the counter. 'That would be sacrilege.' He was a large and untidy man, with a fragment of cigarette paper stuck to one lip and a three-day stubble like a harvested cornfield. He seemed to exude a permanent air of defeat, and had been unfriendly at first, until Rocco had helped him out with three men trying to force him into buying stolen alcohol. It hadn't made him any less melancholy or stopped him playing Georges Brassens endlessly in the café – a musical taste Rocco had never acquired – but he'd at least proved more approachable since then.

'Not yet,' said Rocco, and paid for the juice. 'Early start in the morning.'

'Ah. Tough luck. You around for the *fête nationale* on Tuesday? Lots going on and there's a strongman competition.' He almost smiled. 'Big chap like you would walk it, no problem. The local champion's good but about half your size and, between you and me, he's been drinking a bit recently.' He patted his own considerable paunch. 'Stops him being able to bend easily enough for the big lifts.'

Rocco had seen the posters advertising the events around the countryside and in Amiens, but hadn't given it much thought. Bastille Day was France's biggest celebration of the year, although some deferred to the Tour de France, which had passed through the region not long before. Every community held its own events and parades, some big, some small. Drink and music were a popular component whatever the size, making for a loud display of national pride.

'I can't recall when I last attended one,' he replied honestly. 'Always too busy.'

Maillard frowned, which was much more his usual expression, and scratched deeply at a large armpit. It sounded like scraping mud off the bottom of a bucket. 'That's shocking, that is. They work you too hard. You really should try this one, though; we're having a pig roast, which is a first. If you drop by, I might even go so far as to buy you a drink.' He winked and moved away, sweeping a cloth along the counter. 'You should take advantage of that while you can, know what I mean?'

Rocco didn't ask him to explain, but left and drove down the lane home. As he stopped outside his house, he caught a glimpse of Mme Denis in her garden, hacking at some long grass with a wicked-looking sickle. She looked up in mid-chop, saw him and, to his surprise, bustled indoors without acknowledging his arrival.

He remembered her previous abrupt greeting, which was so unlike her. And now this clear display, as if she were diving for cover. What was going on? One thing he'd learned since being here in Poissons was that leaving things to stew, as so many had done before, led to misunderstandings and extended feuds, some lasting years. Some had even led to violence. He couldn't picture Mme Denis hopping over the fence between their gardens one night and coming at him with her sickle, but it paid not to take chances.

He knocked at her door. It took another rap of the knuckles before she answered. She peered through the gap at him, blinking against the light like a dormouse coming out of hibernation.

'Yes?'

Rocco held up the two bottles of juice. 'I come in peace,' he said. 'Whatever I've done wrong, I apologise, and if it's something I haven't done, tell me so I can put it right.'

The old lady hesitated, then opened the door wider and looked from the bottles to Lucas's face. She batted a hand in the air and opened the door fully. 'It's me who should apologise,' she muttered, her face turning red. She turned away, allowing him to step inside. 'I've been a silly old fool. Come in and I'll get glasses.'

The air inside the house was cool and smelled of soap and vegetables, a heady mix Rocco had come to recognise and enjoy. It was a pleasant place to be: small, consisting of two rooms and a cellar, neat and spotlessly clean. He'd seen Mme Denis chase down a stray piece of fluff like a cat after a mouse on more than one occasion, which put his own housekeeping habits to shame.

She nodded for him to sit at the table, which was covered by a patterned oil-cloth topped by a central laced doily, and placed two thick glasses in the middle. Rocco opened one of the bottles and poured juice for them both, then lifted his glass in a toast.

'Death to our enemies,' he said, and when she smiled and raised her glass added, 'What's the problem? Is it your back? You know you can tell me.'

'My back's fine, thank you. It's not that.' She twirled her glass on the oil-cloth as if marshalling her thoughts. 'All right, I'll tell you. I have a friend here in the village, named Sylvia. Not a close friend but we chat every now and then about this and that.'

'You mean gossip?'

'Call it what you will. She has a nephew in Amiens. He's in the police there and they're close; she helped bring him up, in fact, when his mother fell ill. He's a good boy so I don't want to name him and get him into trouble. I know you could probably find out very quickly who he is by going through the files or whatever it is you do, but will you promise me not to go after him? He didn't mean any harm.'

Rocco wondered what was coming. 'Go on.'

'This... nephew rings Sylvia regularly for a chat, the way good nephews do, and told Sylvia something he'd heard in the office. Sylvia then told me and, well... it came as a shock, I have to say.'

'Go on.'

'You're leaving us.' She said it in a rush and put down her glass with probably more of a thump than she'd intended, slopping juice onto the oil-cloth. She brushed it away with the back of her hand, which was wildly out of character, and looked directly at him with an expression of sadness mixed, he thought, with embarrassment.

'I see. You know that's very serious, passing on that kind of information. It contravenes at least three laws that I can think of and—'

'Forget laws, young man. Is it true?' She stared at him.

Rocco smiled. 'Sorry, I was joking. The truth is, I've been offered a new job in Paris. It's going back to what I used to do, but at a more senior level. They're starting up a new division and want me to join them.'

'I see. That's good, I suppose, moving up in the world.'

'Maybe. I haven't given them an answer yet. There's a lot to consider.' He reached out and touched her hand. 'I'm sorry – that information isn't public yet and I thought I'd have time to make up my mind before talking to anyone. I was clearly mistaken, thanks to Sylvia's nephew.'

'That doesn't mean he's in serious trouble, does it?'

'Well, nothing that a spell in one of our remote Pacific Islands *territoires* won't put right. And yes, I'm joking again.'

'Of course you are. Thank you.'

He leaned forward. 'When I said before talking to anyone, I meant you.'

She smiled and patted his hand in return. 'That's very sweet of you, Lucas. And I shouldn't have jumped to conclusions based on what Sylvia's nephew told her.' She turned and looked at a photo on the wall. It was of her husband, Guillaume, resplendent in uniform on his cavalry charger in 1920, back ramrod straight. 'Guillaume loved horses. He wanted to be a jockey, did I ever mention that?'

'No.'

'Well, he did. It was his dream to ride at Longchamp in Paris. One race. He always said he'd have settled for that: one furious gallop down that famous course in front of all those cheering crowds. Actually, I think he'd have settled for doing it if the stands had been empty, and he'd have provided the background noise himself. He was good, too, which is why he joined the cavalry. He loved and understood horses, you see, knew how they thought, what would make a horse run.' She stopped and shook her head, staring into the distance at a long-held memory.

'What happened?' Rocco asked.

She shook herself. 'Well, the war for one. And... what do they call it – his genes. See that photo? That was taken when he was a young man – and tall. A lot taller than me. Someone once said we looked like a circus act, the two of us, side by side, but I didn't mind. In the end, though, his weight and height counted against him: too tall, they told him. So, he decided to do what he could, still with horses but not in racing.' She sniffed and took a sip of her drink. 'He became a farm worker, driving teams of horses behind ploughs, carts, harrows – anything where a horse could still be useful. Not that it was going to last forever, with those tractors taking over. But not everyone can afford them, even now. There are still plenty of farms where they use horses, and Guillaume, God rest him, would have still been out there if he was alive. He loved it, I could see that, every day when he went out. It was his dream.'

'But he missed his chance to race?'

She shrugged, a slow lift of her shoulders, and smiled. 'Maybe. It's hard to let go of a dream, especially one started so young.' She looked directly at him. 'And the point of me rambling on is that I want to give you one bit of advice, Lucas: you should do what *you* want. Not what your senior officers want, not what society expects… and certainly not what I might prefer. You only get one chance at this life, so don't let yourself be swayed by outside forces or silly sentiment. It's better to regret what you did do than what you didn't.' She nodded and finished her drink, putting the glass down, this time with a decisive firmness. 'If you decide to go, you'll be sadly missed around here, I can tell you. If you decide to stay, well, I'm sure crime will be the same and my hens will still be laying.'

'Even though they don't know they're being kept in the dark?' Rocco felt a tightness in his throat. If there was anyone he was close to in this community, it was this old lady, who had welcomed him from the very first day. He desperately didn't want to upset her.

'Even then. I haven't told them because the less they know the better. They clam up tighter than a banker's fist otherwise. Now, be off with you. Just promise me you'll let me know what you intend to do before anyone else in this village. I'd love to see the look on that Sylvia's face when she finds out I know more than she does.'

Chapter Seventeen

The streets of Le Vésinet were quiet when Rocco arrived the next morning and parked his car at the kerb outside the house named Les Jonquilles. The familiar Ministry car dawdling behind him parked a short distance away. Rocco thought about it for a moment, then walked over to the car and signalled for the passenger to wind down the window. The man complied with a scowl.

'You know whose house this is?' Rocco asked him.

The man nodded, staring straight ahead. His driver appeared more interested in his fingernails and said nothing, his hands flat on the wheel.

'Good. Then you'll know why I'm here. If you get in my way, I'll arrest you – and I have the paperwork to do it, no matter who you are.'

The window was wound back up again, and as Rocco entered the garden of Les Jonquilles he heard the car driving away.

Rocco one, Ministry nil, he thought.

Looking around, he had a faint recollection of having been in the area some time ago, although not to this particular property. Something to do with the theft of some jewellery, he remembered. Investigating the case had been like prising open a box of secrets, with the victim, a retired civil servant, seemingly anxious to keep the police out of his house and willing to write off the theft as a minor thing, really not worth their time or trouble. It had been his daughter who had discovered the break-in and made the call, unaware that her father was in possession of stolen goods acquired through dubious sources.

It was one of Rocco's first brushes with the hidden powers of the higher establishment. He'd been made sharply aware of his limitations when it came to intruding on their lives, even though he was merely trying to do his job. The one bright spot in the affair had been the civil servant finally admitting he'd bought the jewellery from 'a source' currently serving a lengthy sentence for dealing in stolen gemstones and other valuables.

The gates to Les Jonquilles stood open, with a police guard standing on the front steps of the house. He was young and clean-shaven, and his uniform looked as if it had been taken out of the box fresh that morning. A red line ran around his throat where his shirt collar had pressed into the skin, and Rocco felt a degree of sympathy; he'd gone through the same painful transition himself. New uniforms, whether military or police, were one of the many obstacles to be overcome by new recruits, as if the discomfort and tell-tale strangulation marks were designed to test willpower and poise. The young officer shifted his feet as Rocco approached, and finally stepped forward and held up a hand that hadn't yet learned to show the authority that went with the uniform.

'Sorry, but this property is off-limits.'

Rocco smiled and held up his card. 'I should hope so,' he said. 'It's sealed pending my investigation.'

The officer flushed and hopped to one side, throwing up a snappy salute. 'Apologies, Inspector,' he murmured. 'I was warned you would be coming, but I wasn't expecting someone on foot.' He looked past Rocco as if his car might suddenly appear rolling along the drive under its own steam.

'Relax, officer. I wasn't trying to catch you out. What's your name?'

'Mahon, sir. Gilles Mahon.' He stepped towards the front door and said, 'Mme Achard, the housekeeper, is in the kitchen, sir. Straight ahead of you to the rear of the building.'

Rocco nodded his thanks and wandered along a carpeted hallway to a kitchen large enough to do service in a restaurant. It seemed to contain all the latest pieces of equipment for producing meals on a grand scale, and he could have fitted his kitchen in Poissons into it several times over. A percolator on one side was issuing a drift of steam towards the ceiling, and a small woman in an apron was standing at a large double sink, staring out of the window into the extensive rear gardens. She turned suddenly with an expression of surprise, and he saw traces of tears down her cheeks.

'I'm sorry,' she said softly, picking up the hem of her apron and dabbing at her face. 'I didn't hear you come in. Are you the policeman who's come to see the painting? They told me to come in today to talk to you.'

'Inspector Rocco,' he confirmed. 'I'm sorry to disturb you, Mme Achard, and for having to ask you to be back here today. But I have just a few questions for you about Secretary Bourdelet. Can we sit somewhere?'

'Yes. I suppose so.' She looked around in confusion and said, 'Sorry, only I don't normally ask people to sit down in here. I've been trying to decide what to do but they said not to touch anything until you said. It's all so...' She lifted her hands as she ran out of words.

'I understand.' He gestured towards the percolator. 'That smells wonderful; perhaps we could have some while we talk? I know I could do with a cup.'

'Of course.' She seemed relieved to be doing something familiar and busied herself with practised efficiency, placing two coffee cups on a tray with a small jug of cream and a pot of sugar. 'I'll take them through, if you'll follow me?' Before he could offer to help, she had scooped up the tray and was off at a brisk pace, veering left out of the kitchen and along another short hallway to a doorway that led into a wood-panelled room that was part library, part office. It contained a large desk, an ornate sideboard, a card table with four chairs and two standard lamps with heavy lampshades. It felt more office than home, a masculine and formal domain. He checked the sideboard, which held nothing but a few framed photographs, showing group gatherings with some faces he recognised.

A painting – nearly two metres high and a metre wide – completely dominated one wall. What Madame Récamier's enigmatic gaze and the upward curl of her mouth showed was that the photo Dreycourt had given him did her no justice at all.

Mme Achard put the tray on the card table and gestured to a chair, waiting for Rocco to sit before she did. She placed a cup in front of him.

'I'll come to the point, *madame*,' Rocco said, after taking a sip of his coffee. 'As I understand it, Secretary Bourdelet bought this painting about a year ago. Is that correct?' He gestured at the wall.

'Yes, that's right.' She looked at it as if for the first time, her eyes moistening. 'He loved it. He said it was the best thing he'd ever bought… It was something he never tired of looking at. He once said it reminded him of someone he'd once known.'

'His wife?'

'No. Definitely not.'

'Do you like it?'

She looked surprised by the question and shrugged. 'It's not for me to say, is it? I'm just the housekeeper.'

'Personally, I think it's a bit overpowering, but I'm no expert. I'd rather look out of the window. I won't tell anyone what you think, I promise.'

She smiled and seemed to relax at last. 'She's pretty enough I suppose. Too pretty, actually.'

'Really?'

She looked a little guilty and explained. 'Call it a woman's vanity, Inspector. Having that on display is an unkind reminder of the aging process – and I'm just as vulnerable as the next person.' She flushed. 'I think he was a little in love with her, to tell you the truth. You must think I'm talking out of turn.'

'Not at all. We can't all like the same things. What a boring world that would be. Did he say where he bought it?'

'Not to me.' She sipped her coffee. 'It appeared one day and he got a man in to fix it to the wall. He did ask what I thought of it. As if my opinion mattered. But what could I say? He obviously loved it, so I told him it was a fine painting and went about my duties.'

'What about his wife? Did she like it?'

There was a moment's hesitation, then a shake of the head. 'She'd pretty much moved out by then. I think she'd lost interest in anything he did. She came back one day to collect some things, and I found her standing in here staring at it.' A hint of a smile touched her lips. 'She looked

124

as if she was thinking of taking a bread knife to it. In the end she just turned and walked out and never came back. Is it important?'

'Maybe. Maybe not.' Rocco stood up and went over to the painting. He tilted it carefully away from the wall and checked the back. Nothing to show its origins, no gallery name or number. Just a picture, and not one he'd want to hang on his wall. But then, he figured he'd be considered a barbarian by most art lovers, capable of walking past most great paintings with little more than a glance. 'I'd be interested in knowing where it came from, though. Did you see who delivered it?'

'A man in a truck. But I don't recall any details. Sorry.'

Rocco returned to the table. 'Does Monsieur Bourdelet have any children?'

'One daughter, Karine, but they fell out some years ago. She lives in the Netherlands and hasn't been back here since last year. They're not what you'd call a close family.'

'Did he keep a diary in the house?'

She nodded and pointed to the desk. 'It was in there.'

'Was?'

'Two men came yesterday. They looked through the house and took away some papers and the diary.'

'Do you know where they were from?'

'I think it was the Ministry of the Interior. They showed me their official cards, but I don't recall any details. Why they'd be interested in his diary was a puzzle, and I said so. It was his social record, not the Ministry one. Not that he had a busy social life lately. Just a few friends came over occasionally, and some visits he made. The truth is, since his wife left, he hardly went anywhere apart from the office and away on official business, so I don't know what good it would have done them to take it.'

Rocco felt a buzz of curiosity. The Ministry had sealed the house, complete with a guard, pending his investigation, yet that hadn't stopped them sending in a couple of men to check the place out for documents of interest. No doubt they'd been looking for corroboration of the accusation made about Bourdelet using state funds to buy the painting, but he wondered what else may have been spirited away in the process.

He finished his coffee and stood up. If there had been anything of interest here, it was by now beyond his reach. He thanked Mme Achard for her help and was about to leave when he had a thought.

'The diary taken by the two men. That was for the current year?'

She nodded. 'I expect you want the previous year's, don't you?'

'Please.'

She bustled across to the sideboard and opened one of the doors. Inside were a number of books which Rocco recognised as desk diaries. They must have gone back a dozen years. Mme Achard took the one off the top and handed it to him. It was heavy, wrapped in tooled leather, and a quick flick through the pages showed it had more outer substance than inner content. Whatever else Bourdelet may have been, he was certainly no social bunny. He handed it back to her.

'You don't think it will help?' said Mme Achard, 'with what happened to him, I mean.'

'I don't think so.' Rocco wondered how long it would take the men to realise what they might have overlooked and to come back for it. He might as well give them something else to do. 'Were there any other staff employed here, like a gardener?'

'He used a small contract firm, a father and son business. They looked after the place but he rarely spoke to them. They knew what he wanted and got on with it. There was nobody else.'

'One last question: a letter was delivered here on the day he died. I gather you had a medical appointment that day.'

'That's correct. An regular check-up. I have high blood pressure.'

'What time does the post usually arrive?'

'Eight o'clock. It can vary but not by much.'

'And what time did Secretary Bourdelet leave for the office every day?'

'Earlier than that – usually just after seven, but sometimes before. He liked to avoid the traffic and get organised for the day.'

Which meant the sender of the letter must have been aware of his routine, thought Rocco. It had been delivered in time for Bourdelet to take it with him to the office, where he'd arrived by seven-thirty, according to Dreycourt. 'Could it have been placed there the previous day?'

'I don't think so. I was here until gone ten doing some baking.' She flushed. 'He kindly allowed me to use the ovens here whenever I wanted to bake cakes because my oven at home doesn't hold the heat well. But it was always on the understanding that I gave him a slice or two.' She smiled at the memory. 'He had a sweet tooth.'

'How do you know a letter wasn't delivered?'

'Because I always make a point of checking the box as I leave, in case of late deliveries. And occasionally a member of the public might choose to write to him here. I didn't like to think of anything important being left in the box overnight.'

He thanked Mme Achard for her help and wished her well for the future, then walked back to his car, pausing to ask Officer Mahon a question on the way. The officer's answer was all he needed. There had been no moves yet to do a house-to-house check.

As he climbed back into his car, Rocco saw the familiar figure of Detective Desmoulins waiting by his Renault along the street. Rocco gave him a discreet nod, letting him know he should carry on, then drove away, heading towards the centre of Paris.

Chapter Eighteen

Detective René Desmoulins watched Rocco drive away then began his task of talking to the neighbours. Rocco's signal had confirmed what he'd already suggested: that there had probably been no attempt by the local police at canvassing the area for information, presumably on orders from the Interior Ministry. Exactly why he didn't know, but it left Desmoulins a clear run.

The entire street would undoubtedly have heard by now from the rumour mill that something was going on at Bourdelet's house, which was going to make his job a little easier. Rather than having to explain his reasons for being there, and waiting for people to get over the shock, they would probably be in a hurry to get him off the doorstep.

He braced himself before knocking at the first door, which was an impressive chalet-style building with metal shutters. This wasn't his first investigation by any means, but it was the first directly instigated by the Interior Ministry, and he didn't want to let Rocco down.

His knock precipitated a rattle of bolts and the turning of a key, before an elderly woman appeared. She made a lengthy examination of his official card after listening to his explanation for his visit.

She shook her head. 'I'd have been asleep at that time,' she said finally, light flashing off her thick-framed spectacles. 'Like all God-fearing folk. It's a dreadful thing to happen in this area. We're a peaceful, law-abiding community, not like some I could mention.' She thrust his card back at him. 'What are you going to do to make this area safe again, that's what I want to know? Any day now and the criminal masses will be moving in and none of us will be safe in our beds.'

'Madam, it was a suicide, not a crime,' Desmoulins reminded her soberly. 'There was nobody else involved.'

She gave him a vicious stare. 'Really? You think suicide's not a crime? You've plainly not set foot in a church lately, young man.'

Desmoulins felt his control of the situation slipping away. He tried to reassure her that she had nothing to worry about from criminal elements.

'That's easy for you to say,' she snapped. 'You're young and I bet you always carry a gun, don't you? I'm a frail widow barely able to walk.' With that she hopped back swiftly and slammed the heavy door in his face.

This call set the tone for the day. Each house brought no answers, long tirades about unstable politicians, crooks, conspiracies and suggestions that weren't far short of insane. In all, it was a normal day's police work as Desmoulins knew it, occasionally interesting, sometimes good-willed but mostly unproductive.

Eventually Desmoulins approached a house in which an elderly man was clipping a small bush to certain death in his front garden, while pretending not to watch the policeman's slow progress down the street. The local watchman, Desmoulins figured. Every neighbourhood has one, male or female, self-charged with keeping an eye on all the goings-on around them.

'Ah, I figured you for a *flic*,' the man said, eyeing the official card. 'I've been waiting for one of you lot to turn up. You'll no doubt be wanting to ask if I saw anything to do with Bourdelet at Les Jonquilles, won't you?' He stood up straight and brushed a stray leaf off his belly, before glancing around to see if he had a neighborhood audience. He didn't and huffed in disappointment, slipping his clippers into his pocket.

'That's very perceptive of you,' said Desmoulins. 'And did you?' As he spoke, he felt something tugging on his trouser leg and looked down to see a tiny dog, the size of a wet rat, sinking its sharp little teeth into the hem of the material.

'Filou, stop that,' the man muttered mildly. 'Sorry – he's harmless. Just don't let him cock his leg at you, that's all. He can pee for the Fifth Republic when he gets going. You wouldn't believe how much piss comes out of such a small dog.' He showed twin rows of yellowed teeth in a humourless smile. 'After hearing Bourdelet blew his stupid head off, I've been expecting the place to be crawling with uniforms. Instead of which there's just been the pimply youth on guard over there. He looks as if he's hardly begun shaving. And now you. Not exactly a convincing response is it, for such a big cheese? What kept you?'

Desmoulins bit his tongue and resisted the temptation to flick the rat-dog away into the flower border. 'You sound as if you weren't a fan.'

'What? Of Bourdelet? Damn right. Useless as a secretary of state and looked down on the rest of us as peasants. I never liked him, no. Is that a crime?'

'Did you see anything that day or the day before?'

'Like what?'

'I don't know. You seem the kind of person who might notice anything unusual in the area.' A nosy, self-righteous bastard in other words, he wanted to add.

The man stuck his chest out and nodded proudly. 'Well, I am known to be more on my mettle, as it were, than most of the old fossils around here. Sleepwalking to their graves, most of them, if not outright *cou-cou*.' He made a circular motion to the side of his head with his finger. 'Unlike them I've still got all my marbles and I like to keep an eye out.'

'And...'

'A yellow van, PTT yellow, drove by while I was out walking with Filou. Seven a.m. it was. I checked my watch. Served in the navy as an observer/gunner, you see, so I got used to logging things. The strength of any fighting force, observers, did you know that?'

Desmoulins didn't; he'd always figured on cooks being the centre of the military universe but he decided to keep that to himself. 'I have heard it said. Is seven early for the postal delivery in this area?'

'Well, yes. It's usually about eight. At least, it would have been if it had been a PTT van.' He said this with knowing emphasis, as if Desmoulins was mentally deficient, and smiled as if he'd just come up with the answer to solve the problem of Bourdelet's suicide.

'But you said it was PTT yellow.'

'Indeed I did. And it was. But it was only when it had gone that I realised it didn't have any of the usual markings on the doors. Right colour and all that, but no letters.' He took out his clippers and chopped off another branch. 'Being an observer, you see, I notice that sort of thing. But before you ask, I didn't get the registration number. To be honest, I had a swine of a headache and Filou here was holding on to his pee, so I wasn't fully focussed, you might say. Sorry.'

'Never mind,' said Desmoulins. 'That's very helpful of you, M—'

'Dupannet. That's one pee and two enns. Du-pann-et. Glad to be of service.'

Desmoulins left the ex-navy observer despoiling the bush and walked down the path with Filou snapping at his heels. He waited until the rat-dog followed him through the gate, then slammed it shut and walked quickly back to his car, leaving the dog barking excitedly as it took off along the pavement in the opposite direction with Dupannet calling it back without success.

Chapter Nineteen

While Desmoulins' lower leg was being assaulted by Filou, Rocco was making his way through the layers of security and bureaucracy at the Louvre Palace. It was a slow process. His police card appeared to carry less weight than he'd expected in these hallowed quarters. Responses varied between uncertainty and outright suspicion. So far, however, the letter of authority given to him by Dreycourt had been enough to get him through two levels to the third-floor landing, where he found another security desk.

Word had evidently gone out about his impending arrival. On his way up, he'd been aware of people looking at him with sombre expressions and standing aside as if he had a communicable disease. It was a common reaction to a police presence where death had occurred, and he didn't let it bother him. In a close-knit working environment like this, the death by suicide of a senior figure and a subsequent police investigation would create more ripples than a snap election.

'How do I know this is genuine?' said the latest security officer, stepping out from behind his desk. He flapped the letter of authority in a dismissive manner, having given it barely a glance. A lanyard hanging from his neck showed his name to be Brasseur C. 'You could be anyone.' His expression was deliberately blank and it was clear he was playing to the gallery of two other officials standing nearby, dressed in identical suits and lanyards.

Rocco struggled to hold his temper. He'd been fine with the first two checks, waiting for self-important bureaucrats to pass him on to the next level of official obstruction, but now his patience was growing thin. 'I'm a police officer investigating the suicide of a secretary of state, and that letter should be enough to confirm the fact.' He waited for a response but there was none. 'You could, of course, try ringing the telephone number in the letter to confirm my status – if that isn't too much to ask.'

The man looked at the letter more closely, his lips moving slowly as he did so. 'Inspector Lucas Rocco,' he read out, his voice echoing around the landing. 'From Amiens. Bit out of your jurisdiction, aren't you? Or maybe you don't have enough to do up there. What do they do up in Amiens, apart from growing sugar beet?'

Rocco said nothing as the man gave him a careful up-and-down look, focussing on his long coat. 'Feeling the cold?'

Before Rocco could reply, one of the other security men stepped forward and took the letter out of Brasseur's grip. He was neat and compact, and walked with a slight limp. 'I'll make the call, Inspector.' He threw Brasseur a warning look but it failed to register. 'Can you wait here, please?'

Rocco watched him hurry away. The man looked vaguely familiar but he couldn't recall where from.

Brasseur, meanwhile, was enjoying getting in Rocco's path too much to move. 'I'm sure it won't take long,' he said with studied insolence. 'If it's genuine, of course.'

Two minutes later the other man returned, slightly red in the face, and handed the letter back to Rocco.

'It's confirmed, Inspector Rocco,' he said quickly, glaring at his colleague. 'You're cleared to go. Last door on the left. My apologies for the delay.'

Rocco took the letter and folded it into his pocket. 'Have we worked together?'

'That's right, sir.' The man looked pleased at being remembered. 'Officer Tellier I was then, attached to the Clichy district. It was a while back, though. I was invalided out.'

'What happened?'

Tellier slapped his leg. 'I got in the way of a bank job getaway. It smashed my thigh and that was it.' He shrugged pragmatically. 'Dangers of the job, right?'

'I'm sorry to hear that. Good to see you again.' Rocco nodded and went to move on but found Brasseur still barring his way and now looking at his colleague with a venomous stare.

'Are you going to move,' Rocco said softly, 'or do I have to kick you down the hallway?'

After a momentary hesitation, Brasseur swallowed and stepped aside.

–

In contrast to the rest of the building, where activity was evident, the suite of offices assigned to the late Jean-Pascal Bourdelet were empty save for a woman in her sixties sitting quietly at her desk, staring into the distance. She was what some would call *soignée*, with elegant hair, a smart suit and careful make-up. She gave a start when Rocco appeared, and quickly dabbed at her eyes with a white handkerchief.

'I'm sorry,' she said softly. 'Inspector Rocco, isn't it? I was told you were coming.' She stood up and pointed towards an ornate wooden door across the way. A pair of wooden stands joined by a length of thick rope stood across it, barring entrance. 'You'll be wanting to go in there, I expect. Give me a moment and I'll move the rope and unlock the door.'

'No need, Mme Boyesse,' Rocco said, lifting a hand to stop her. He felt certain the last thing the poor woman wanted to do was to go anywhere near that door. As the first person on the scene, it undoubtedly hid an image she would remember for the rest of her life, and he was surprised she had come in to work at all.

She looked grateful and sank back in her chair. 'Can I get you anything, Inspector?'

He shook his head. 'No. Thank you. I won't be long. I believe nobody else has been in here since he died?'

'No. Well, just two men earlier, just before you arrived. Security, they said.'

Rocco felt a faint drumming in his chest. No doubt the same two men who'd cleared out his desk at home. 'What did they want?' According to Dreycourt, Rocco himself was to have sole access.

'I don't know. They showed me their security passes, so I had to let them through. Did I do wrong?' She looked concerned and he quickly moved to calm her down. She would have been following orders, so it was pointless blaming her.

'No. Not at all. Did you see if they took anything with them?'

'Some papers, I believe. They had a large cardboard box with them; it looked heavier going out than going in.'

'Fine. Please don't let anyone else in, will you?' He moved the rope and stepped inside the room, closing the door after him. The lock mechanism had been torn from the wood, he noted.

The office was spartan compared with some Rocco had seen, holding little in the way of furnishings and no personal touches such as family or official photos. Having seen Bourdelet's home, Rocco came to the conclusion that, apart from the painting in his study, Bourdelet had simply preferred unfussy minimalist surroundings.

He stood for a while, absorbing the atmosphere. The air was heavy with a smell he'd come across too many times in the past, in battle and in peacetime, and he quickly pushed it to the back of his mind. Death always carried a lingering atmosphere, but violent death held an aroma all of its own.

The desk was covered with a grey blanket. He lifted one corner. There had been no attempt at cleaning it or the floor in the immediate vicinity. The blood had dried to a near-black hue where it lay thickest on the desk's leather-inlaid surface, with heavy brown spots on the floor and on the chair where Bourdelet had been sitting. The chair had been pushed to one side, no doubt while removing the body.

Rocco checked the ceiling and walls, but they were devoid of any blood, thanks to Bourdelet's thoughtful covering of his head with his jacket.

The jacket and the gun were gone, along with the letter, a copy of which Rocco had in his pocket. He checked the desk drawers, but they had been emptied of all but office stationery, pens, a large ink bottle, writing pads and paper clips. The doors of a tall cupboard against one wall hung open, revealing a bare interior, and he wondered what had been removed so completely. Secrets of state not even an investigator should see? Or was someone higher up the chain of authority being ultra-cautious? He would probably never know.

He took a tour around the room but saw nothing worth pursuing. The windows were shut fast and didn't appear to have been opened in a long while. That did away with any possibility of a locked room mystery and another's hand in Bourdelet's death. And now it wasn't even a crime scene in the normal sense, since there was no longer a body or a weapon. The removal of evidence had happened, so it was too late to do anything about it now; he would have to accept what the first people in the room had seen and take their word for it.

He was about to leave when the door opened in a rush and a tall man in a smart suit stepped inside. He was in his early fifties, Rocco judged, tall and fit and, by the look of him, an ex-cop, probably early-retired and on his second career. He wore no lanyard, but carried the authoritative bearing of a man in charge. Behind him Rocco could see Mme Boyesse looking agitated.

'You're Rocco, I take it,' the newcomer announced, and extended a hand. 'Captain Goubier, head of security. Any problems?'

In other words, Rocco read, how long are you going to be here and when are you getting out of our hair?

'Nearly finished,' he replied, and shook the man's hand, then gestured at the desk and cupboard. 'There's not a lot left in here. Why is that?'

'Ah, yes. We removed a few items of a sensitive nature, such as files and folders, that kind of thing. It's standard procedure when an outsider comes in.' He gave a thin smile. 'No offence, of course.'

'But it's a crime scene.'

'Really? I thought it was suicide.'

'I was tasked with investigating a death. It's the same thing, with the same rules of procedure. The office should have been sealed with all access barred. Or was the gun sensitive, too, in a locked room?'

'That wasn't my decision.' Goubier coloured slightly. 'Orders came from on high. Bad enough having a body with a hole in the head on the premises, let alone a weapon lying around.'

'Where is it now?'

'The body?'

'The gun.'

Goubier said nothing and Rocco realised he wasn't about to get an answer. After an awkward silence, he asked, 'As head of security, answer me this: there are at least three security checks on the way into the building, yet Bourdelet managed to bring in a loaded firearm. How could he do that?'

Goubier looked uncomfortable. 'The checks are – or were – fairly basic in nature. In any case, as secretary of state he wouldn't have been subjected to a search. But after what happened,' he shrugged, 'we've been told to be more thorough in future. Is there anything else?'

'Who was first on the scene?'

'Well, Mme Boyesse was nearest, of course, although the door was locked from the inside so she couldn't get in. She summoned one of my security officers and he broke in.'

'I'd like to speak to the man involved.'

'What good would that do?'

Rocco sighed. 'It's called crime scene detail. The room has been extensively disturbed and it's important to confirm what the first arrival saw.'

'Sorry, but he's on sick leave. The whole thing hit him rather badly.'

Rocco stared at him, unsure if the man was joking. He concluded not. 'You must be so proud.'

Goubier frowned. 'I don't understand. Proud of what?'

Rocco nodded towards Mme Boyesse in the outer office. 'To know that at least there's someone around here with the courage to carry on with their job regardless.' He ignored the way Goubier flinched. 'Bourdelet was assigned a driver. I'd like to talk to him.'

Goubier gave an almost imperceptible shift of his eyes. It wasn't much but enough.

'What?' Rocco snapped. This was a farce.

'I'm afraid that won't be possible. Lopez has been reassigned.'

'That was quick. On whose orders?'

Goubier looked towards the ceiling but said nothing. Instructions from on high, was what he meant. He just couldn't bring himself to say it out loud.

'Where has he gone?'

'I don't know. They don't have to tell me these things.' He actually managed to look embarrassed at the admission and looked away. 'Sorry.'

'Me, too,' said Rocco. 'Me, too.'

–

Rocco left the Louvre Palace with more questions than answers, and a feeling that too many doors had been slammed shut too quickly. But, judging by the way Bourdelet had lived, both professionally and privately, with few unnecessary embellishments other than a dubious work of art, he doubted there would have been many clues for him to discover. What had driven the man to go to his office to kill himself, however, was probably something only Bourdelet could have answered. Was it some sort of stab back at his former place of employment, like an end-of-term schoolboy prank?

By the time he got back to Amiens it was late. He found Desmoulins waiting for him with a report on his trawl of the neighbourhood around Bourdelet's home. The only high point was the reported sighting of a yellow van.

'It's a lead,' Rocco assured him, 'and worth keeping in mind. Bourdelet's housekeeper said there was nothing in the postbox when she left at ten the night before.'

'So the van could have dropped off the letter earlier that morning.'

'Yes. As your man said, right colour and easy to mistake for a genuine PTT vehicle. Ring the local depot, will you, and ask if they have any unmarked vans in their fleet.'

'Already done,' said Desmoulins. 'They haven't any and it was definitely too early for a delivery to that area.'

Rocco smiled. 'Good work, René. It's a step forward.'

Desmoulins acknowledged the compliment with a nod. 'So what next?'

'Mers-les-Bains. The same exercise in the neighbourhood around Gambon's house. See if someone noticed anything.'

'And Abbeville, near Petissier's home?'

'That, too, as soon as you can.'

'Will you be coming?'

'Not immediately. I'll be visiting Gambon's place at some stage, too. But first I need to speak to a master forger.'

Before leaving the office, he rang Sébastien Cezard. Eliane answered.

'Hello, Lucas. I'm sorry, but Pa's in the middle of a project. I don't want to disturb him unless it's absolutely urgent, but I will if you want me to.'

'No. I just wanted to see if he's going to be in tomorrow. I'd like a chat.'

'That's fine. He'll be here, since he rarely goes out. I'll tell him to expect you. Can I tell him what it's about? It's not more shooting, is it?'

'No. Not that. I'd like to seek his expertise on a subject.'

'Oh, very well.'

Next, he rang Claude and arranged to pick him up the following morning.

'Sure. Where are we going?' Claude asked. 'Will I need my gun?'

'Not this time. I think we've frightened enough people. We're going to make another call on Cezard and show him some photos. I'd like you to watch his reaction.'

'Suits me,' Claude replied, a laugh in his voice. 'This has nothing to do with Eliane being easy on the eye, has it? You being single and she being... well, also single?'

'You're an old romantic and the answer's no.'

'Damn. You're going to die a lonely old detective, you know that?'

Chapter Twenty

The third-floor security guard, Brasseur, had watched from along the landing as Rocco left Bourdelet's office and walked back down the stairs. The investigator hadn't been inside very long, which meant he'd found nothing to speak of or had quickly discovered something important.

He saw Tellier approaching and called him over.

'What's the idea, being all pally with the big cop?' he muttered. 'You made me look a fool – you should have backed me up. I was only having a bit of fun.'

Tellier shook his head slowly, not intimidated by Brasseur's bullying approach. He'd come across the type too many times before. 'You should learn to read people better,' he said bluntly. 'Rocco's not someone you want to mess with. And given that he's been handed the authority to investigate Bourdelet's death, he carries more weight than you or I will ever do. On the basis of that letter he could have had you arrested for obstruction.'

Brasseur didn't get the message. 'Are you kidding? He's a country cop, that's all. That letter just makes him think he can punch above his weight. Or do you know better? You seemed cosy enough the two of you, like a kid with his favourite teacher.'

'All I know is he was decent to work with and a good cop.' He started to walk away, then stopped and turned back. 'You weren't on the force so I don't suppose you'll have heard of a man named Samir Farek.'

'No. Should I have?'

'He was a gang leader here in the city, had a base in the Belleville area. He was a vicious bastard and was heading for the top of the tree, disposing of anyone who got in his way. He had a brother named Lakhdar, who was just as bad but with more brains.'

'So?'

'Lakhdar hired an assassin to take him out. Rocco took them all down. There were others, too, before that. The reason he got transferred up north was on some Interior Ministry assignment, not because he was stupid or incapable.'

Brasseur wasn't impressed. 'Yeah, yeah – now I'm bored. Look after the desk, I'm going for a smoke.' He walked away along the landing and entered the small room where the security personnel rested when they weren't on duty. He checked nobody was approaching, then picked up a phone on the desk and dialled a number in the southwest of the city.

It rang twice before being picked up. As usual there was no greeting. Brasseur licked his lips before saying, 'I've got the information you wanted. The cop handling the Bourdelet suicide is called Rocco. Lucas Rocco. He's based in Amiens. It's up north.'

'I know where Amiens is. Go on.'

'He's been and gone. Showed up all important and throwing his weight around but didn't get much. The security section had been in just before he got here and removed anything important from Bourdelet's office.'

There was a pause, then the man on the other end said, 'You know for sure that he found nothing? Were you in the room with him?' The voice was soft, but something in the tone made Brasseur go cold around the shoulders. He realised he'd said too much.

'No. Sorry, I mean… I don't think he'd have got much.'

'You're paid to report, not to think.' There was a click and the line went dead. Brasseur put the phone down and remembered to breathe again. He took out a cigarette and sucked in a lungful of smoke, his hand shaking. He needed a drink. Just a small one. He also wanted to turn the clock back and not be involved with the man on the other end of the phone. But it was too late for that. A bad gambling habit had been enough to put him in debt with no way out.

Less than eight kilometres away from where Brasseur was steadying his nerves, Yuri Serban stood up and stared out of his window at his base in Ivry-sur-Seine. There wasn't much to look at, but that was the way he liked it. Ordinary buildings in an unremarkable neighborhood where nothing much ever happened. It allowed him to operate without wondering if the doors were going to be kicked in at any minute by the heavy boots of the CRS. The *Compagnies Républicaines de Sécurité* were well known for their forceful methods. Being made to hand responsibility to people he didn't trust, such as Brasseur, was never easy, but staying ahead in the information game was vital. Gathering information from a variety of sources to which he didn't get easy access was part of the business he was in. Information was like gold: difficult to come by, but worth the investment if it produced results. Sometimes the sources and informants failed at the simplest of tasks, sometimes they came up with something worthwhile. Right now, he was trying to decide on which side of the divide this latest information fell.

Serban had heard the name Rocco before. He couldn't recall the precise facts, but he had a feeling Rocco had been a thorn in the side of certain gangs in the north of the city. He rang a contact in a research section of the local police. This man was an officer who enjoyed regular payments into a bank account in return for useful nuggets of information. He gave the man Rocco's name and waited for him to call back. It didn't take long. He listened in silence, making an occasional note, then thanked his contact and replaced the phone.

Another key aspect of his business was deciding when to get involved and when to pull back. Even more critical was knowing when to cut his losses. With a small operation like his, it would be easy to overstretch his resources, placing him in a vulnerable position and open to attack. He wasn't sure about this man Rocco. To continue with the project meant dealing with a tough investigator not known for giving up easily, if his contact was to be believed. On the other hand, calling time on a potentially useful source of income risked having another group step in and take over. And his pride would not allow that to happen.

His pride.

It was something which burned bright inside him, demanding much, seeking more, but always kept in check due to an innate sense of caution. He'd seen too many others in his position end up face down in a gutter after overestimating their abilities. There were many routes to success, but the man who found a new method of sourcing money from, or influence over, others was likely to come out on top. Until recently he'd been happy to trundle along doing his own thing his own way, staying out of trouble. But this scheme brought to him by the man known as *Maître* had stirred something inside him. He wanted more, even if things so far hadn't gone quite as planned.

Caution told him that if Rocco was as good as his reputation, it might be safer abandoning the project and getting out. But something inside him wouldn't let go that easily. What if he could take it over himself? As part of the original proposal, he'd made sure of learning more about the background behind the three letters. On seeing the names of the targets, he'd been instinctively wary. They were all high profile, and only the president himself, surrounded by a phalanx of bodyguards and the best resources France had to offer, would have presented a greater risk.

He dialled another number.

'Rocco?' The man sounded surprised, his cultured tones unaffected. 'Yes, I've heard of him. He has a reputation for fighting criminal organisations much larger than yours, but I believe he's been posted out into the middle of nowhere. I wouldn't concern yourself, Yuri. If they brought in such an outsider it's because they want to make sure the investigation falls flat and stays out of the media. From what I've heard Rocco is no lover of the press, so I doubt he'll talk. In the end, when he gets nowhere, the Interior Ministry will tell him with great relief to drop it. Case closed, end of a potentially damaging scandal.'

'I hope you're right,' said Serban. 'What about the other targets?'

There was a slight pause. 'What about them?'

'You said there would be others if these first three failed to make a return.'

'Ah, those. They're of little interest to me. I'll have to think about it.'

'Are you saying you're willing to pass up a lucrative business?'

'Let's say they don't have quite the… relevance of the first three. They were in the background as make-weights. Don't worry, Serban, you won't lose out. If I decide not to proceed further, you'll still be paid, I promise. I think you'll be pleased with the amount.'

There was a click and the line went dead.

Serban dropped the phone into its cradle and breathed deeply. The other man had just made a big mistake: he'd underestimated Serban's ambition. Serban stood up, forcing himself to remain calm. He'd see how the other targets played out first, before making a decision. Perhaps he needed to make the man who called himself *Maître* a surprise visit.

Maybe it was time, he thought, eyeing the distant horizon. Time to spread his wings and move up in the world.

Chapter Twenty-one

Detective Desmoulins had never been to Mers-les-Bains. His occasional days out *en famille* as a child had been limited to the neighbouring town of Fort-Mahon-Plage, 30 km to the north. Given a fast turn of speed when his parents weren't watching, its wide stretches of sand allowed him and his brother to get far beyond calling range before they could react. Since then his wife, Sandrine, had ventured the occasional wish to try somewhere different, like Mers, but pressure of work had never allowed it.

Right now, he was wishing he'd brought her with him; he could have left her to enjoy the beach while he did the detective bit around the neighbourhood home of Jean-Marie Gambon.

It soon proved to be a re-run of his visit to Le Vésinet, with few people willing to talk, most claiming they hadn't seen anything worth mentioning and only a couple happy to dish any dirt on their neighbour, the former Director General of the *Sûreté Nationale*.

'He'd been fooling around with that young house-keeper of his for a couple of years – even before his wife left him,' said a Mme Challonnet. Her face twisted in disapproval at the idea and she nodded towards the Gambon house just along the road, where a uniformed officer was pacing up and down. 'And him a senior policeman, once. Is that why he tried to hang himself – because of the shame?'

Sensing the absence of helpful information, Desmoulins asked a few more questions before moving on. Another neighbour suggested that Gambon was part of a secret cabal of politicians, senior cops and civil servants trying to overthrow the state from within.

'It's blatantly obvious to the rest of us.' M. Medioni was a scarecrow of a man with liver spots and a nasal voice, and the shrewish look and narrow face of a zealot. 'So why you lot haven't been able to see it is beyond me. What the hell do we pay you for, tell me that?'

Desmoulins stepped back a pace from the powerful smell of brandy emanating from the man, feeling his willpower beginning to slip away. Many more interviews like this and he'd throw himself in the sea.

'Don't worry,' he said quietly. 'We know all right – and we're keeping an eye on all of them.' He touched the side of his nose with his forefinger.

'Ah.' Medioni's eyes went wide and he brightened up considerably, his mad suspicions vindicated. 'Of course. That's good to know, officer. Excellent. I knew I was right.'

Desmoulins said, 'But keep it to yourself, understood? We don't want to tip our hand too early and ruin the chances of an arrest.'

'Absolutely.' Medioni frowned. 'Sorry – you asked about something else.'

'A yellow van. Have you seen one in the area in the past few days?'

'Only the PTT van. It comes every day. Like clock-work.'

'Are you sure it was the PTT that you saw every time?'

'Absolutely. The driver is my niece's boy, Allain, so I always watch out for him, to give him a wave.'

Three doors along, after ringing the bell, Desmoulins found himself confronted by an excited-looking individual in a bright yellow shirt and red trousers who virtually leapt out to greet him.

'Have you got the papers?' the man demanded, grabbing him by the arm. 'Coulibay's the name. Philippe Coulibay.' He spelled it out. 'Court papers… they should have been here by now.'

'Sorry,' said Desmoulins, gently prising the man's fingers from his arm. 'But I'm not here to deliver any court papers.'

'What? Christ, when are they going to get here, eh? When?' Coulibay slapped a hand against the side of his head in obvious frustration and stared wildly each way along the street. 'I'm going through a bastard of a divorce,' he muttered angrily, even though Desmoulins hadn't asked. 'Being fleeced, I am. Robbed. Mugged. She wants eighty per cent of everything. *Eighty!* I need to sign the final papers before she gets any other ideas and hires some crooked private detective to cook up more lies against me. The way things are going right now I might as well save everyone the effort and put a gun to my head, except she'd probably want the cost of the bullet, too.'

'You need to calm down, M. Coulibay,' Desmoulins advised him. 'You'll make yourself unwell. And, believe me, that's no way to solve the problem. In any case,' he added, 'I believe the usual division in divorces is fifty-fifty.'

He made his escape while Coulibay was trying to think of an answer, and was fifty metres down the street when he heard someone puffing up behind him and turned to find the stick figure of M. Medioni trotting along the pavement.

'Officer. Officer,' he gasped nasally, and slowed to catch his breath. 'Sorry – I was wrong earlier. I did see another yellow van the other day. I didn't really give it a thought until you mentioned it just now, but I remember seeing it stop at Gambon's house. I thought it was Allain, my niece's boy, at first, but then I noticed it didn't have the proper insignia on the side, like they're supposed to. I was going to mention it to Allain, but it slipped my mind.'

Desmoulins felt a thrill run through him that he wasn't about to let go. This was better than anything so far, supporting the sighting by Dupannet in Le Vésinet. 'Okay,' he said. 'Slow down, sir. Deep breaths. Did you get a look at the driver or the registration?' It was too much to hope for, he thought; around here they all seemed to be a bottle short of a full crate.

'I did. Both.' Medioni breathed deeply, then in a rush added, 'The driver was a sallow individual, like those types who haven't had a touch of sunshine in their lives. He had on a peaked cap but it wasn't the official issue. He reminded me of a skinny version of... what's that comedian who does the Don Camillo films?'

'Fernandel?' A vision of a big face and a wide smile full of teeth popped into Desmoulins' head. God on a bicycle, he thought, he should be easy enough to find.

'That's him. Only skinnier and paler and not so many teeth.' Medioni laughed. 'Maybe he didn't look so much like him at all, now I come to think of it. Anyway, I'm glad I remembered that detail. I bet it helps, doesn't it?'

'I think it might.' Desmoulins kept his expression blank and wondered how on earth he was supposed to find a face that looked nothing like the actor comedian, except in Medioni's insane imagination. 'What about the registration?'

'Sorry, that went right out of my head.' He scowled. 'I mean, I did see the registration, so you'd think I'd be able to call it to mind… but no. Sorry. It was a Paris number, though, I remember that much.'

Ten minutes later, after leaving a phone number for Medioni to call if he remembered anything else, followed by a phone call to the office with details of the second appearance of a yellow van, Desmoulins was on his way back to Amiens. It might turn out to be nothing, but he hoped and suspected not. Bigger cases had been solved because of more slender clues, and if whoever was delivering the letters had made a slip-up, it could all hinge on finding the vehicle.

Chapter Twenty-two

A new blue Mercedes with a soft top and whitewall tyres was parked at the front of the château when Rocco and Claude arrived the next morning. It carried a Paris registration and looked polished and buffed to an eye-watering shine, in stark contrast to the state of the ancient building and its sagging structure. There was no sign of the sporty blue Renault.

'Not Cezard's car,' said Claude, before Rocco could ask. 'I checked. He doesn't go out much but when he does, he drives a banged-up old Peugeot 203. Probably keeps it out back somewhere.'

Rocco knocked on the front door. Sébastien Cezard opened it, wearing a paint-spattered shirt, trousers and carrying a cheroot.

'Lucas… Claude,' he greeted them. 'Eliane told me you were coming. I'm afraid she's had to go out – but not to avoid you, though, I promise.' He laughed nervously, his eyes shifting to the Mercedes outside. 'What can I do for you?'

Rocco said. 'May we come in?'

'Sure. Of course.' He stood back and waved them inside. 'I've got a visitor with me at the moment from Paris. But if you don't mind joining us, you're welcome.' He turned and set off along the hallway to the room where they had first met.

As they entered, a figure turned towards them from the window overlooking the rear gardens. He was tall and upright, with carefully coiffed grey hair swept back on either side of his head. Clean-shaven, he was dressed in a smart navy-blue suit, a white shirt and maroon tie, and carried the confident and prosperous air of a big city businessman.

Sébastien made introductions, scattering ash from the cheroot onto the carpet. 'Inspector Rocco and Officer Lamotte. Laurent Vauquelin, my agent and lawyer.'

The three men shook hands and Rocco wondered what the other man was doing there. From the way Vauquelin was looking at him, he got the impression the lawyer wasn't surprised to see him.

'So, you're not local,' Rocco said, to break the ice.

'Heavens, no.' Vauquelin lifted an eyebrow, as if the very idea was ridiculous. 'I come out here only when absolutely necessary, to see my client. And it would appear that my timing might be appropriate. May I ask the reason for a visit from two officers of the law?'

'That depends. Are you asking as an agent or a lawyer?'

'I ask as a lawyer. Is that a problem?' Vauquelin appeared unruffled by Rocco's response, knowing he had the upper hand if his client wanted him present. 'Perhaps we can start with seeing some documentation.'

Rocco held up his ID card so that Vauquelin had to move closer to see it. He'd met individuals like this before. In the Paris courts they held sway like dangerous big cats. Smooth, educated, well-heeled and with a carefully culti-vated arrogance, they exuded authority, especially when defending clients of a dubious nature. Their approach was to treat the police as the enemy, with barely-concealed contempt. In the close confines of the wood-panelled courts with their sombre, lofty atmosphere and rituals, which few policemen were able to confront on equal terms, it often worked.

'I don't want to interrupt your meeting,' Rocco said, 'but I have a couple of questions to ask Monsieur Cezard.'

'About what?'

'I need his professional opinion.' Rocco could see he wasn't going to get past the lawyer for long, so he took the envelope Dreycourt had given him from his pocket and extracted the photos of the paintings. Addressing Sébastien, he continued, 'Have you seen these three paintings before?'

Sébastien took the photos and leafed through them, lifting his glasses to study them more closely and humming as he did so. He looked up at Rocco. 'I think so, almost certainly. They're quite well known, of course. But I can't recall exactly when and where I saw them last. Why do you ask?'

Rocco was aware of Vauquelin edging closer, like a cruising shark looking for someone to bite. Before the lawyer could intervene, he said, 'You've no doubt heard about Secretary of State Bourdelet's suicide?'

'Yes.' Sébastien nodded. 'A ghastly business. So sad when someone takes his own life.'

Vauquelin showed no such empathy. 'What has that got to do with my client?' he demanded, as if anxious to regain some measure of control over the conversation.

There was little point in Rocco pretending the main issue behind Bourdelet's death was anything other than the painting, since the news about it was now in the public domain, so he tapped the relevant photo with his finger and said, 'This particular item is hanging on the wall of Bourdelet's home. It's a copy of the original. On the day of his death he received a blackmail letter accusing him of using government funds to buy it. It's believed the accusation led to him taking his own life.'

It didn't shift Vauquelin's demeanour one bit. 'Again, I ask the question, what has that to do with my client? You're seriously overstepping your authority here, Rocco. What has Secretary Bourdelet's death got to do with... well, a rural police force?'

Rocco ignored the slight. 'I've been given the responsibility to investigate the death by the Interior Ministry. I could show you my letter of authority but I won't.' He turned to Sébastien. 'It's been suggested that you may have produced this painting. Is that true?'

Sébastien opened his mouth to reply but Vauquelin beat him to it, chopping the air with his hand to cut him off. 'Who suggested such a thing?'

'I'm not at liberty to say.'

'Are you accusing my client of forgery? Is that what this is about?'

Rocco looked at the lawyer. 'I'm not accusing him of anything. Unless you know better?' He turned back to Sébastien. 'It's not a crime to produce copies of old works of art... not unless it's meant to fool someone into buying it as an original, which doesn't appear to have been the case here. But since this painting was central to the letter and Bourdelet's reaction to receiving it, it might help my investigation if I could find out where he bought it in the first place. Monsieur Cezard?' He was careful to observe a formal approach, aware that any lack of correctness with Vauquelin there could come back to bite him.

The lawyer's mouth snapped shut, unable to counter Rocco's question.

Sébastien looked lost for words, his eyes darting between Rocco and the lawyer. 'I… I don't think so. To be honest I can't remember.'

Vauquelin gave out a hiss of breath. 'You don't have to answer that question, Sébastien. Inspector, this is deplorable. Either you suspect my client of something, in which case you should say so and make a formal charge, or you should leave.'

Rocco said nothing, his eyes on the artist, whose cheroot had gone out. The fact that Sébastien had said he couldn't remember painting it was not an outright denial, merely an agreement that he might have done. Either way it didn't incriminate him unless Rocco could find a trail to follow.

'Without accusing you of anything, is there a possibility that you did paint it?'

Sébastien took a drag at the cheroot, and looked puzzled when it didn't produce any smoke. 'I… I might have – a long time ago. One does many things when one is trying to get a name—'

'Enough!' Vauquelin jumped in and glared at Sébastien. 'This has gone far enough and I strongly advise you to say nothing else unless you're charged with a crime. Inspector?'

'No charge,' Rocco said calmly. 'I'm done, thank you.' He smiled and stepped back, nodding towards Claude. 'Although there is still the question of the gunfire we last spoke about – but that's a question for Officer Lamotte.'

Vauquelin sighed and waved the matter aside as if he were bored with it already. He looked at Sébastien. 'You'd better tell them if you know anything, Sébastien, then we can let them get on with some serious policing. My apologies, but I have other business to attend to. Call me if there are any problems.'

On that pointed note, after a brief handshake with his client, he turned and walked from the room without so much as a glance at the two officers. Moments later they heard the front door closing, followed by the sound of the Mercedes driving away.

'Friendly sort,' murmured Claude, and went over to the window and stared out into the garden. 'Wish I had a garden like this. How many rows of potatoes and onions I could get in there. I'd make a fortune.'

'I'm sorry,' Sébastien replied, nodding towards the departing lawyer. He seemed genuinely regretful and tried to explain it away. 'I'm afraid Laurent's very protective on my behalf, always has been. He tends to see everything as some sort of threat to my livelihood.'

Rocco wondered if that was the reason Sébastien seemed a little on edge, and why he'd felt it necessary to defend the lawyer. Or was there something else? 'His livelihood also, if he's your agent,' he suggested.

Sébastien grunted. 'I suppose. I never thought of it that way. He probably looks on me as a naïve and gullible paint-splasher who's going to get taken in by anyone who comes along. Or maybe he thinks I might start selling my work behind his back and cutting him out of the deal to save on the commission.'

'Did you tell him we were coming?'

'Well, not deliberately. He happened to be here about another matter and I mentioned your intended visit. He said he would stay on until you called. I told him it wasn't necessary but he's what you might call a force of nature: difficult to put off when he's concerned on a client's behalf.'

'You've known him for a while, then?'

'A few years. He helped me out over a non-payment which went to court, and another case when I was accused of breach of copyright. He got me my payment and the case against me was dismissed, so you could say I was very grateful. After that, he offered to represent me and has done so ever since.' He relit his cheroot, puffing a cloud of smoke into the atmosphere with a deep sigh. 'Would you like some tea? Eliane would never forgive me if I didn't offer. She's a stickler for etiquette, although,' he winced slightly, 'not where Laurent's concerned, I'm afraid.'

'Not keen?'

'Sadly, no. She's never taken to him, which is why she decided to go shopping when I told her he was coming. My daughter's headstrong, like all young women these days. Sorry – did I ask if you wanted tea?' Sébastien's mind seemed to be somewhere else, and Rocco wondered if it was a typical artist's manner or a reaction to the visit from Vauquelin.

'Not for me,' said Rocco. 'I didn't know artists used agents. Although I suppose having someone with connections might be an advantage.'

Sébastien shrugged. 'Way of the world, Inspector. Way of the world. It's what Laurent calls a commercial imperative these days. Stuck away out here I can't get to the galleries as much as I used to, so it helps to have him dropping my name into wealthy ears whenever he can. He's got a wide range of contacts and he's also better at negotiating terms than I am. You might be surprised at how tough it can be to prise a decent fee out of the wealthy elite. They like to think they're doing the artist a favour by giving them a commission, then pay as late as they possibly can when it's finished. Still, I suppose that's how they got to be rich in the first place.' He looked at his now diminished cheroot and dropped the stub in the fireplace. 'Now, you wanted to ask about the shooting.'

Claude, studying some books on a shelf by the fire, looked confused by the sudden change of topic but recovered and said, 'Only if you have any news.'

'None, I'm afraid. I haven't seen or heard anything.'

'Fine. Case closed. We'll put it down to sun spots.'

Back outside, after bidding goodbye to Sébastien, Rocco looked at Claude. 'Sun spots? Really?'

'Sorry.' Claude looked unabashed. 'It caught me on the hop. It was the best I could do at short notice.'

'What did you think?' He'd brought Claude along because he valued his opinion. Unconstrained by trying to impress any superiors or a mountain of other cases calling for his attention, Claude relied on a more basic internal antennae to judge the words and actions of others. Some would have called it gut feeling.

'That Vauquelin's a bit of a *connard*, isn't he? I told you I should have brought my gun.'

'No argument there. Maybe next time. And Sébastien?'

Claude pulled a face. 'He's harder to judge. He comes across as a nice bloke, a little odd, I suppose, but nice enough. If he's crooked, he's a good actor.'

Rocco nodded. He was finding it hard to place Sébastien in the role of a master blackmailer. A possible forger, yes, since the man almost certainly possessed the skill. And he'd definitely seemed a little uneasy when he and Claude had first arrived. But did that make him guilty of having turned the screws on clients who'd bought his paintings?

Claude climbed into the car and began fiddling with the radio until he found a music station. Rocco let him play. His mind was firmly fixed on the lawyer. He felt a sense of unease about Vauquelin's attitude. Not the way he had leapt to his client's defence, which was fairly normal for any lawyer; it was their job, after all. But he couldn't help but get the feeling that there was something else going on in the background, something he couldn't put his finger on. If Vauquelin had indeed stayed on because he'd heard Rocco was coming to see Sébastien, it made him wonder why. Was he trying to get his defence in quickly and, if so, why the rush?

–

On his way back to Paris, Laurent Vauquelin stopped at a café on the outskirts of the town of Breteuil to make a telephone call. The place was fairly busy and nobody gave him so much as a look. Secure in the knowledge that nobody there would know him, he decided it would be better to deal with this now rather than leaving it until he got back to his office. He found the phone and dialled a number from memory. It was answered with the customary silence.

Vauquelin said, 'Serban? It's me.'

'Yes.'

'I believe we may have a small problem.'

There was a lengthy pause, then, 'How so?'

'I spoke to Rocco, the inspector dealing with the Bourdelet case. He was at Cezard's place, asking questions about the paintings. I pretended ignorance about his being involved, of course.'

'And?'

'I don't think he's the type to back off as easily as we hoped. I've met his sort before.'

A sigh came down the line and Serban said, 'That's unfortunate, *Maître*.' The use of the title felt more like a slap than a mark of respect, but Vauquelin gritted his teeth and remained silent. 'But, unless you make any mistakes, I can't see how he'll discover links to either of us. That said,' Serban added pointedly, 'the only one in danger of taking a fall is the painter.'

'Well, yes, I suppose so. But can we not do something?' Vauquelin asked. 'What if he finds a link through the letters?'

'Are you suggesting that will be of my doing?'

'No. I'm merely saying there ought to be some way of dissuading him.'

'What do you want me to do – shoot him? Place a bomb under his car? Offer him a bribe?'

'No... I don't know.' Vauquelin was startled by the suggestions and wondered if, deep down, they were serious.

'I suggest you line up another target,' said Serban. 'And try not to panic. We have a business arrangement, nothing more; we need to recoup our losses on these first three because so far they've brought no returns whatsoever.'

Vauquelin protested. 'That's hardly my fault. Their reactions to the letters were unforeseen. In any case, as I said before, you will receive payment.'

'Are you saying there won't be more?'

'No. I'm saying this is a small setback. That's all.'

'I hope so, *Maître*. For your sake I hope so.'

Vauquelin heard the words, followed by a soft click, and wondered what he had got himself into.

Chapter Twenty-three

Rocco returned home to find a cloth-covered dish on his doorstep. The smell as he unwrapped it told him all he needed to know: it was from Mme Denis. Gifting him with eggs and fresh vegetables from her own abundant plot was her way of ensuring that he did not forget the basic principles of eating to stay alive. But a pie? And a meat pie at that, with a golden crust peppered with holes and releasing a tantalising aroma of meat and herbs. He sensed this might be a further offer of apology for her curtness of the other day. He decided to walk round to the old lady's small cottage. A personal thank you was required along with, no doubt, a snippet of detail about his latest case.

'Thank you, *madame*,' he said warmly, when she came to the door. 'I shall eat well tonight. But you really didn't need to go to such trouble. And meat is expensive.'

She brushed off the words with a *pouff*. 'There's no need to concern yourself. I have an arrangement with a friend at the other end of the village. Her husband's a farmer and produces his own excellent meat. He supplies several restaurants in the area.'

'An arrangement?'

She gave a chuckle. 'Yes. I let drop a few choice details of your past cases in return for some of her husband's meat cuts. It's called bartering. It's a lost art – you should try it sometime.'

'I do, often,' said Rocco. 'Only I barter not to shoot criminals if they come quietly.'

She gave him a sideways look. 'I don't believe that for a second. Eat the pie and be grateful; you're looking a bit peaky, if I may say so. You need feeding up. That *commissaire* of yours is working you far too hard.'

'Thank you. I'll tell him you said so.'

'What you don't eat, keep cool, otherwise it will go off.'

'How do I do that?' Rocco didn't have a refrigerator and hadn't yet seen the need.

She frowned. 'Use the *cave* – the cellar – of course.' Then her face cleared. 'Wait – you don't know about the cellar?'

'Didn't know, never had cause to look,' he replied honestly. It was the truth. He'd never been concerned with storing anything so hadn't ventured to search.

'Honestly, you men.' She grabbed him by the wrist. 'Come with me. I know there is one because the previous tenant used to complain about the steps being too steep.'

She bustled off, and led him to his kitchen, where she pointed to a cupboard door beneath the stairs. 'It's under there – a trapdoor in the floor.'

Rocco opened the door and sure enough saw a square cut-out in the floorboards. When he lifted it, he saw a flight of stone steps going down into the dark.

'It's not very deep so you'll have to stoop,' said Mme Denis. 'It's perfectly dry and there's room for some bottles and vegetables and what-not and…' She turned on him. 'And I can't believe you didn't find this already!' She slapped him on the arm. 'How do you think we store food in the countryside without all the modern *trucs* you city folk use?'

Rocco shrugged. 'I don't know… I assumed you just hung it from a tree wrapped in a dead animal skin.'

This earned him another slap, this time accompanied by a smile. 'Idiot. Eat your pie and put the rest down there.'

When she had gone, he inspected the pie. It was quite heavy and looked substantial enough for at least two hearty meals. He cut a wedge out of it for his dinner and prepared some potatoes, then put them on to boil while he placed the rest of the pie on a ledge in the cellar, which was little more than a brick-lined two-metre square hole in the ground, and surprisingly cool after the heat of the day outside. Then he took a walk around his garden and thought about his future.

Leaving this place would be getting back to what he knew best, which was the city and its fast-moving atmosphere, with little time to relax or wonder what was coming next. Crime in Paris was like nowhere else, fuelled by a cultural mix from all over France, North Africa and the rest of Europe. Given the correct documentation, people were now able to travel legally more easily than ever before in their search for work and a new life. And, for those who cared little for constraints or social conventions, there was ample opportunity to feed off the more law-abiding of its citizens and the increasing wealth around them.

Thoughts of Paris reminded him of Vauquelin. The lawyer had behaved no differently from most of his kind when a client was confronted by the police. He'd been suspicious, coolly aggressive and defensive. But there had been something in the man's demeanour and even his presence at the château that made Rocco wonder at his hostility.

He went inside, picked up the telephone and called a Paris number. If anyone could find information about the lawyer it would be Captain Michel Santer, his old boss and mentor in the Clichy-Nanterre district. A fount of knowledge on all matters of justice in the Paris metropolis, what he didn't know he could usually find out very quickly from his legion of contacts built up over many years. Overweight and tough as a Seine barge-master, he would no doubt make Rocco pay for the favour in some way – usually with food – but it would be worth every centime in the end.

'Vauquelin?' Santer echoed, once they had got past the customary exchange of friendly banter. '*Maître* Vauquelin?'

'That's the one,' said Rocco. 'You know him?'

'Of him, yes – and not much of it pleasant. I've never crossed swords with him, if that's what you're asking. I'm far too low down the ladder for that. Why do you ask?'

'He's popped up in this area, representing a local artist who might be mixed up in a case I've been asked to look at.'

'An artist, huh? They're said to be a passionate lot. Probably all the paint fumes and lack of good food. Anything juicy?'

'Bourdelet.'

There was a pause, then Canter swore softly. '*Mère de Dieu!* You mean *Secretary*—'

'That's the one.'

'How the hell did you get lumbered with that? They might as well have given you a stick of dynamite and told you to shove it down your trousers!'

'I think the Interior Ministry must like my sparkling wit and go-get-them attitude.'

'I hope you don't live to regret it. You know cases like that can be a killer, don't you? Especially if you stumble on the kind of information the people at the top don't want to hear. It's called shooting the messenger.'

'So I've been told. Anyway, this lawyer Vauquelin also calls himself an artist's agent.'

'Fancy that. Artists have agents, too, do they? Like film stars. They'll be making records next. Listen, the short answer is, I don't know anything definite, but I'll ask around and get back to you.'

'Thanks, Michel. I appreciate it.'

'How much?'

'Pardon?' Here it comes, thought Rocco, and smiled to himself. He hadn't seen Santer in a little while, so it would be good to get together again. But his captain was about to make him pay for the privilege.

'You heard me.' Santer laughed. 'If you remember the last time we spoke, over that Vieira killing a little while back, I mentioned a new restaurant I'd heard was doing a nice line in seafood. I could do with trying it out – just for research, you understand.'

Rocco laughed. 'I remember. Langoustine in garlic butter followed by smoked salmon, I think you said.'

'And a nice Chablis – *premier cru*, of course. That's the one. Glad there's nothing wrong with your memory, even if your choice of work is a bit suspect. The restaurant's on the outskirts of Montigny, in an old mansion, so not far from your place. It's called Le Vieux Poêle. I reckon I can spare some time to meet up with one of my star pupils.'

'It's a deal – but don't blame me if your heart explodes one day.'

'There are worse ways to go, my friend. I'll call you first thing tomorrow. Luckily tomorrow's a half-day off for me, so let's meet up in Montigny for lunch, say twelve-thirty?'

'You'll have something that soon?' He'd expected to wait forty-eight hours at least for Santer to tap into the grapevine of police contacts. Plainly he had underestimated the man.

'I already know who to ask. I just need to pin him down – he's a busy man. Don't worry, Lucas, it'll be worth it, I promise.'

Rocco couldn't argue with that. With his current workload, anything he could learn from Santer would be useful. It could well be that any snippets about Vauquelin were purely gossip and unhelpful, but that was police work: some you won, some you lost.

Chapter Twenty-four

Commissaire Francois Massin had never been one for mixing at the kind of social levels of Secretary Bourdelet, Judge Jules Petissier or even former Director General Gambon. He had never been much of a socialite and, after his fall from military grace in Indochina, any kind of interaction with such people had become too much of a potential ordeal. Many senior members of the establishment had served in the military and were likely to be amply acquainted with Massin's past. The military world was small and tight-knit, and chatting to men whom he suspected would look at him with barely-concealed distaste was something Massin preferred not to do. He didn't fail to see the irony in this additional lack of courage, but was prepared to live with it.

Yet still there was buried away inside him a need to know what his contemporaries and those above them truly thought of him. Had his service in the police helped to gloss over the memories of the disgrace? Or was his reputation following him around still, like a noxious smell, to be revived and chewed over the moment he put in an appearance?

The answer was, he didn't know. And since nobody had come out and voiced an opinion over the years, about which he was both grateful and a little suspicious, he wondered if this exercise he had decided to undertake in place of Rocco might provide some answers, whether positive or negative.

In any event, this evening would be the first test, prompted by an embossed invitation he'd found in his personal mail, and felt like jumping off a cliff. It was one of the regular gatherings of senior police personnel which he'd previously been happy to avoid, held at a plush venue outside Versailles. They were designed to instil a sense of comradeship among the officer corps while smoothing over any inter-regional problems that occasionally occurred. He knew that many of the officers attending, including some retired high-ranking members invited as a courtesy, had contacts high up in the establishment, and were not the kind to hide their lights under a bushel, especially when alcohol was flowing and everyone felt comfortable in the company of equals. If there was any gossip circulating, it would be a useful place to start.

He handed the invitation card to a male receptionist at the front desk. The man took it with a faint frown, shrugged and placed it to one side without looking at it.

Massin took a glass of champagne from a table and walked into the main hall, where he did a tour of the room. Nodding occasionally, exchanging a greeting here and there, gradually he felt himself settling in among them while resisting the urge to turn and flee for the obscurity of the darkness outside.

'Ah, Massin.' A voice sounded in his ear. He turned to find himself face to face with a man he hadn't seen in a long while. *Contrôleur Génóralde Police Nationale* Alexandre Ceyton had always been genial, especially when he was first assigned a position in the force. 'It's good to see you,' Ceyton said, and shook his hand with no evident censure.

'Thank you, sir.' Massin noticed a few looks from officers around them. With the confident manner and good looks of a film star, Ceyton's approach immediately placed Massin among the ranks of the accepted.

'You've been absent too long from these gatherings. How is Amiens treating you?'

'Very well, sir,' said Massin. 'It suits me very well.'

'Good. I'm glad you decided to come this evening. It's always useful to have a full house at these events.'

'Thank you.'

'I heard you've had some interesting occurrences up there, including the death of a gang leader and that planned attempt on de Gaulle last year. I always thought it would be too remote up in Picardie for there to be such problems, but apparently not. What was the name of your officer who dealt with those? I should know the name but it escapes me.'

'Rocco, sir. Inspector Rocco.' Massin hid his surprise that this senior officer had such instant recall of the events, among all the other crimes throughout the country. He felt rather than saw other men bending an ear nearby, no doubt wondering about his friendship with such a senior member of the hierarchy.

'Rocco. Yes, I remember now. Isn't he the one handling the Bourdelet thing?'

'That's correct.'

Ceyton pulled a sympathetic face. 'Rather him than me. Like being thrown into a bed of nettles in one's underwear. Still, he sounds capable and you've clearly got a good hand on the tiller, so I'm sure he'll survive.' He leaned forward and said, 'Good thing he weathered the de Gaulle thing, though. It would have been a real stinker for his promotional prospects if the big man had gone down, wouldn't it?' He gave a grim laugh and was joined by chuckles from two other men who had moved closer, attracted by the topic of conversation.

'So, you're Massin,' said one, eyeing him appraisingly over his glass of champagne. 'I've heard things about you.' He murmured his own name and introduced the man next to him. Both names Massin instantly forgot. He shook their hands and wondered if what they had heard was good or bad.

'I'm in Nantes district,' the newcomer continued. 'I've had a couple of men recently interested in moving somewhere else, and both enquired about transfers to your region. What do you do up there to arouse such interest? I know you don't pay better than anywhere else, and the weather's no better, so what's the secret?'

'No secret,' said Massin. 'We're just doing our jobs. No different from yours, I suspect. And we got lucky a couple of times.' He hoped that didn't sound stuffy or self-deprecating. People at this level were suspicious of pomp or false modesty, and neither did he wish to downplay Rocco's part in the investigations.

The man nodded in acknowledgment. 'Good point. Luck plays a big part. But you have to be able to capitalise on it when it comes along – as you and your team evidently did.'

The third man joined in. 'I'm in Touraine and our analysis is that the wider corridor between Paris and the ports of La Manche is going to see a surge of growth in the coming years. And you're sitting bang in the middle, Massin. Of course, a lot depends on whether Britain is allowed to join the Common Market.'

Ceyton gave a chuckle. 'Somehow I can't see that happening, although you're right: if trade grows then so will a need for effective policing to cope with the increased infrastructure.' He looked at Massin. 'Do any of your men speak English, as a matter of interest?'

'A couple,' he replied easily. 'I do, a little, as does my deputy, Perronnet. Rocco, too. In fact, he went over to Scotland Yard last year to discuss the English gang suspected of involvement in the de Gaulle issue you just mentioned.'

'Damn,' the second of the two officers muttered with a wry smile. 'You've got the territory sewn up already, haven't you?' He laughed. 'I'll be contacting you for help if I need to send anyone to England, you can be sure of that.'

Later, having circulated and noticed only one or two signs of recognition in men's faces, Massin found himself back again with Ceyton, who was standing on the edge of the room studying the crowd and looking, thought Massin, faintly bored.

'You look as impatient to be away as I am,' Ceyton commented. 'Don't misunderstand me, I enjoy these functions as much as the next man, but they can be rather wearing. The Americans swear by it for sounding people out. They call it pressing the flesh.' He gave Massin a sideways look. 'Tell me, what's your real reason for being here? Is it anything to do with Rocco's potential move back to Paris?'

The question caught Massin off guard. He had no idea that the subject of Rocco's new job was common knowledge. His reaction must have been visible because Ceyton looked around and said, 'Don't worry, it's not public yet, which is why I didn't mention it earlier.' He grinned. 'Mind you, it was tempting with those two so eager to listen in to our chat. That would have ruined their evening.'

'I see.' Massin didn't, entirely, but didn't know what else to say. This conversation was moving far above his head, perhaps a result of his not having been to these gatherings before.

'You won't be aware,' Ceyton continued smoothly, 'but I've been on the planning panel from the beginning in discussions about the proposed *Brigade de Recherche et d'Intervention* or BRI. It's something of a touchy subject in some quarters. There's the cost, of course, of setting up the force, and there are libertarians in the establishment who feel it's merely a subversive way of expanding the powers of the police, a sort of addition to the CRS. It's not, believe me.'

Massin nodded. From what little he'd heard, the new BRI would be like a scalpel compared with the blunt hammer of the CRS. 'I'm glad to hear it. I doubt Rocco would be interested otherwise.'

Ceyton nodded, and looked at him as if searching his face for clues. 'Why have you never been to one of these before?'

'It's never been my thing, to be honest.'

'Nor mine. I'd get out of it, too, if I could, and my wife would certainly appreciate me spending more time at home.' He had a sharp twinkle in his eyes and gave Massin a friendly smile. 'Yet you suddenly turn up out of the blue and manage to look as if you've been a regular. What are you after? Come on, you can tell me. I came here deliberately to make contact with a couple of specific individuals, so you're not alone in having an agenda.'

Massin felt a drumming in his ears. He swallowed. He might as well be honest with this man. After all, what was the worst that could happen? 'It's a work question,' he replied. 'I'm looking for inside information, I suppose you'd call it… of a sensitive nature.'

'Sounds interesting,' Ceyton said, and snatched up two fresh glasses from a passing tray. 'A senior uniform doing some detecting. How unusual. Do tell, is it a current case?'

Massin hesitated, but since Ceyton had already mentioned Bourdelet, it was pointless trying to avoid it. And refusing to answer questions from such a senior officer would look highly suspicious.

'It's partly the Bourdelet case,' he said, 'but Rocco's been assigned to two more just like it. Judge Petissier and Director General Gambon were victims of the same blackmail letter.' He gave a brief summary of the reactions to the letters and Rocco's search for the blackmailer.

Ceyton lifted both eyebrows. 'I heard about that. What is it you're after, specifically?'

Massin told him. Links, he explained, between the three men. Someone had to have known the backgrounds of all three, specifically that they had purchased forged or copied paintings of old works of art. It wasn't the kind of information one could stumble on by chance, since none of the men would have been keen to have their peccadilloes aired outside their close circle of friends. 'Find the links, is Rocco's belief,' he finished, 'and we could be a lot closer to finding out who knew all three men. Who could be responsible for sending the letters.'

'And why,' Ceyton suggested heavily. 'What is it they say – follow the money? Find out who would benefit most from financial gain?'

Massin nodded. 'Unless it's simply a way of ruining their reputations.'

'Revenge? I hadn't thought of that. You could be right.'
Ceyton peered into his glass. 'Well, I'm not going to get
any husband of the year award for going home now, and
I could do with a bit of excitement.' He looked around at
the crowd. 'Tell you what, Massin, I'll give you a hand. I
probably know more people here than you do, so let me
do a bit more mixing, and I'll give you a call tomorrow if
I find anything. That do you?'

Massin nodded. He wasn't sure if he hadn't just made a
disastrous mistake, but he had a feeling that Ceyton's offer
of help was genuine. 'That's very kind, sir. I appreciate it.'

'No problem. It might lead nowhere, of course, but
that won't reflect badly on Rocco. As long as he puts on
a good show, eh?'

'Show, sir?' Massin was puzzled.

'Yes. It's all about public perception, you see. This
entire Bourdelet affair is a scandal waiting to explode.
If we do nothing we're accused of a cover-up; if we
go overboard we're accused of wasting money. But, by
focussing certain special resources on the case – a well-
known investigator with a proven record – even for a short
time, we're seen as being even-handed.'

'I see.' Massin didn't quite, but he decided to let it ride.

But Ceyton hadn't finished.

'The advantage to this approach,' Ceyton continued,
'is that there's nothing wrong with a failed investigation.
They happen, as we all know. And sometimes, as might be
the case here, you have to know when to cut your losses.
Job done but nobody loses.'

'Failed? Sir, I'm not sure Rocco will fa—'

'I'm sure he won't, Massin. I'm sure he won't.' Ceyton
leaned forward, his wine breath touching Massin's face.
His expression had turned almost chilled. He said softly,

'As long as your boy does what he's told *when* he's told. Get my meaning?'

'Told what?'

'Told to write it off. Shove it in a bottom drawer somewhere and forget it.' He finished his drink. 'If he does that, he'll have a prosperous and successful career ahead of him, mark my words.' He tapped Massin on the arm. 'Make sure you remind him, though, won't you?'

Chapter Twenty-five

Rocco got to the office early, prior to a drive to Mers-les-Bains to visit Gambon's house and, later, if he was conscious, to see Gambon himself. He wasn't sure what either would produce in the way of answers, but it was work that had to be done. He hadn't yet heard from Desmoulins about his visit to the coastal resort, so left a note at the duty desk about where he would be and walked round to the Café Schubert, the nearby watering hole of choice for officers from the station.

The café smelled of fresh pastries, strong coffee, serge uniforms, with a harsh overlay of cigarette smoke. It was half-full, having seen a recent changeover of shifts, and he made his way through the few officers and support workers, shaking hands on the way. He ordered a coffee and two croissants which he took to a corner table. Although he'd arranged to have lunch with Michel Santer, they were both experienced enough to know that meals and appointments meant little in the midst of a police investigation, and you simply had to grab food whenever you could.

He was halfway through the second croissant, enjoying the soft, buttery pastry washed down with black coffee, when the *patron* of the Schubert called out to him and pointed over the heads of the other customers towards the corridor at the rear.

'Inspector Rocco? Telephone call.'

Rocco found the phone hanging by its cord down the wall. The caller was Michel Santer, sounding pleased with himself.

'I struck lucky,' he announced. 'I spoke to a friend of mine in the Ministry of Justice. I figured he'd know more about current lawyers than anyone else.'

'That's quick work. Anything useful?'

'Well, depends what you call useful. He told me Vauquelin's a real scrapper and makes no secret of his dislike and distrust of cops. He takes on any case where he thinks he can question the integrity of the arresting officers or investigators, and doesn't mind dragging them through the mud if it means he gets his client off.'

'Scoring points, in other words. He's not the first.'

'Exactly. He's been hauled up in front of the Inspector General's panel on more than one occasion for making claims about the conduct of officers which subsequently turned out not to be true, and has weathered at least three investigations regarding his 'unprofessional' relationships with certain criminal types.'

'And he's still practising?'

'Just about. The last one nearly finished him. He got too close to a fraud case in Lyon, and was accused of attempting to bring the judicial system and the police into disrepute. They took a soft line on that one, but he began to appear less and less. Now he only takes on particularly high-profile cases where he thinks he can stick it to the judges by winning spectacularly.'

'There aren't many of those, surely.'

'You're right. The fact is, anyone facing a big court appearance only has to ask around and they'd soon hear that Vauquelin's not the most popular of defence lawyers with the judges. And who wants that kind of representation? They'd be at a big disadvantage from the word go.'

Rocco thanked Santer and told him he'd see him at the restaurant. He returned to his table and finished his coffee, before setting off for Mers-les-Bains. His mind was a jumble of questions about why a legal brawler like Vauquelin would want to represent a jobbing artist like Sébastien Cezard, both as agent and lawyer. Was he that desperate? Cezard hadn't appeared to be any kind of star, more like a man who was getting by. And that would put him a long way from being able to meet Vauquelin's level of fees.

—

In the station just around the corner from the Schubert, Detective Desmoulins stared in frustration at the report he was trying to compile. It didn't amount to much and, in the cold light of day, even the yellow van seen in Le Vésinet was looking like a dead end. It often happened that leads would fall away to nothing, leaving a case no closer to being solved. But it was a major part of the job to keep going even when it seemed the odds were stacked against you.

He jumped when his phone rang, and snatched it up, grateful for the interruption.

'Is that Detective Desmoulins?' He recognised the nasal sound of M. Medioni, the madman conspiracy theorist and brandy drinker from Mers-les-Bains.

'What can I do for you, Monsieur Medioni?'

'I remembered that number – the one on the yellow van. I was sitting here, having a little drink and... there it was, plain as you like. How about that, eh? I wrote it down as soon as it came to me. I was going to mention it to Allain but I thought I'd better call you first.'

'Best not tell him, if you don't mind,' said Desmoulins. He grabbed a pen and waited. 'What was it?'

'Oh, right.' Medioni sounded disappointed but he read it out anyway, and Desmoulins felt a burst of relief. He thanked the man for his help and made him promise not to discuss the details with anyone.

'But – not even with Allain? He'd be very interested, I know he would. He's very proud of the PTT.'

'Not even him.' Desmoulins dropped his voice. 'You've been very helpful, sir, and we value the co-operation from members of the public such as yourself. Unfortunately, we need to ask for your absolute discretion on this matter for the time being. It's what we call a strictly need-to-know issue, if you understand what I mean.'

By the sudden silence on the line he thought Medioni had fallen over in shock. But then the man spoke, his voice dropping conspiratorially. 'Of course. Perfectly under-standable. Need-to-know. Got it.'

Desmoulins thanked him and dropped the phone back on the rest. He stared at the vehicle number on his pad. A Paris registration meant nothing – there were thousands of those around and no doubt among them lots of yellow vans, too. This could either be nothing at all… or a step forward in the investigation. He consulted his directory and snatched up his phone again, dialling the number for the vehicle registration centre headquarters. It would take time to go through the system, but eventually the machinery would grind it out and he'd have an answer.

–

Rocco arrived at Gambon's house and found a uniformed officer outside. The local police inspection of the property would have taken place by now, and a copy of any resultant paperwork would be on their way to him. But he wanted to make his own inspection to get a feel for the place.

The officer used a key to let him in, and Rocco set about checking the rooms. As he might have expected of a senior policeman, the interior was neat, tidy and almost spartan in appearance, everything arranged just so for the minimum of fuss. Furniture was aligned around each room rather than in it, and ornaments were few, other than several framed photographs of Gambon with colleagues and prominent members of the establishment. Rocco gave them a passing glance, recognising a former defence minister, two army chiefs and a current senior member of the civil service who'd been in the news discussing policing matters.

There were none with Secretary of State Bourdelet, he noted. It was a pity but not surprising; that would have been too easy.

He checked drawers and files, finding several albums and yearbooks charting Gambon's steady rise through the police service. The man had evidently been keen to record his successes. Yet Rocco didn't get the feeling that there was anything missing. Sometimes when searching properties relating to criminal activity, it was soon evident that the place had been culled of anything incriminating. Gaps in records were inexplicable, cardboard folders showing signs of once-bulging sides were disturbingly thin or empty. Gambon's paperwork, however, looked perfectly normal.

He took out the copy of the letter received by Gambon. As Dreycourt had said, it referred to two paintings, one of which he had sold to an American buyer in California for an undisclosed sum. By itself that wasn't a crime, but if Dreycourt managed to prove that the American had been sold the painting as a genuine article, it was fraud.

He found the other painting in the living room. 'Mademoiselle O'Murphy' was, like Bourdelet's painting, the centrepiece on an otherwise bare wall, to be seen and admired. Much lighter in tone than the photo had suggested, predominantly gold and tan, it demanded attention without the need for extra light.

He checked the back of the painting, but there was nothing to suggest where it had come from. No discernible signature either, he noted, just a squiggle at the bottom which could have been anything.

He checked the notes from Dreycourt and saw that Gambon's housekeeper, Anne-Marie Guillard, lived nearby. He left the uniformed officer to lock up and made his way there. If there was any evidence to find, it might well be the mistress/housekeeper who had been cast aside who provided it.

Guillard was small, neat, pretty and in her forties. Dressed in a tight skirt and scooped-neck blouse, she wore high heels that just about brought her head level with Rocco's chest. She flashed a ready smile and her two-handed welcome drew Rocco into her home as if she had been starved of company. Her home was small, comfortably furnished, fluffy, flowery and predominantly pink, and she virtually pushed him into an armchair and insisted he take coffee.

'That's not necessary, Madame Guillard,' he assured her, feeling the stuffed cushions sucking him down like quicksand. 'I won't disturb you for long, I promise.'

She made a moue with her lips. 'But you already have, Inspector,' she said softly, and gave a tinkling laugh as she turned towards a small kitchen. 'I won't be a moment. Just make yourself comfortable and we can have a nice long chat.'

In what seemed a few seconds she was back with a tray of cups and a pot of coffee. She set the tray down in front of Rocco, the blouse moving to reveal an ample expanse of sun-bronzed skin. 'There,' she murmured. 'I hope it's to your satisfaction.' She held the pose for a moment, making him wonder to what she was referring, and fluttered her eyelashes before taking a cup and sitting down across from him.

Rocco sank half the contents of his cup in one gulp, wondering how many unsuspecting souls had come through the front door recently never to leave. To cover his thoughts, he took her through the details of the letter, asking how much she had known of M. Gambon's affairs.

'Affairs, Inspector?' she queried with a coy smile. 'Why, the only affair I know of was the one he had with me. If that's the kind of affair you mean, of course.' She gave another tinkling laugh and patted the skin at the base of her throat.

Rocco kept his face carefully blank. 'Business affairs, *madame*. Like the purchase of the paintings.'

'Oh, I see. Silly me.' She looked up at the ceiling and took a deep breath, her bosom lifting. 'All he told me was how he'd got them through a contact at a very good price. I must admit I liked the one he kept. Very... sensual,

I thought it was.' She switched her gaze to Rocco and blinked twice. 'He said she reminded him of me.'

Rocco felt heat building up around his neck. 'Did he say who he'd bought them from?'

'No. He was very guarded about that kind of thing. But he did say he'd found a buyer for one of them – an American he'd known in Paris many years ago.' She sipped her coffee. 'He was very pleased with himself about that, I remember, because he said the arrogant Yank knew nothing about art and had more money than sense. I told him that wasn't very nice and that surely he was committing fraud.'

'What did he say?'

'Not much, but I don't think he was very pleased. Well, mention the word fraud to a policeman and they're bound to get a little jumpy, aren't they?' She looked momentarily crestfallen. 'I shouldn't have said it, I suppose, but it was too late. However, what he did was wrong and I thought I was in a position to say so. My mistake. I should have let it rest and kept my mouth shut. But just recently we had a little… disagreement, and I called him a fraud. I didn't mean to, but he took it that I meant about the… you know, the painting.'

'And did you?'

'I suppose so, yes. But it was out before I could stop it.' She fluttered her eyelashes. 'You know how it is, Inspector. You say things in the heat of the moment and suddenly it's too late.' She sighed. 'It wasn't long after that that he told me our little "arrangement" was over.'

'Arrangement?'

She said candidly, 'I wasn't there just to clean his house, Inspector.' She held his gaze as if daring him to comment. 'Don't tell me you're one of the moral majority in this country who pretend people don't ever have sex for fun instead of procreation?' She blinked slowly. 'You don't seem that way, if I might say so.'

'Not at all, *madame*. It's none of my business what people do as long as it isn't a crime.'

'Please, call me Anne-Marie.'

'Is that why you handed the letter to the local news-paper instead of the police? You were angry at him for ending the affair?'

'I was bitter, I admit. It was so brutal, the way he cast me aside as if I'd never mattered to him. So maybe I did want a bit of revenge, yes. The thing is, he still expected me to keep house for him!' A delicate handker-chief appeared out of nowhere and she dabbed at her eyes, which Rocco thought looked perfectly dry. 'I thought if I handed the letter to the police they'd simply sit on it, him having been a senior officer. That's how they protect each other, isn't it – all boys in the same club?'

Rocco said, 'My coming here is to prove otherwise. Did he ever mention any names or receive any visitors in connection with the paintings?'

'No. He just said he'd got them from someone he knew. They were delivered one day, but I wasn't there at the time. The next time I went in they were on the wall and he was admiring them. But the smaller one was sold not long after.'

'Do you know if he received any phone calls that might have upset him recently?'

'Before he tried to hang himself, you mean?' She looked away and shook her head. 'Not as far as I know. He didn't use the telephone much. But he used to go into town nearly every day so I suppose he might have used a public telephone down there. He was quite secretive like that, although I don't know why.' She paused and wiped her eyes again. 'Perhaps I was stupid and he'd got another woman hidden away somewhere. Am I going to get into trouble for giving the letter to the press? Only that seems very unfair. I thought I was doing a public service.'

'I can't answer that. My guess is you won't.'

Rocco stood up and thanked her for her help, then left.

As he climbed back in his car and headed back towards Amiens, the radio crackled. It was the police operator with Desmoulins waiting to speak with him. The young detective sounded upbeat.

'I got a registration number for a yellow van seen in Mers-les-Bains, in the same street as Gambon's house,' he said. 'I don't know if it's the same as the one in Le Vésinet, but it's worth following up.'

'I agree. Did you get a name?'

'I have now. It's registered to a garage in Sarcelles. I checked with the local police. They said the owner's a local criminal with a reputation for some dubious connections. But so far they've never been able to pin anything on him.'

'What kind of connections?'

'He runs a line in cheap cars for hire, some used by local riff-raff. A couple of the vehicles have been spotted close to the scenes of robberies, but the trail didn't go back directly to the garage so they had to drop the investigations.'

Rocco chewed on the information as he drove. As leads went it was tenuous at best, but better than nothing. He checked his watch. He was meeting Santer at lunchtime in Montigny, and from there to Sarcelles was going to be tight. But he'd make it. 'Let's lean on him. Can you be at the garage at four?'

'Can do. I'll get there early and scout around, see if they have any yellow vans in evidence.'

'Good idea. Let the local force know we're going. If you get any problems get Massin involved and he'll clear the way.'

Chapter Twenty-six

'I still don't understand why they asked you to conduct the investigation,' said Santer. 'It doesn't make sense.' It wasn't the first time he'd mentioned it, and Rocco had a feeling he was leading up to something.

'They just did and that's it,' he said. 'Not mine to reason why.'

'Really? Well, I have my suspicions.' Santer picked up his glass and gave an almost delicate sip, pursing his lips to fully savour the flavour of the pale wine. It was a fine Chablis, Rocco could tell that by the look of satisfaction that glided across the captain's face. Not for nothing did he have a reputation among his colleagues as something of a gourmet, although it wasn't often that he could indulge himself like this.

They were sitting in Le Vieux Poêle on the outskirts of Montigny, and had dispensed with the first course, a delicate langoustine. They were now waiting for the salmon, which Santer had expressly ordered the evening before to make sure they weren't out of it. The captain was being deliberately cagey about telling Rocco what he'd learned, but Rocco wasn't concerned. He'd spill the information eventually, once the wine had loosened his tongue and his appetite had been dented. It was a game his former boss liked to play in return for the reward he was about to enjoy.

'Go on, thrill me,' Rocco encouraged him and tasted the wine. It was crisp and fruity, with a subtle aftertaste that hung on the back of his tongue and lingered in his throat.

'Think about it.' Santer leaned forward, nearly upsetting a basket of bread. 'The Ministry is huge. They've got investigators coming out of their ears: military, civil, intelligence, security, scientific – quite apart from people like the Dreycourt character you told me about. It's an ants' nest of experts, that place.' He looked abashed. 'Not that I'm saying you're not expert, of course I'm not – you'd put them all to shame. But still—' He broke off as the salmon arrived, and sat back with a look of reverence as it was served. 'God, I love this place.'

Neither of them spoke until the waiter had gone and they had each taken the first forkful of pale pink fish. For a few seconds Santer looked as if he were in heaven, eyes closed and a soft smile on his face. Then he continued: 'They've also got reach, in the Ministry, you know that. They control every corner of this country, with informants round every corner.' He checked that nobody was close enough to overhear and said, 'It's a police state, only nobody likes to call it that because who the hell wants to live in one of those? We're not the USSR, after all, controlled by those shovel-smacked faces in the Politburo.'

'Does all this have a point?' said Rocco mildly, playing his part. 'Fish good?'

'Fantastic. Beautiful. I must bring my wife here – she'd love it. And yes, it has a point.' He poked his fork at Rocco. 'The point is I worry about you, Lucas. How far do you have to go in any town before you see a uniform? Tell me.'

'Not far.'

'Correct. And that's not counting the non-uniforms, the ones you don't see.'

'Now you're sounding paranoid. Does this fish contain mercury?'

'What?' Santer stared at his plate. 'What makes you say such a thing?' Then he smiled. 'Ah, one of your jokes. You had me worried for a moment. You're thinking of the Japanese thing a few years ago, aren't you? Well, forget it – these are freshwater fish from Aquitaine, absolutely clean, no impurities. What was I saying? Oh, yes. But you're right. I am paranoid – and with reason. You've been chosen, my fine young friend, to do this job for one reason and one reason only.' He scooped up another mouthful of fish and chewed with relish.

Rocco knew what was coming. 'Go on.'

'You've been set up to fail.'

'You think?' Rocco could see what he was driving at because he'd had similar thoughts himself, especially after Dreycourt's warning that nobody else wanted to touch it. 'If that was true,' he countered reasonably, 'they could have chosen someone inexperienced.'

'Ah, but that's where they've been clever, see. Bourdelet is a scandal in the making. They can't have that. It would be bad for the government if everyone knew the finance secretary had been dipping into secret state coffers. He'll be written off... but as a suicide while of unsound mind due to stress. It happens all the time: a casualty of events for the sake of the country. They'll read eulogies about what a fine chap he was, a loyal servant of the state, hardworking, blah-blah-blah. Then you'll hear no more about it.'

'What about the other two?'

'Exactly my point. Bourdelet alone, that can be explained away. But throw in two more top dogs buying forgeries and being blackmailed for specified crimes, and it's got enough combustion to lift the roof off the Élysée Palace. That's not so easy to hide. So they have to have a main whipping post... which comes back to poor old Bourdelet. Tough on him but he wasn't that popular, anyway. So, what to do? They can't not have an investigation, as that would set tongues wagging. So, who will do it? Choose one of their own insiders and they could be accused of trying to hide something, to control events. I'd be surprised, anyway, if any of their own people wanted to go anywhere near it for fear of the result. Bourdelet being an obvious exception, and forgive me for being tasteless, but government employees are not known for committing professional *hara-kiri* if they can help it.'

'True.'

'On the other hand, if they chose someone inexperienced, they'd have the press and the opposition parties on their backs for not taking the matter seriously. By choosing you, a detective with a top record of successful investigations, they can demonstrate that they've put their best man on the job... and Bourdelet will still be written off and everyone will be happy. Job done. A big shame but he was a bad one, but...' He shrugged and set about clearing his plate.

'There's only one thing wrong with that theory,' said Rocco. 'If I'm supposed to be so good, what if I solve the case and find the painter and the blackmailer and his accomplices?'

'Same thing, my friend. That's when they'll shut the case down and bury it, because that way they can prove they did their best but without any huge scandal. You won't ever let the cat out of the bag because that's the way you are. You'll go back to your day job and forget all about it.'

Rocco couldn't fault Santer's logic. He'd gone through the various possibilities himself more than once. Even he knew there were scandals that the government could not possibly allow to become public, not at the present time. It made him wonder if Santer was aware of his new job offer. The timing of the offer and his being handed the investigation were a pure coincidence, but others might not see it that way. In any case, he figured Santer didn't know, since that would have been the first question the captain would have hit him with today.

'What about Vauquelin?'

'The painter's agent and lawyer? Well, I already told you about him. My friend says to be very careful of that one. Vauquelin's lost a lot of credibility on the court circuit recently, which must have put a serious dent in his case load and income. But he's got friends in low places who don't mind playing rough, so you should watch your back.' He eyed Rocco's plate, which still wasn't clear, with interest. 'Are you going to eat that fish or not?'

Chapter Twenty-seven

Moteurs Gregnard was in a ramshackle building in a back street away from the centre of Sarcelles, and Rocco was hard pushed not to form preconceptions about the place before he saw the inside. The jumble of buildings in the surrounding area were dilapidated and looked mostly deserted, and there was an air of defeat hanging over them that seemed to emanate from the ground up, as if the area was waiting for the wrecker's ball to move in and lay waste to every brick and timber. Aging vehicles were parked along the front of the premises, and two men in grubby vests and oil-stained trousers were sitting outside next to a single fuel pump, puffing on cigarettes.

So far Rocco had seen no through traffic of any description, and it wasn't difficult to see why: who would want to risk coming down such a dead-end street in what was surely a road to nowhere? He saw Desmoulins climb out of his car further down the street and waited for the detective to join him.

'I've walked past a couple of times,' said Desmoulins, sliding into the passenger seat, 'but couldn't see a yellow van. That's not to say there isn't one – there's a space at the rear where they could probably get a dozen vehicles or more.'

'Are those two oily vests the only employees?'

'I think so. They came out after three men arrived about fifteen minutes ago. They've been out there ever since.'

'Under orders, I expect. What did the three visitors look like?'

'Cheap suits, street swagger and trying to look tough. Late twenties to early thirties. They pitched up in the green Simca across the street, and an older man met them at the door. I think it was Gregnard himself. Looks as if they were expected.'

Rocco studied the Simca. It didn't look new but was highly polished and sat low on the springs, with a row of fog lights across the front as if it had been prepped for the Tour de France Automobile Rally, idiot amateur division. 'How did the local force feel about you coming here?'

Desmoulins pointed down the street. 'The ratty blue Peugeot with the red wing? There are two detectives inside in case we need any help.'

Rocco looked at him. 'Did you ask them to come?'

Desmoulins smiled. 'I didn't have to. The moment I mentioned Gregnard, they almost jumped in their car before I'd finished speaking. They've been trying to pin him down for a long time. They're pretty sure he's been moving stolen goods around the city, quite apart from providing vehicles for raids and fake documentation to just about anybody who can stump up the cash. It must be a lucrative business because, although the garage is a dump, the locals told me Gregnard has a very nice house at the posh end of town, and can be seen splashing money around on a regular basis.'

'So, we're among friends?'

'We are. I told them it's just a chat for now but they said if we need help, just whistle.'

'Come on, then. Let's go and disturb Monsieur Greg-nard's day, shall we?' Rocco climbed out and led the way along the street. They were watched every step of the way by the two men, who stamped out their cigarettes and got to their feet. One of them, the taller of the two, scooped up a length of metal bar and swung it experimentally from side to side with a swishing sound.

'Sit down, boys,' said Rocco, and flicked back his coat to show his gun, while Desmoulins held up his ID card. 'We're here for a chat, so why not be sensible and have another smoke? I'm sure your boss won't mind.'

The men sat down again, the tall one dropping the bar on the ground. The shrug as he did so was a face-saver which said they could have done something if they'd wanted to, but they weren't paid to confront the cops.

The interior of the garage smelled of oil, damp and cigarettes. Compared to the outside it was surprisingly clean, the floor oil-stained but clear of rubbish. There were two ramps, an inspection pit and long benches along the side walls covered in tools and car parts. Racks above them held a variety of tools and above them a selection of colourful automobile plaques. The overall appearance was of a professional set-up in sharp contrast to the second-rate exterior.

Rocco had seen this kind of place before: a dump to outsiders but capable of turning out high-level work for the right kind of customers.

An office was visible through a glass-panelled screen covered in auto parts stickers. Four men were seated around a desk, the air around their heads clouded with smoke. Whatever they were discussing looked serious. The odd man out was a heavy-set, older individual in his fifties dressed in an expensive-looking sports jacket and shirt. He was stabbing the air with a fat forefinger.

Gregnard, thought Rocco, and he was laying down the law about something. It was a good time to catch him off-guard. He stepped up to the door and knocked, then pushed it open.

'Sorry to interrupt,' he said calmly. 'But we need to talk.'

Gregnard dropped the pointy finger and growled, 'Who the hell are you? Piss off and come back next week. We're busy.' He glared towards the outside, no doubt wondering why his men hadn't intercepted these intruders.

The three visitors weren't quite so patient. They took it as their cue to stand up and look tough. Rocco did the trick with his coat while Desmoulins flashed his card. It worked wonders. They went to sit down again but Rocco stopped them.

'Don't bother staying,' he said. 'We don't need an audience.'

Gregnard looked surprisingly untroubled at this and didn't argue. He nodded at the three younger men and said, 'Just think about what I said, right? Not here, not now, not ever.' He stood up and watched them leave, then turned to Rocco and shook his head, 'I was about to toss them out anyway. You saved me the trouble. Young punks think they can come in here and make a silly offer for my business? They need to grow some balls first. What is it you two want? Rocco, isn't it?'

Rocco was surprised. 'Have we met?'

'No, but I've seen you around. Down in Clichy, wasn't it? It's been a while.' He sat down and gestured at the empty chairs. 'Why not make yourselves comfortable? Where have you been?'

'I've been working elsewhere,' said Rocco. 'My colleague is Detective Desmoulins. Are you having trouble with those three?'

Gregnard gave a spit of laughter. 'You're joking. Them? They're *voyous*, that's all. Street thugs. Good on talk and scaring old ladies, but nothing in the tank.' He scratched at his face, which was covered in a three-day stubble. 'They're looking for a base and for some reason thought I'd be ripe for a takeover. They were wrong. What can I do for you, Inspector?'

'I hear you have some vehicles for hire, is that correct?'

'Sure. Why – you looking for a wedding limousine?' His smile didn't reach his eyes. 'I don't have one in the yard but I can always get one for the right kind of money.'

'Thanks, but not yet. How about a small van, a 2CV in PTT yellow?'

Gregnard pursed his lips and slowly shook his head. 'Not sure I can do that. Why so specific? You thinking of a change of profession?'

'The registration records show you as the owner,' said Desmoulins. He took a slip of paper out of his pocket and pushed it across the desk.

Gregnard didn't bother looking at it, playing the cool customer. 'I hire out lots of vehicles, but I don't recall every one. It might be mine, it might not. So what?' His tone was still civil but getting harder, and Rocco recognised a man trying to think fast on his feet.

'We've had reports of that vehicle having been seen in connection with two suicides and another near-fatality. All three incidents appear to lead right back here. To you, Monsieur Gregnard. What do you say about that?'

Gregnard shrugged and tilted back on his chair, his belly rising above the desk. 'So what? A vehicle hired from me just happened to be in an area when a couple of losers decided to kill themselves. Doesn't mean I know anything about it. Do you go after the SNCF when some idiot walks across the track in front of an express?' In spite of his brash words he didn't sound overly confident.

'You admit it does belong to you?'

His eyes flickered nervously. 'Yeah, but so what? I hire them out, I don't see what people do with them. I didn't even know about any suicides.'

'Not personally, no,' said Rocco. 'But you'll have heard of one of them. And that's where a whole load of trouble is going to come down on you. Believe me, we're the polite squad, unlike the ones coming along behind.' He was bluffing, because it was ten to one that nobody would be coming along after him and Desmoulins. But he was counting on Gregnard not knowing that.

'What's that supposed to mean?' Gregnard stared at them in turn. He was beginning to sound edgy, as if realising that this had been a build-up to something he hadn't seen coming.

'Jean-Pascal Bourdelet. Late Secretary of State for Finance. Does that ring a bell?'

There was a long silence, with Gregnard's mouth forming into an 'o' while he digested the words. It took a few seconds, then he fell forward on his chair, the feet slamming into the floor as the implications finally hit home. He'd evidently read the newspapers.

'*Putain!* What's that you say? Are you winding me up?'

'Your car,' said Desmoulins, pointing at the piece of paper, 'was seen to deliver a letter to Bourdelet's house just minutes before he drove to his office and shot himself in the head.' He smiled and leaned forward. 'Come on, you know how it works: if there's a connection, all we need to do is look closer. A lot closer. Can your business stand that kind of scrutiny?'

Rocco stood up, deciding on a bit of play-acting of his own. They'd got Gregnard unsettled, now all they had to do was push home the advantage. Gregnard looked surprised by the sudden move and reared back in his chair.

'I'd like to take a look round your yard,' said Rocco. 'See what you've got for hire, check a few vehicles over. Desmoulins here was a master mechanic before he joined the force.'

Gregnard looked faintly alarmed at the idea. He shook his head but didn't move. His expression had turned sour, as if he'd been backed into a corner. He muttered, 'That won't do any good. It's not there.'

Rocco sat back down. 'Now we're getting somewhere. Where is it?'

Chapter Twenty-eight

Rocco headed for home after telling Desmoulins he'd see him in the morning. He radioed the office and got patched through to the Lille police station, where he asked to speak to officers Pouillot or Maté.

'Sorry, sir, Maté's out,' said the operator. 'Pouillot's here, though. I'll just get him for you.'

Seconds later Pouillot came on. 'Inspector Rocco? Is there a problem?' He sounded calm enough but with a hint of unease, as if something might have gone wrong with the arrest of Fontenal and his colleague.

'Not at all,' said Rocco. 'I need your assistance. Are you still holding Fontenal?'

'Yes, sir. I'm not sure of the progress, though. It's in the hands of the magistrate.'

'Good. I need to speak with Fontenal about an unrelated matter. It won't undermine his case so there's no conflict. Who do I need to talk to in your office?'

'I can check that for you, Inspector. Can I call you back?'

Rocco thanked him and cut the connection. Standard procedure would have involved going through Massin to the Lille *commissaire* for permission to visit a prisoner in his care. But with no provable connection to the Bourdelet case it would have encountered too many obstacles, and the Ministry's letter of authority would count for nothing.

He'd figured Pouillot would be anxious to be seen as proactive, and that might cut a couple of corners and save time.

His sole rationale for speaking to Fontenal was expediency. The gun-toting criminal's usual area of operations was in the outer reaches of Paris rather than the inner districts where the bigger gangs held sway. But Fontenal was a jackdaw, picking up names and contacts all over because that was the way his larcenous mind worked. If a person seemed useful, Fontenal would slot their name into the back of his head because you just never knew when a name could be turned into a profit. And the name Gregnard had finally spilled – that of the man who'd hired the yellow van – was one Rocco was pretty sure Fontenal would know.

While he was waiting for the young officer to call him back, he checked with the station and found he had an urgent message from Dreycourt.

'Sorry to load your case burden even more, Lucas,' said the art expert when he got through. 'I just received a call about a house fire involving a work of art just outside Compiègne. The local brigade commander thought there was something a little off about the owner's attitude and wondered if it was a potential fraud case. The Compiègne police knew about my involvement from a previous case and called me.'

'Go on.'

The fire had occurred in the living room of a house, Dreycourt explained, destroying most of the room and half of a large painting on one wall. The fire brigade was summoned by a neighbour who saw smoke coming from an open window. But the owner, Olivier Bajon, refused to talk to the police who attended and insisted it was an accident with a room heater.

'In high summer?' said Rocco.

'Exactly. I mean, if the owner doesn't want to make a fuss about a fire, that's up to him and his insurance company. It could be nothing, but it was the involvement of a work of art so soon after the other three that got my attention.'

'Quite right. I'll take a look. Is there a letter involved?'

'No. At least, if there is, Bajon isn't saying. But the brigade commander said he seemed unusually agitated, while saying it really wasn't worth anything.'

Rocco thanked him and pulled into the side of the road to check his map. He was closer to Amiens than Compiègne and the diversion would take a further bite out of his day, but any new potential lead was worth checking.

As he got back on the road Pouillot came through on the radio. The officer sounded pleased at getting the co-operation. 'I've passed word to the duty officer to expect you.'

'Good of you, Pouillot. Thank you.'

Rocco dumped the map on the back seat and headed for Compiègne.

He found the house easily enough, on a small estate of upmarket detached properties. It was easy to spot, with a damaged fence where the fire brigade had dragged their hoses through, leaving behind a layer of water that had turned the front garden into a swamp.

He knocked at the door. It was snatched open by a small man in his sixties with tufts of white hair above his ears and an aggressive expression on his face.

He stared at Rocco's card and muttered, 'Mother of God, when do you people let up? I said it was an accident. Why can't you accept that?'

'We like to make sure you're certain before we close the file,' said Rocco easily, and pinched his nose at the smell of smoke hanging in the air. 'It's all part of a public safety initiative. May I see the damage?'

Bajon stepped back with a huff of impatience. 'If you want to waste your time, be my guest. It's a fire-damaged room, that's all. I'm sure you've seen worse in your time. Anyway, why are the police involved? It's not a crime to be careless in one's own home, is it?'

'Of course not.' Rocco followed him through into a room blackened by smoke and smelling of burnt plastic and wood, where the air was gritty on his tongue. The damage seemed mostly confined to one wall, where half of a large oil painting lay propped at floor level, presumably where it had fallen or been dislodged by the fire hose. The burned remains of an oil heater lay nearby, mixing the air with the pungent smell of paraffin. The subject of the painting was difficult to make out through a layer of soot, but it looked like a woman in a long, floaty dress smiling at someone in the section burned away by the fire. The style was vaguely familiar, like a host of other paintings he'd seen in the past.

'Nice,' Rocco commented. 'Family heirloom?'

'Huh. I wish,' said Bajon. 'It's worthless if you must know. Not that I'd know the difference. I bought it because my wife liked it. Nothing wrong with that, is there?'

'Of course not. But why were you using the heater?'

Bajon scowled. 'Because I feel the cold, Inspector, that's why. I used to work for the foreign office overseas,

206

and caught a dose of pneumonia, followed by a fever. It was some years ago but I haven't been able to get warm ever since, even in this hot weather. My wife thinks I'm off my head but she doesn't know what it's like. I like to stay warm, that's all.'

'How did it happen?'

'I was an idiot, if you must know. I was lighting the heater when I dropped the match. It fell onto a spilled patch of paraffin and went up like a bomb.' He pointed to his eyebrows. 'See there? I lost some of the hairs. I was lucky I didn't lose my eyes.'

'Are you insured?'

Bajon laughed. 'You mean for the painting? Forget it. I got it from a man I know who owed me a favour and I hope I never see him again. He said an antique dealer had told him it was decent enough so he offered it to me for a few francs.' He leaned close and stared up at Rocco. 'Even I know it's rubbish. I'm not an art lover; I wouldn't recognise quality art if it bit me on the arse!'

Rocco bent and peered down at the bottom right-hand corner, but could see no signature.

He looked at Bajon. 'Does the name Cezard mean anything to you? Sébastien Cezard?'

'No. Should it?' The old man looked irritated by the question and Rocco got the feeling he wasn't acting. 'There's no provenance, if that's what you're looking for. If it was worth anything the dealer would have made an offer, wouldn't he? Now, is that all? Only I have a lot of cleaning up to do.'

Rocco thanked him and walked out to the road, relieved to be out in the open air once more. An elderly man was standing by the gate to the property next door, pretending to be checking the hinges. When he spotted

Rocco, he shuffled across to intercept him. 'Are you the police?'

'I am. Can I help, Monsieur—?'

'Oh, my name doesn't matter, *Commissaire*.'

'Inspector, actually. Inspector Rocco.'

'Sorry. I just wanted to tell you something. It was me who called the fire brigade. If it hadn't been for me the whole place might have gone up in smoke, and yet old Bajon had the cheek to criticise me for sticking my nose in, would you believe? I was simply being a good neighbour. I mean, what kind of person would just stand by while a neighbour's house burned to the ground?' He ended on a breathless note, as if it had taken some effort to let out his grievance and he'd finally run out of puff.

'Perhaps,' Rocco suggested, 'he's feeling embarrassed about it. People do sometimes, when this kind of thing happens.' He put his hand on the door handle of his car, but the man hadn't finished. He stepped closer, bringing with him a smell of fried food.

'Hold on – there's something else. It's just... something about the painting that got burned isn't right.'

'In what way?'

'Well, he told me and my late wife not so long ago, God rest her soul, that it was an inexpensive piece he'd acquired from his father just recently. Yet I heard him telling one of the fire brigade men that it was a work of art, a family heirloom left to him by his father who died before the war.'

'Memory plays tricks with people when they're under pressure,' Rocco countered. It was more likely that Bajon had been confused, even lying for the sake of appearance and wanting to impress his neighbours.

'If you ask me, there's something funny about it,' the man insisted. 'I mean, if it was that special why did he tell us differently? Did he think we'd steal it?'

Why indeed, Rocco agreed. But people had their reasons. He decided to get Desmoulins to look into it. If there was an insurance angle, it shouldn't be too hard to get hold of the details. In the meantime, he had to get this man off the scent before he got himself into an argument he couldn't handle. 'Maybe he's too upset to know what he's saying.'

The man pulled a face, as if realising that Rocco wasn't going to be drawn into his game. 'If you say so, Inspector. Only don't blame me if it turns out he's perpetrating some kind of fraud, that's all I've got to say.' With that he stomped off and disappeared behind his gate, where he glared back at Rocco before turning and walking out of sight.

Gossip or truth? Rocco wondered, as he drove to the office. Misremembered detail, perhaps. Neighbours occasionally fell out and previous confidences often became weapons to be used in the subsequent war of words.

--

As he drove away, his radio buzzed. It was Pouillot calling from Lille.

'Inspector, I think you should know that if you want to speak to Fontenal it has to be today… that's to say, this evening.'

Rocco checked his watch. It was already six. 'Why the hurry?'

'We've been advised he's going to be moved to one of the Paris stations first thing in the morning. There's an outstanding warrant on him and they're claiming priority.'

Damn. Someone with more muscle was grabbing him, no doubt because of the gun involvement. He had no choice; he'd have to see Bam-Bam now, before he got dragged into the Paris system and out of reach.

Chapter Twenty-nine

The interview room at the Lille station was small, airless and grim, as if any hint of life or colour had been drained out of it by the years of bad news, violence, death and stories of lives gone horribly wrong. When Rocco stepped through the door, he saw Fontenal slumped in a hard-backed chair looking aggrieved, with a uniformed officer standing behind him.

The prisoner brightened up visibly when he recognised his visitor. '*Alors*, Rocco,' he murmured, and went to stand up, but the officer clamped a hand on his shoulder, forcing him back down.

'It's all right,' said Rocco. 'You can leave us.'

The officer nodded and left the room, and Fontenal heaved a sigh of relief. 'Thank God. It's good to see a friendly face at last. That one was getting on my nerves. They're a nightmare up here, I swear. Anybody would think I was Al Capone, or that I'd slaughtered a bagful of kittens!'

'You were carrying a gun, you moron,' said Rocco. 'What do you expect? If I hadn't recognised you in time at that old café, you'd be dead by now. How would Edith feel about that?' He sat down in the other chair. 'I haven't come to get you out, so don't get your hopes up. But I might put in a good word for you if you can help me out.'

Fontenal assumed a criminal's stock expression of instant suspicion. 'Yeah? Who do I have to turn in for that? You know I'm not a snitch, right? Not for anything or anyone so don't even ask.'

'Yes, I know,' Rocco said with heavy sarcasm. 'You have such high moral standards.' He took a packet of cigarettes and matches out of his pocket and tossed them on the table. 'Have a smoke and listen because I don't have long.'

Fontenal grabbed both and lit up, puffing eagerly, then gave a satisfied smile. 'Thanks, Rocco – you're a gentleman. How can I help?'

'Georges Peretz. What does the name mean to you?'

'Peretz? I know him, yes. Never worked with him, but I see him from time to time. He's been around a while. Does a bit of driving and odd jobs here and there. Why?'

'Driving and odd jobs. So not what you'd call a gang leader, then. A planner. An ideas man.'

Fontenal laughed. 'What old Georges? God, no. I mean, he's not stupid but he was never top of the class at school, if you get my meaning. He's more your simple follower of orders, not like us independent operators.' He smiled and took another puff of his cigarette.

Rocco was tempted to point out that Georges, the follower of orders, was currently out and free to do what he liked in the world, unlike certain independent operators he could think of. But he decided against it. Rubbing Bam–Bam's nose in it wouldn't help.

'Whose orders does he follow?'

'Eh? What do you mean?'

'Let me put it more clearly.' Rocco did so carefully, tapping the table for emphasis between each word. 'Who does he work for?'

'Ah, that. I don't know. Seriously. I mean, I've been out of the loop down there for a while. Ivry and that area. People and circumstances change. It's a constantly shifting scene, you know?'

'Who said anything about Ivry?'

Fontenal's Adam's apple bobbed wildly. 'Pardon?'

'You said Ivry. Peretz lives in Bercy, in the 12th arrondissement, the other side of the river.'

Fontenal dragged in a large lungful of smoke, playing for time, and coughed violently, leaning forward and banging his chest. When he regained his composure, he said, 'Okay, so he lives in Bercy. I don't know why I said Ivry. They're next to each other, of course. My mistake.'

Rocco wasn't fooled; he'd seen Fontenal and too many others go through the same performance, hoping to come up with a convincing answer to a tricky question. 'You're right, Bam-Bam. Your mistake.' He picked up the matches and cigarettes and made to stand up. 'Good luck tomorrow, because you'll be in Paris first thing, alongside all your independent operator mates. Let's hope they're still feeling friendly towards you.'

'Eh? Why shouldn't they?'

'Well, think about it: they'll all know about your latest little escapade here in Lille, won't they? Word travels fast about that sort of thing, especially a guy with a gun bringing down the ceiling of a bank. That'll give them a laugh.'

Fontenal looked sour. 'Yeah, don't remind me. It was bad luck, that.'

'I'm sure. But what will they say when they hear you've been chatting to the *flics*?'

'What? Rocco, wait.' Fontenal's mouth worked hard, as if it were an effort to force the words out. 'That's a bit low, isn't it? You know what would happen if they thought I was a snitch. I'd end up in the river tied to a block of concrete!'

'Undoubtedly. So talk.'

'All right, I'll tell you – but only because you've always played straight with me. If it gets out that I said anything I'll be dead before the day's out. This is a serious person I'm talking about.'

'As long as you tell me the truth.' Rocco dropped the cigarettes back on the table as a sign of good faith.

'Sure. Of course.' Fontenal scrabbled for a new cigarette and lit it with the stub of the old one. He blew out the smoke in a nervous gust, eyeing Rocco with a squint as if he might suddenly disappear. His voice dropped as he said, 'Georges works for Yuri Serban.'

'Never heard of him.'

'Seriously? Christ, Rocco, you have been out of circulation. Serban's bad news. Not like some of the bigger boys, the Africans or the Corsicans, but he's got a short fuse and doesn't let anyone get one over on him. He runs a couple of small clubs, some gambling dens, a few girls, a taxi firm – lots of small stuff. But between you and me I reckon he's got his eye on the big time.'

'What makes you think that?'

'Because I know the type – and I've heard stuff.'

'What sort of stuff?'

'He's clever. He's been playing it small so far, see, so nobody gives him a second glance – cops or the bigger gangs. But, bit by bit, he's building a busy little empire for himself. You know what it's like: it's never long before a crim like that starts to get more ambitious. And Serban's ambition is to move closer to the centre and take over someone else's turf. Why do you want to know about him, anyway?'

'Where does he operate?'

'So far, strictly on the outskirts, south-east suburbs. Ivry-sur-Seine area. He puts out the picture of not wanting to mix it with the bigger boys, preferring to do his own thing, so they leave him alone.'

In Rocco's experience, most big city gang leaders liked to consolidate wherever they could, which meant taking over smaller groups if they thought a territory showed promise. Leaving one operating nearby long enough to get more established was almost unheard of.

'Why haven't they moved in on him?'

'Because they know he's got friends who'll back him up. Not gang members, but guys from the same background who aren't afraid of a fight.'

'Why would that worry them?'

Fontenal shrugged. 'Because most of them are head-cases and out-of-town and nobody knows what they look like. You can't fight faces you don't know, can you? And none of the big boys want to start an international fight because it gets the cops interested and doesn't make a profit.'

'You say background. What does that mean?'

'I don't know for sure, but I've heard Serban's family's from Romania, a long way back. The way I heard it is they do feuds in a big way over there. Hurt one family member and you get the whole clan on your back for ever.'

'Has he ever been inside?'

'I don't think so. He's clever, makes sure he doesn't get too ambitious and hurt the wrong people. Not unless they cross him, at least.' He seemed to realise what that statement implied and looked alarmed. 'Hey, remember

– you won't tell anyone about this, will you? He'll go after Edith if he can't get to me. I'm not kidding, Rocco – he's got a thing about people talking out of turn.'

Rocco waved a hand to calm him down. He stood up, realising that Fontenal was unlikely to say anything more. 'Nobody will know outside this room, I promise.' He nodded at the cigarettes. 'You can keep those. I'll see what I can do about putting in a good word with the magistrate. It won't be much, though, because of the gun.'

Fontenal nodded, subsiding in his chair. 'Fair enough. My own fault, that. Thanks, Rocco. I appreciate it.' He grinned and squinted through the smoke. 'You couldn't give Edith a call for me, could you? Just a quick one to let her know I'm all right? She probably doesn't know about this yet and she'll be worrying.' He told Rocco the number to call.

'I'll see what I can do. You don't deserve her, you know that?'

'That's what she's always saying. I'm starting to believe it.'

–

Rocco thanked Pouillot for his help and got the name of the magistrate handling Fontenal's case. Her name was Laure Ordon. He asked for the use of a telephone and gave her a call.

'You're optimistic, aren't you, Inspector?' said Ordon. She sounded young and confident, clearly unfazed by a call out of the blue. 'He and his friend were armed. That's not going to help their case.'

'I know. But Fontenal has given me information that might help with another case I'm working on. It should be worth consideration, don't you think?' He was guessing he didn't have to tell her that informants were key in solving many cases, and the knowledge that 'an informant' had received some consideration in a sentence for providing inside information might persuade others to come forward in future.

'I suppose, although it depends what this other case is, frankly.' Her tone of voice lacked enthusiasm, and he decided he had to take a chance on giving out a name. He'd been ready for that very question and figured it was worth the risk to mention it. 'Jules Petissier.'

'What? The Assize Court Petissier?' Her tone went up a peg or two. 'You're investigating that? I thought it was attempted suicide.'

'It probably was. But there are secondary circumstances which may have driven him to it.'

'What sort of information did Fontenal give you? Did he name someone?'

Rocco smiled. She must have known he wasn't going to tell her, but it hadn't stopped her asking. Magistrates loved gossip as much as anyone else. 'I can't say at this point. Let's call it a possibility.'

'Well, I've met Fontenal, Inspector, and I'd be amazed if he moves anywhere near the right circles for that kind of detail. Still, if it's a possibility, I'll put the fact forward in his defence but I'm not promising anything.'

He thanked her and rang off, grateful for magistrates who were prepared to consider the bigger picture.

Next he rang Edith, Fontenal's long-suffering partner, and told her the bad news. She responded with the expected wail of despair, but rapidly became pragmatic and asked for details of where he was being held.

'Did you say Rocco?' she asked. 'François mentioned you before. He said you were okay.'

'You mean for a cop?'

'Yeah, for a cop.' She laughed. 'Thank you, anyway. I'll see where he ends up and pay him a visit. If you see him, tell him he'd better be wearing a crash helmet when I get there because he's going to need it.'

Chapter Thirty

In Amiens, Commissaire Massin was working late, trying to catch up with paperwork while dwelling on the police officers' function near Versailles. He was still feeling vexed by the turn in the conversation with Ceyton, and couldn't get rid of the feeling that somehow the senior officer had deliberately found him and steered the talk towards the Bourdelet case. He'd tried telling himself that it was rubbish, that it had been his decision to attend the event, so there was no way Ceyton could have known he'd be there.

And yet… why did he feel that the last few words uttered by Ceyton had come across as a threat? That if Rocco didn't do as he was told, which by implication meant call a halt to the investigation when ordered, it would be the end of his career – and by association, Massin's, too.

On the other hand, hadn't Ceyton offered to help him investigate potential links between Bourdelet, Petissier and Gambon? Why would he do that if he wanted it to fail?

Even as he thought it through his telephone rang. He snatched it up. 'Massin.'

'Ah, François. I'm glad I got you.' It was Ceyton. 'I thought you'd like to hear about my investigations on your behalf following our little chat.'

Massin's heart pounded. Had he been wrong about the man's intentions? 'Yes, sir. Of course.'

'Well, a big zero, is what I discovered. By that I mean no connections at all.'

Massin felt his belly go cold. Ceyton's voice sounded oddly relieved, as if it had been a sticky subject that could now be forgotten and filed away, a dead-end case with no result.

'Not even Gambon and Petissier? I'd have thought a judge and a senior policeman would have had some passing professional acquaintances in common.'

Ceyton chuckled. 'You'd think, wouldn't you? Believe me, there's not as much contact between the police and the judiciary as you might think at our level. We're all too busy watching our backs. I did a thorough job, I can promise you. Enjoyed myself, too, rattling a few bones and raking in favours owed. But the answers all came back the same: as far as anyone can tell, they all moved in different circles, belonged to different clubs and would not have studied together due to their different ages. The short answer is Bourdelet was a snob and loner, Petissier was the most God-awful career-hound and social climber, and neither of them would have acknowledged Gambon if he'd been on fire in the courtyard of the Élysée Palace.'

'I see. Well, thank you for your efforts, sir. I appreciate it. I'll tell Rocco.'

'Good. You might want to tell him something else, too, while you're at it. While I was rattling a few bones, I happened to get a call from high up in the Interior Ministry – and I mean nose-bleedingly high.'

Massin didn't like the sound of that. 'About what?'

'There have been calls to impose a time limit on how long this investigation can go on.'

'I hope that's not going to be unreasonable, sir. These things take time. And Rocco's investigation has barely got off the ground.'

'I'm sorry, Massin.' That hard tone in his voice was back, the one Massin had heard at the function. 'Certain people high up in the government are getting impatient. They need answers soon in order to bring the Bourdelet investigation to a close. The longer it goes on the more likely it will be for rumours to build and for stories to begin circulating. And the government can't have that. I did warn you.'

'What's the sudden rush?'

'Simple. A new secretary of state for finance is about to be appointed and they can't have an unresolved investigation involving the misuse of departmental funds hanging over the newcomer's head. It's bad for government business and won't help public confidence in such an important element of the state.'

'What about the other two cases – Petissier and Gambon?'

'Those, too. I think you should advise your man to report what he has found so far and we'll see what the response is.'

Massin felt a sense of unease. Unless Rocco had moved further along in his assignment than he was aware, and had somehow triggered a sensitivity in the machinery of government, this went against all the normal protocols of a criminal investigation. He'd read the blackmail letters and in each one there was a clear criminal intent in the threat to the reputation of the victim. Were some elements of the government playing at following the rule of law while deciding to sweep the three cases under the carpet? If so, it confirmed what Ceyton had suggested.

He already knew that Rocco's first response would verge on the unprintable. But his first question would be entirely rational. 'How long do we have?'

'Days,' replied Ceyton. 'Two or three at most. Candidates for the post are already being lined up. I'm sorry to be the bearer of such news, but there's nothing more I can do.' He hesitated. 'It has been put to me that the view in the Ministry is that Rocco would be a most useful asset to the BRI here in Paris. He has the right experience and background and is a natural choice to be a senior member of the team. You might like to remind him of that while he makes up his mind about this case. Good luck.'

The call was ended, leaving Massin staring at the wall. He was appalled. In his years in the military and the police he had witnessed pressure. You toed the line or you could forget reaching any further in your career. But the pressure had usually been subtle, a suggestion rather than a heavy threat, understood and accepted as a normal part of being on a career ladder surrounded by competitors. This was beyond direct; it was an open reminder that if Rocco wanted to advance further, he should remember where his future lay.

He got up and paced around his office. Even before speaking to Rocco, he knew the detective's contention would be that if the three men had had nothing in common and were unlikely to have even known each other, then the common factor, the *connection* bringing them together in the blackmail scheme had to be through someone else. An outsider. Somebody who knew them all, or knew their individual history.

How the hell Rocco was going to find that person in a couple of days was hard to imagine.

He picked up the phone and called the radio room. 'Get Inspector Rocco to call me. Urgent.'

Chapter Thirty-one

Rocco was just finishing another section of Mme Denis's pie when his phone rang. It was the operator at the station. 'Sorry to disturb you, sir, but Commissaire Massin wishes to speak with you.'

Rocco was surprised. For Massin to be calling this late it was unlikely to be good news. 'Put him through, please.'

'Sorry, sir. The *commissaire* wants to see you in person. In the office.'

'Now?'

'Yes, sir. Sorry. He says it's important.'

'I'm on my way. Thirty minutes.'

Rocco stood up, put on his coat and headed for the car. All the driving was beginning to catch up with him but there was no arguing with a direct order.

Thirty minutes later he joined Massin in his office. Other than a couple of night duty officers downstairs, there was nobody around and the building felt like an empty shell, devoid of its usual hustle and bustle.

'Thank you, Inspector,' Massin said, and held up a coffee pot, steam issuing from the lid. He had taken off his uniform jacket and looked unusually casual, with his top button undone and his shirt cuffs turned back. 'Just made. I know it's late for coffee, but I think we might both need it. And you'll have to excuse the lack of formal dress, but it's been a long day. I'm sure you feel the same.'

'Thank you,' said Rocco, noting the sombre tone in Massin's voice. 'I won't say no. Is there a problem?'

Massin finished pouring, then sat down and leaned back, flexing his shoulders. 'You could say that. We're on the edge of your investigation being closed down, and I wanted to warn you in person. It seemed not to be the kind of discussion to have by telephone.' He sipped his coffee, then launched into a replay of his talk with Ceyton and the officer's subsequent warning.

Rocco listened in silence. It came as no surprise, given Santer's grim prediction, but it was still disturbing to hear that there were now strict conditions attached to his handling of the case. Even more so was the implied threat to his future advancement if he didn't follow orders.

'I may have precipitated this, I'm afraid,' Massin confessed, 'by getting Ceyton involved. It could have been a step too far in letting them know how you were proceeding. I shouldn't have put myself in the position.'

'Unless it was him who approached you.'

Massin looked at him. 'What do you mean?'

'You said you decided to go to this senior police officers' event. Was that normal?'

'No. I've never been before. But seeing the invitation gave me the idea to see what I could discover.'

'Have you had an invitation before?'

'Not that I can remember. They usually place a piece in the officers' bulletin.'

'But not this time.'

'No.' Massin chewed his lip. 'Not this time.' He frowned. 'You think it was a deliberate ploy to get me there?'

'I'm suggesting it seems unusual, since they've never bothered to ask you before.'

Massin stood up and took a tour of his office. 'Now you mention it, I handed the card in but the man on the desk didn't seem to know what to do with it. Others were walking straight in. But why?'

Rocco assumed he was wondering why the subterfuge. 'If you want to drop a word in a contact's ear without making it look deliberate,' he said, 'then a chance encounter in a crowd is the safest bet. In this case, you were there, Ceyton was there; what could be more natural than a chat... followed by a little timely advice.'

'To what end?'

'To warn me off.' Rocco stood up to join him. 'They didn't want this investigation from the start. This was their opportunity to send in a torpedo to get it stopped.' He waited for Massin to say something, but the senior officer seemed conflicted at the idea of such an open piece of skulduggery from the high command.

'So far,' he continued, 'two other people have said pretty much the same thing to me. Both suggested this investigation was riddled with danger and would go nowhere, that finding out the truth behind the letters would stir up too many problems they didn't want broadcast.'

'Such as?'

'Bourdelet by himself was a shock but explainable: a case of stress, a moment of weakness, but not unheard of. Throw in the other two and suddenly you have intrigue on your hands involving senior members of state bodies – the finance ministry, the police and the judiciary. That's too much.'

Massin nodded and looked disappointed. 'Somehow I expected more of Ceyton. He could have been more direct and I'd have understood. But to pretend to help while shooting a line…'

'He didn't exactly put himself out, though,' Rocco pointed out.

Massin smiled thinly. 'You're right. There's no way he could have got to many who knew all three men in such a short space of time.'

Rocco thought about Santer's prediction at the restaurant. 'So this is their way of shutting it down without losing face: get me to have a stab at it, then call it off.'

'It would seem that's the intention. My question is, what do you have so far?'

'Not a lot. We have some leads. Why do you ask?'

'That depends on you. Talk me through what you've got so far and we'll see where we go from there.' He hesitated, then added, 'For some reason I don't feel the desire to roll over like a performing dog. Do you?'

'No. How much time do we have?'

'Ceyton said three days at most. I'd say more like two.'

Rocco told him about the yellow van and the man named Serban. 'It doesn't amount to much but it could be a link in the chain.'

'Can you mount surveillance on him?'

Rocco shook his head. 'Probably not, if he's connected with any of the Paris criminal network. Even if he didn't recognise me someone else might.'

'How about Desmoulins?'

'Possible. But I have a better idea.'

'Do you want to tell me?'

'He's an old friend of mine. He's better than me at this kind of stuff.'

A light dawned in Massin's eyes. 'You mean Caspar? Is that wise?'

'He's a good man and, yes, I trust him. I'll have to pay him, though.'

Massin nodded. 'Do it. But tell him it has to be forty-eight hours, no more.'

Chapter Thirty-two

The first thing Rocco did on exiting Massin's office was to call Dreycourt. It was late but he needed to check with the art consultant that nothing else had cropped up.

'Lucas. I was just thinking about you. How's it going?'

He told Dreycourt about the calls for the investigation to be called off. Dreycourt wasn't surprised.

'Don't say I didn't warn you, Lucas. There's a bad smell about this business and they want rid of it. The way they see it, if you haven't pinned anyone down by now, you're unlikely to do so. It's the way their minds work, as if villains walk around in black masks and striped jumpers. But the excuse about the replacement is rubbish. The incomer won't give a damn about rumours about their predecessor. He or she will be too busy picking up the reins and getting on with the job. I can think of several ministers who've taken over office during a scandal, and it never stopped them from doing what they had to do and making a success of it. It's a requirement of the job.'

'Could there be another reason for wanting it shut down?'

A brief hesitation. 'Political expediency, you mean? Entirely possible. One man's mistakes can easily rebound upwards, enough to make the opposition sharpen their teeth and start talking about poor judgement and a weak administration. Let it go far enough and it becomes a feeding frenzy. If that's the case, nobody's sharing it with me.'

Rocco let it slide. Political ripples following a scandal were inevitable, but if there was an underlying reason it would be buried layers deep and he had no chance of finding it in time. He mentioned the clearance of papers from Bourdelet's office just before his visit, and the fact that he was being watched.

Dreycourt didn't seem concerned. 'They're watching you because that's what they do. Just because they've given you an assignment doesn't mean they trust you entirely. It's called paranoia. Ignore them. As for the paperwork, they're using the opportunity to clean up in case Bourdelet left anything behind that they don't want anyone else to see. Have you made any progress with Cezard?'

'Not much.' Rocco didn't want to mention Vauquelin's presence. He had nothing concrete to say about the lawyer, and throwing the man's name out there could rebound on him with unfortunate results. 'He denies any involvement but I'm going to have another chat with him.'

A sigh came down the line. 'Pity. We're running out of time.'

Rocco hesitated. Dreycourt was clearly under pressure, too, and was looking to see something solid to feed up his chain of command. He decided to give him something to use to keep the dogs off their backs. 'We've come across the possible involvement of a criminal group in Paris who may have delivered the letters. I'm looking into that right now.'

'Really?'

'Don't get too excited,' Rocco cautioned him. 'It could be nothing. They might have been acting for someone else and they'll be unlikely to share that information with us.'

'Can you bring them in and question them?'

'What, and use a rubber hose? Tempting, but no. We'll try proving connections first.'

He ended the call and thought about where to go next. He still had to check the Petissier house, but first he had to get Caspar on board. He dialled a Paris number.

Chapter Thirty-three

Marc Casparon, known as 'Caspar', had spent many years working undercover in and around the capital, running informants among the various criminal gangs, working his way in among members and becoming a part of the community. It had been dangerous work and over the years the stress had taken its toll. A breakdown had nearly blown his cover and had meant the end of his career in the police. Too well-known a face in certain areas, he'd been forced to take on a new kind of work and ease himself out of the criminal *milieu*, advising companies and private individuals on security matters.

Rocco had worked with him on occasion and admired him. Now, if any jobs came up where his specialist skills could be used, he had no hesitation in calling him. Caspar himself still yearned for the old excitement and, if the kind of jobs Rocco called on him to do were a far cry from his old work tunnelling deep into the lives of the criminal elite, neither man mentioned it. Rocco's main concern was keeping him safe and not exposing him deliberately to the kind of people he used to know so well.

'Give me the details,' Caspar said as soon as Rocco told him what he wanted. 'Work's a bit slow at the moment so I could do with some excitement.'

Rocco told him everything, from Bourdelet's death to the information he'd gleaned so far.

Caspar whistled. 'That's pretty heavy. I've heard of Serban but he wasn't on anybody's radar when I was out there. He was too small and we had bigger fish to go after. What are you looking for?'

'Anything you can get. Connections, mostly. If Serban's acting for somebody else in delivering the letters, it would help if I knew who that was.'

'Well, he won't know me and I've never heard of Peretz, so at least I'll be able to get up close and see what he's up to. This is urgent, you say?'

'Very. I've got a couple of days before they close it down. If I can get something solid it might be enough to stop them doing that.'

'I'll get on it first thing.'

–

Caspar had tracked down Serban's center of operations on the outskirts of Ivry-sur-Seine by calling an old colleague the night before, and was now parked nearby. It was just gone nine a.m., allowing time for the street to be populated with adequate cover, and for Serban to show himself.

The front of Serban's base was an old two-storey redbrick block inside a courtyard, part of a former local government workshop closed down and sold off two years ago for development. Serban's name wasn't on the deeds, his contact had said, but he was generally considered to be the owner, having purchased the block through a third party.

Caspar did a walk-past, stepping into the courtyard and checking the entrance foyer for signs of occupancy. There were no lights on to show that anyone was inside, as the day was bright and sunny enough not to need them. A spread of posters, envelopes and newspapers lay across the tiled floor inside the glass front door, a visual deterrent to any callers hoping to make a sale. A layer of dust on an ancient reception desk and a tattered chair with the stuffing leaking out of the cushion completed the sad picture of a building unoccupied and unloved.

He made a tour of the block, which consisted of small commercial warehouses side-by-side with a spread of cheap bungalows. He came up on the rear of Serban's building along a narrow street scattered with dustbins, a couple of ancient cars with no wheels and an accumulation of rubbish that looked many years old. A few shopfronts were boarded up and it seemed a place where time had stood still and was unlikely to get going again any day soon.

The exception to this was the rear door to Serban's block, which had a new Opel Rekord parked outside. Tan-coloured and shiny, it probably didn't stand out so much out in the city, where fancy cars were more the norm, but right here it screamed out not to be touched.

Caspar caught sight of his reflection in the car's bodywork and remembered to slouch his shoulders. He was dressed in a battered cap, faded trousers and an old leather jacket that had seen better days, and carried a bag slung across his back. His general appearance was in keeping with his gaunt face and dark features, which had seen him blend in all over the city, easily overlooked and difficult to remember. In the past, he'd been described variously as an Arab, as Mediterranean, maybe Italian or Spanish. Right now, he was playing the part of a street rat, scouring bins and corners for anything he could trade for a few francs, a common-enough sight among down-and-outs and those in between jobs.

He veered close to the Opel, peering inside but not getting too close. If Serban was the kind of man described by his contact, he'd probably have someone watching the streets in the area, especially where his car was parked. Having a heavy come bursting out of the building with a baseball bat was something Caspar wanted to avoid, so he continued up the street – but not before eyeing a new lock plate on the rear door of the building and a reinforced metal strip running down both sides of the door itself. He'd seen this kind of set-up before: it meant nobody was going to batter that door in without making a lot of noise. They'd be delayed long enough for those inside to make an exit from another part of the building.

Back in his car he checked the street. On his left was a high wall covered in cracked, grey rendering, behind which he'd glimpsed a dilapidated factory. On the other side of the street, apart from Serban's place, were a garage, two small shops and what looked like a collection of small workshops. It was the kind of area that offered good cover for the sort of operation Serban was running. Not many close neighbours and the kind of mixed spread of businesses where his comings and goings could go on without attracting the wrong kind of attention.

Caspar sat and waited, sipping water sparingly. He'd done so many stakeouts like this over the years that the routine was familiar. Find a spot to watch, settle down and wait to see what happened. Occasionally nothing did, which was unfortunate. But whoever was under observation had to move sometime, and that was when all the waiting paid off. He had no idea if he could take anything back to Rocco, but he was here to get whatever he could.

An hour ticked by with grinding slowness, the street scene barely changing. Pedestrians came and went, delivery vehicles drove along and parked or passed through. Lives were being lived and people followed their routines, the same as always.

Then a man in a suit stepped out of the courtyard. He was in his late twenties or early thirties, heavily-built, with swarthy skin. He wore heavy shoes and his head swung left and right, checking the street, eyes flicking quickly over faces, vehicles and windows. Despite this, he seemed relaxed. His suit was cheap and creased as if he'd slept in it and, as he turned, the jacket opened slightly, revealing the butt of a pistol in a holster under one arm.

Caspar stayed where he was, breathing easily, motion-less. If the man was any good at his job he would already have a picture in his mind of the surroundings. To move now would be bound to attract attention.

The watcher took a last look around before turning his head and giving a nod. Moments later a second man stepped out from the courtyard and turned immedi-ately right, walking along the narrow pavement with the watcher following closely behind, off to one side and close enough to intercept any threat from passing traffic.

Serban was bulky across the shoulders, with the lumbering gait of a wrestler who'd spent too many hours in the gym and was carrying muscle that he didn't need. Soon that weight would turn soft and the belly would spread. His hair was thick and dark on the top, cut short at the sides, and his heavy chin bore a rash of dark stubble above a startlingly white shirt and blue tie. His suit looked expensive and hung easily about his frame.

Made to measure, thought Caspar, but worn by a thug. A rich one, too, whose sole goal in life was to scare people and make himself even richer. He was willing to bet that both men spoke Romanian along with most of Serban's close retinue. Keeping it in the family, like the Turkish, Algerian and African gangs. Protective. Intimidating. Deadly when threatened. Outsiders were rarely admitted to the inner ranks, suspicion quick to close against them like the jaws of a vice.

Caspar was in a dilemma: he could follow the two men and see where they were going, or he could slip inside Serban's place and have a quick shuffle through to see what he could come up with. He decided to stick with what he had; the office wasn't going anywhere but it might be useful to see who Serban met up with.

After a quick change of clothes, he climbed out of his car and set off along the street. He'd done away with the cap and now wore a differently-coloured jacket and smart but unremarkable trousers taken from his shoulder bag. The down-and-out was gone and he now carried a briefcase, the leather worn with use, a newspaper held by a strap on one side. Office pen-pusher said the image, running errands for a boss and enjoying the brief outing in the fresh air before he had to go back inside his cubicle.

Up ahead of him Serban slowed and turned right into a short street populated by shops, cafes and neighbourhood eating places. He entered one of these while his watcher stood against the building with his hands folded in front of him, eyes scanning the street. Caspar crossed the street to get a better view of the door Serban had gone through. It was the entrance to a restaurant named Bacau, its name embellished with two flags: the Italian on one side and what Caspar guessed was a Romanian flag on the other.

Caspar walked on down the street for fifty metres, then re-crossed and came back. He walked past the watcher without making eye contact and pushed through the door of the restaurant as if he did it every day. A scattering of tables ran down the middle with a long counter down one side and the other wall covered in mirrors. It was simple, colourful without being flashy, and the clientele looked as if they had been born there.

Serban was taking a seat at a rear table. A waiter was fussing about him and giving the table top a quick wipe with a cloth. Personal service for an important customer. Serban sat with his back to the room, an unusual position in Caspar's experience of gang leaders, who liked to see everything that was going on around them while feeding their paranoia about possible threats from rivals or cops. But a mirror on the wall in front of him served to give him a view of the rest of the room and the entrance, and he undoubtedly felt comfortable there and safe from harm.

Caspar caught the eye of the man behind the counter and made a sign for coffee and pointed at a pastry behind the glass front. Then he indicated a table near the rear but along the side wall, and the man nodded.

Serban was alone, drinking coffee and sipping occasionally at a glass of water while flicking through a newspaper. Every now and then he'd glance in the mirror but seemed relaxed. If he was waiting for someone he was in no hurry.

A man entered and walked straight down the room to the rear. He was young, thin, unshaven and pale, with the poorly-fed look of the street. He wore green trousers and a mismatched blue jacket, and his shoulders were hunched as if the weight of the world was beating down on him. He bent to Serban's side and spoke softly for several seconds. He wasn't invited to sit and made no move to do so.

Moments later he straightened and moved away, leaving the restaurant without buying anything.

A runner, thought Caspar, recognising the type. Not what the gangs called soldiers, who were generally younger, fitter and more assertive, but the lowest rung on the gang ladder. The runner's job was to carry messages or packages, act as a spotter or lookout, even play decoy and take a fall if that was required.

Three more similar men followed in quick succession, speaking to Serban for a few moments before leaving. Like the first man, they were in their twenties, servile and unremarkable. This was Serban conducting his daily business: receiving news, sending messages, spreading instructions this way because like a lot of his kind he didn't trust the telephones. Caspar had observed too many meetings like this not to be aware that, although they all had their own formats and procedures, in the end they followed a pattern, no matter how big or small the gang. The main man held the reins and everyone else who came near him had a part to play. Gangland democracy in action, thought Caspar ironically.

–

A few minutes ticked by and Caspar was beginning to think business was over, when two more men entered the restaurant, seconds apart. The first was tall, fleshy, with grey hair and dressed in a smart suit, as different from the runners as it was possible to get. He couldn't see the man's face from this angle, though. Business type, thought Caspar, upper salary bracket, probably on his way to a meeting but with time to stop for a quick shot of caffeine. The man stepped over to a spare table in the centre and made a sign to the man behind the counter.

The second man entered moments later. He walked down the centre of the room and stopped alongside Serban, waiting with his hands down by his side. This time there was a nod of the head from Serban and the man sat down.

Better clothes than the runners, Caspar noted, and an air of confidence the others had lacked. Probably a trusted worker bee because he'd been invited to sit. Otherwise unremarkable to look at. Whatever they were talking about created a low-level buzz. Caspar had long ago learned the art of lip-reading but it needed two mouths to make a conversation, and the newcomer's lips barely moved. Probably a former convict, he would have picked up the habit during exercise yard conversations where discretion was an absolute must. Moments later, the newcomer stood up and left the restaurant without looking left or right.

Caspar's coffee and pastry arrived and he took the newspaper from the straps on his briefcase and pretended to read. To his surprise, the smartly-dressed business type stood up and moved down the restaurant, stopping at Serban's table. This time there was no waiting for permission, no sign of servility. The two men shook hands and the newcomer took the seat across from Serban.

As the man turned to face back up the restaurant, Caspar's gut went cold. He lifted the paper, blocking out a direct view of his face. He swore silently. Christ, of all the people to run into: Laurent *tête de merde* Vauquelin, cop-hater extraordinaire and lawyer to the criminal elite. Too late, Caspar realised his face was visible in the wall mirror, and that Vauquelin was looking at him. The lawyer had a faint frown etched on his handsome features. Was it a frown of recognition or a response to something Serban had just said?

Caspar took a sip of coffee with his free hand and focussed on the paper, trying to breathe evenly, while seeing flashbacks of his life before leaving the police. He'd been forced to surface from a deep undercover assignment to give evidence on a case from several months earlier. A prostitute had been slashed by a pimp and drug dealer in a row over money. She'd been courageous enough to bring a complaint against her attacker. But the investigation hadn't stopped at the violence; by chance it had revealed a network of dealers operating across the city, and two of the leading organisers had been charged with offences ranging from drug importation to intimidation, arson and murder. Caspar had been watching both men.

It had been a tough time for him, forced into the daylight under a court order, the stress adding to his already fragile state of mind. He'd been allowed to appear in court in disguise to avoid compromising other ongoing investigations, but the one person who had been permitted to see him out of the shadows had been the counsel for the defence, *Maître* Laurent Vauquelin.

Like most of his colleagues, he'd already known of Vauquelin's intense antipathy towards the police and had been very careful with his testimony. But it had been a gruelling time being constantly on guard against the lawyer's attempts to prove that he and his colleagues had acted unlawfully. Later, long after the trial, the lawyer had been suspected of becoming just a little too close to some of the criminal clients he had defended, to the extent that he'd been accused of manufacturing evidence against the police to get them off the charges on a technicality and, likely, to bring the justice system into disrepute.

Caspar's hand was shaking, threatening to slop coffee on the table. He clamped his fingers tightly together and forced it to be still, hoping Vauquelin hadn't noticed.

In the wake of the trial and his subsequent decision to leave the police, he'd managed to wipe Vauquelin's face and supercilious smile from his mind, safe in the knowledge that he would never have to see the man again. And now here he was within a few metres of him.

He finished his coffee and risked a quick glance in the mirror. The two men were deep in conversation and Vauquelin was no longer staring at him. Whatever Serban was saying had got his full attention, but the words were too muffled to make out.

Not for the first time in his life, Caspar wished he could have been a fly on the wall. He couldn't see Serban's face but Vauquelin was suddenly very tight-lipped, as if he'd discovered something unpleasant taking a swim in his coffee cup.

Whatever they were discussing was going to remain a mystery. No words heard meant nothing to report, save that once again the *maître* with the dubious reputation was mixing with a well-known crook. By itself it wasn't a crime; defence lawyers represented criminals, it was what they did, all legal and above board. They could be discussing property deeds for all Caspar knew.

He stood up and picked up his briefcase, turning his back as he did so. He stepped across to the counter and deposited some coins in a dish. The man behind the counter nodded and Caspar moved towards the door.

'*Monsieur?* One moment.'

He froze, a familiar cold grip of alarm taking hold of the back of his neck. He turned slowly, and found a waiter holding out a newspaper.

'You forgot your paper, sir.'

Thanking the man and not daring to look towards the rear of the room, Caspar took the newspaper and made his exit, feeling Vauquelin's eyes drilling into his back all the way.

Chapter Thirty-four

Behind him, Laurent Vauquelin was only half-listening to what his client, Serban, was saying. He was staring after the gaunt figure with the briefcase. He was certain he knew him from somewhere. Vauquelin prided himself on his memory for faces, a necessary skill in his line of work. Surprises and lack of knowledge were a sure-fire killer in the cut and thrust of defence debate, and he'd schooled himself to stay at the top of his game.

He ran back in his mind to a gallery of snapshots featuring adversaries and witnesses, experts and prosecutors, the cream and dross of cases he'd worked on. The man had the look of a criminal, he decided, although the clothes and briefcase didn't quite fit. Certainly not a member of the legal profession, but possibly a lawyer's runner. Or an investigator.

'Are you listening to me, *Maître*?' Serban's bark dragged him back to the topic in question, before he slapped a hand on the table. 'You think I'm happy wasting my time here while you go off into dreamland? Pay attention or piss off – frankly at the moment I don't care which!'

'My apologies,' Vauquelin murmured. 'I saw someone I thought I knew.'

'Yeah, well since you probably know half the lowlifes and undercover parasites in Paris by now, that's no great surprise. But just remember who's paying your fees.'

Serban shook his head and pushed back in his chair. '*Merde*, I've forgotten what I was saying now, damn you.'

'I'm sorry.' Vauquelin wasn't, but he had to play the part with this ignorant gutter rat.

Serban snarled. 'It'll have to keep; I've got other things to be doing.' He leaned forward as he got to his feet, looming over Vauquelin with a tangible air of menace. 'Just bear in mind, our business isn't over yet. I want some return on my investment but without any further problems. So, you'd better come up with some alternative names to the last three washouts. What was it you called them – makeweights?'

'What about Rocco?' said Vauquelin. 'He's getting closer, isn't he?'

'Not to me he isn't,' said Serban bluntly. 'He's got nothing on me. You, however, I reckon he's got in his sights.' He smiled mirthlessly. 'Why not use your influence to make him go away? I'm sure you can pull some strings with your high-and-mighty mates in the police. Maybe get one of your legal snitches to find some dirt on him. After all, that's what you're good at.'

'I have no influence in the police or the Interior Ministry. None at all.' Vauquelin's voice skidded up a couple of octaves as he saw the look on Serban's face. The Romanian wasn't kidding. He'd heard often enough how dangerous this man could be, but he hadn't witnessed it this close before. The realisation was enough to bring out a fine layer of perspiration on his neck.

'You're not serious.' Serban looked sceptical.

'Absolutely.' God, thought Vauquelin, why did crooks like Serban always assume that being a lawyer meant you had access to every high office in the land? 'If I try sticking my nose in, I'll be accused of trying to undermine the investigation – and that will get me suspended. If they take me down, the first thing they'll do is look into my recent client list to see who I've been working for. Do you really think you can find another *avocat* who'll help you the way I do?' He swallowed hard, suddenly realising that he'd gone too far. 'Not that it would come to that, of course.'

Serban shook his head, his eyes like flint. 'I see. So that's how it goes, is it? You've left a safety letter behind, have you, ready to implicate me if anything happens to you?'

Vauquelin realised his mistake. 'No, that's not what—'

Serban leaned close again. 'What if I burn your office down and put a torch to your home? Would you enjoy that? Would that make you feel any safer?'

'No, Yuri – I didn't mean that.'

'Forget it.' Serban snapped his hand through the air, cutting him off. 'I'll deal with it myself. But I'll need Rocco's home address.'

Vauquelin felt a stab of alarm. 'Why? What are you going to do?' He had an instant vision of Serban taking extreme action to stop Rocco, and it coming back to haunt him.

'That's none of your business, *Maître.*' Serban's breath was damp against Vauquelin's cheek as he spat out the title, more insult than courtesy. 'For a start I don't think you have the balls to want to know what I'm capable of.'

'How do you expect me to get his address?'

'I don't care how – just do it. I want it by the end of the day. Oh, and it will cost you. Call it a protection fee.'

'What? But why should I pay for… for this?' Vauquelin went to stand up in protest but Serban clamped a meaty hand on his shoulder and pushed him back into his seat, his fingers creasing the rich material of his jacket and digging in painfully to his flesh. If any of the staff or customers noticed, they studiously paid no attention, although there was a noticeable drop in the conversation level. It was a stark reminder to Vauquelin that he was in enemy territory here, a long way from the civilised courtroom circuit he enjoyed. Showing his teeth in this place was likely to earn him far more than a sharp retort from a testy judge.

'You charge me for putting my signature on a document for you, don't you?' Serban countered softly. 'Every time I ring you there's an additional charge to my monthly bill, a fee for disturbing yourself on my behalf. So why should I do anything that benefits *you* for free? You're up close to the really rough side of my business now, Vauquelin. Don't you dare go gutless on me.' He paused. 'And if you ever, *ever* threaten me again, it will be the last thing you ever do!'

With that he turned and strode out.

Vauquelin felt shaken. Was he out of his depth? He drained his coffee cup and was tempted to ask for something stronger, but decided it would be too easy to give in to a brief weakness. Anyway, during their exchange a word uttered by Serban had sounded vaguely familiar. And alcohol wasn't the way to make it clearer. Something Serban had said had given him a hint about the identity of the man he'd seen earlier. *Undercover.* Damn. That must be it. He closed his eyes the better to think back. During his career he'd forced the courts to bring in more than one undercover cop. In so doing he'd found examples of shortcuts and of behaviour bordering on the misuse of power. Several clients had cause to thank him for his diligence on seeing the cases against them thrown out of court. That must be it: the man was an undercover cop! But which one – and what was he doing there?

Caspar was sweating as he hit the street, and it wasn't from the heat of the sun. He'd blown it, pure and simple. He'd got close but was still no nearer to finding out if Serban was connected to the yellow van and the blackmail letters. He breathed deeply and let out the air slowly, then walked back towards where he'd left his car, wondering what the hell to tell Rocco.

He was really not cut out for this game any more, he decided. For that he needed ice in his veins, and he didn't have it any longer. Perhaps it really was a good thing he had to give it up. But even as he returned to where his car was parked, he realised that the last few minutes, a chilling reminder of what he used to face on a regular basis, had given him a jolt of electricity, a feeling akin to a parachute jump he'd made in the army years ago. And he'd missed that buzz.

He was so focussed on his thoughts that he almost collided with a man who suddenly stopped right in front of him and turned round, muttering something and cursing to himself.

It was the man who'd sat down across from Serban just before Vauquelin.

Instinctively Caspar switched into survival mode, his brain recovering swiftly from the shock of seeing Vauquelin. He looked at the other man, dredging up the name of the driver of the yellow van. It was worth a try. Who else would have been trusted to take a seat? If he was wrong, he could apologise and be on his way, a stranger mistaking another's face. It happened all the time.

'Georges?' he said, assuming an expression of vague uncertainty. 'Georges Peretz?'

The man stopped, suspicion washing across his bland face. 'Might be. Who's asking?'

'It's Jomi. Don't you remember? Jean-Michel. We met a couple of times and you put a couple of tips my way. How's it going?'

The name Caspar used was one from the past and untraceable. Jomi or Jean-Michel Cabanas had been a petty criminal who'd made the decision to go straight and leave the area, drawn by a woman he'd fallen for in a big way. The power of love, Caspar had thought, which he knew well himself, could move mountains and change lives. Cabanas was still living somewhere in the Jura region with his lady as far as Caspar was aware, working a small-holding and enjoying the rural life.

'Oh. Jomi. Of course, yeah.' Peretz looked unsure, but in the face of such a convincing act, having feigned recognition, he couldn't back-track. 'I'm doing okay. It's been a while. You?'

'Excellent. Just in town for the day.' Caspar was about to see how far he could push the conversation when Peretz looked past him and said, 'Look, I'm sorry but I have to go – I forgot to give something to my boss and he'll kill me if I don't deliver.'

'Don't worry. We all have burdens, right? Good luck – and nice to see you.'

As he walked away, Caspar wondered if he'd really made the kind of connection Rocco was after. Serban, Peretz and... *Vauquelin*? Mother of God, that would be sensational. But what would it prove? Vauquelin was a defender of criminals... and the other two were most likely his clients. So what?

He reached his car and dumped his briefcase inside. Then he walked across the road and into the courtyard opposite. An empty building lay on one side, with windows missing and wind-blown leaves piled around the entrance. On the opposite side was a smaller, two-storey block with a clean entrance and a full complement of glass. He walked up to the door and listened. Too much background noise from the street to tell. He tried the handle. Locked.

A scrawny ginger cat twined its way around his ankles. He nudged it gently to one side, then turned and walked along the front of the building. He turned left at the end and saw a frosted window on a latch at the bottom. The cat followed him, purring like a small engine. Ten seconds later Caspar was inside and standing on the tiled floor of a washroom, holding his breath against the pungent ammonia smell of uncleaned toilets and listening to the drip-drip sound of water in the pipes. He eased the door open and cocked an ear. Nothing. He breathed out.

He was facing a set of stairs. First things first, in case he ran out of time. He made his way up, light on his toes, and stopped at the top to listen and called out, 'Hello?'

Nothing. There were four doors. Three of the rooms were empty, with a layer of grit on the floor. Electrical wires trailed from sockets and ceilings and the place smelled of mildew. The fourth room was an office, furnished with a desk, table and filing cabinet and three unmatched chairs. It was clean and smelled of cologne and cigarette smoke.

He went downstairs. Four more rooms; three were empty, the fourth was a small kitchen with a sink and a fridge on which sat a kettle and a coffee percolator. The only room in the whole building being used was upstairs. A bolt hole, in other words, but one that could be abandoned at short notice, no great loss incurred. He'd seen buildings like this before.

He checked the desk first, flicking through a couple of notebooks and skimming through papers: bills, reminders, meaningless clutter, the usual kind of desk rubbish along with pens, pencils, paper and folders. There was nothing useful, like a list of associates or a plan of crimes committed. He opened the drawers. Also empty... except one. It contained three photographs and some sheets of paper. Names – one he immediately recognised – addresses... and three letters that made the hairs move on the back of his neck.

He knew he didn't need to look any further, but he was nothing if not thorough. He moved across to the filing cabinet. Locked, which was no surprise. He jiggled the frame, hoping to pop the drawer open, but it was a sturdy unit with no give.

A rattling sound echoed along the corridor, and the rumble of voices. A man's laughter. The front door.

Time to go. The breath caught in his throat and he slipped out of the office door and back along the corridor to the washroom. Pray to heaven that whoever it was didn't want to wash their hands in a hurry.

The ginger cat was sitting on the floor waiting for him. Its tail swished happily and it gave a soft mew of pleasure.

Caspar whispered, 'Sorry, cat, but I have to go.' As he hoisted himself onto the sill and slipped through, his jacket caught on the latch and the window banged shut behind him. It sounded horribly loud in the small room and a voice called out, followed by heavy footsteps hurrying along the corridor.

Caspar ducked away and hoped the cat would be all right. Seconds later he was jumping over a fence into an adjacent lot and making his way back to his car.

–

Ten minutes after that he stopped at a café and downed a quick brandy and coffee. He wasn't sure which was better for his frayed nerves, but he didn't care. He'd made it out, albeit just in time, but at least he hadn't been caught. He had to tell Rocco what he'd found. He checked the time and was surprised at how quickly the hours had gone by. It was early afternoon. He tried calling him but the switchboard operator at Amiens said the inspector was out and wasn't expected back until five.

'If you leave a number, sir, I'll get the inspector to call you as soon as he can.'

'Never mind,' Caspar told him. 'I'll catch up with him later.'

He went back to his car and headed north. His fiancée, Lucille, was out of town for a couple of days visiting her niece who'd just given birth, so he had time to spare. And he could do with a change of scenery.

And what he'd found was better relayed face-to-face than by telephone.

–

Back in the comfort of his city office, Laurent Vauquelin dialled a number in Ivry with shaking fingers. This was going too far, he knew, and could only end badly. But so would going against Serban, who was turning into something of a monster before his very eyes. From small-time criminal with self-set limitations whom he'd managed to keep clear of the law by skilful means, the Romanian was morphing into the kind of gangster Vauquelin was more accustomed to defending. They, too, had started out small, building their base street by street, extending their reach and scope until suddenly they had a territory, a turf, with everything that entailed, including men at their command and a burning need to make their mark on the world and repel all comers, police included. Few of them lasted long. If the competition didn't get them, their own greed and arrogance making them think they were unstoppable usually did.

He stopped in mid-dial. He'd already decided against mentioning the cop he'd seen in the restaurant. On the way back to his office he'd recalled where they'd met. A quick flick through his files had confirmed the man's name. Casparon. A deep-cover officer no doubt buried for extensive periods in the underworld, ferreting out information on the gangs operating in Paris. If Serban thought he was under surveillance there was no telling how he'd react, and Vauquelin didn't want to be caught in the blast.

The fact was Serban was moving too fast. He'd seen it before when criminals overstretched their capabilities and came to believe themselves untouchable. Their arrogant self-belief invariably took down others with them in the fallout, the collateral damage of another's ambition. But how do you stop a runaway train? And what would Serban's response be if he tried to stop him anyway? The thought made Vauquelin feel sick. He continued dialling. Get this over and done with, that was all he had to do. Then get out of the city for a while.

'Yes?' The hated voice, soft and bland, like a king on his throne.

'I got the address you wanted. It's on its way round to you by courier.' He was wishing he could get out of fulfilling this obligation but it was far too late. With luck, maybe Serban's men would get caught going after Rocco and blow their boss out of the water. The thought gave him a small measure of satisfaction. Let Serban try taking him on as his defence counsel then.

For once he managed to put the phone down before Serban did, and felt a small measure of triumph at that.

Chapter Thirty-five

The track from the road to Petissier's house was narrow and deserted. The grass verge on each side brushing the wheels of the Citroën demonstrated the lack of regular traffic. Drivers coming down this way were either lost or here by invitation.

It was a peaceful haven in a pleasant setting, Rocco concluded. After driving through many kilometres of undulating fields dotted with small villages and an occasional farming cooperative depot, he reached a lake in a hollow. Through the surrounding trees, he counted two, maybe three large properties, each with its own fenced-off space. A rich man's paradise, secluded enough to guarantee privacy.

Petissier's house was the first one he came to. He opened the gate and drove up to the main building, twin porthole windows in the roof like eyes observing his approach. No uniformed officer on watch this time, simply a strip of police tape across the front door, one end flapping vaguely in the slight breeze. As he got out of the car, a squat figure in a leather jacket emerged from behind an outbuilding at the back, adjacent to a double garage. As the man approached, he jingled a bunch of keys in one hand. He looked to be in his early fifties, with short-cropped hair and a military bearing.

'Inspector Rocco?' he queried. 'You're here to inspect the house, sir.'

'That's right. Who are you?'

'Officer Hubert, Abbeville station.' They shook hands. 'I'm sorry about the informal clothes, sir, but I'm supposed to be on sick leave. Walking wounded, you might say. They drafted me in to come down because of a severe shortage of staff. They said to leave you to it.' He smiled and held up the keys, selecting one. 'This is to the front door, the others are to the back and side doors and the outbuildings. When you're done, if you could close the door behind you and leave the keys on the bench in the shed over there, I'll pick them up later.'

'Thanks. Do you know anything of what happened here?'

'Only what I heard at the station, sir. They said the judge lost it and tried to kill himself.' He shook his head. 'I don't condemn anyone who's that desperate; you never know what goes on in people's lives, do you? But they reckon he'd used dirty money, so we shouldn't feel too cut up about it, eh?' He nodded towards the shed. 'Before he went, he had a big burn-up behind the shed. Paperwork, they reckon. It's all gone now, though. Anyone's guess what that was all about.' He added heavily, with a tug of cynicism at the corner of his mouth, 'Guilty conscience, perhaps?'

Rocco didn't comment. He'd thought he'd detected a smell of smoke in the air, but assumed it was from a farmer nearby. He was surprised it had hung around this long.

With a brief wave Hubert stumped away to a powerful-looking motorbike leaning against the garage wall. He put on a crash helmet and kicked the engine into life, then headed off down the drive, the engine noise echoing around the house and trees in a crackling farewell and growling up the narrow road out of earshot.

Inside, the house was cool and smelled of furniture polish and something infinitely less pleasant: death. The shutters had been left hanging half-open, no doubt by the emergency team and police, letting in just enough light to see. Rocco did a walk-through first to get a sense of the place. From the hallway he checked a long galley-style kitchen with a tiled floor and heavy wooden cupboards, then moved to a large living room followed by a dining room and a study overlooking the lake and gardens at the back.

To Rocco, each room had the familiar feel of a space that had been well-searched by the police, with drawers not quite closed and, in the study especially, a few scattered papers lying about.

A rich man's house, Rocco thought. Expensive tastes. It was stylishly furnished but somehow lacking in feel, as if rarely lived in. A place for display rather than comfort.

He returned to the living room, where a now familiar picture was propped against one wall. It was 'The Toilette of Esther' by Chassériau, and looked somehow diminished down on the floor. A hook on the wall above showed where it had been hung, and he wondered who had moved it. Petissier himself, possibly. From regret or guilt? Or maybe both at being found out?

There was a signature, he noted, at bottom right, but it was indecipherable and too short for the artist's full name. If it was meant to be Chassériau, maybe he'd run out of paint. He studied the painting from a few paces away, then compared it with the photo Dreycourt had given him. Interesting.

He looked at an array of family photographs around the room. Dreycourt had been right about one thing: Petissier's late wife had looked nothing like Esther. Not that she'd been in the back row when it came to looks, but a strong chin and a direct, unsmiling stare gave her an unforgiving, though handsome, look. He wondered if she had approved of her husband's choice of art or whether she had died before he'd made the purchase. It couldn't have been easy for an older companion or wife, living with a picture of a beautiful young woman with a come-on look and no clothes to conceal her youthfulness.

He walked through to the study and made a rapid search of the desk. It contained nothing useful and he decided that whatever else Petissier had done here, he hadn't left anything behind that might come back to haunt him or his family.

More photos were dotted about on the desk, walls and side table, set in silver frames. Rocco checked them through, then looked again. Most were collegiate group shots, taken at functions or with neutral backdrops, in which Petissier held the centre spot, the successful man among his peers. Rocco recognised one or two faces from government circles or the judiciary. Then he stopped, seeing one familiar face in particular, and checked again. It appeared more than once, and one photograph showed the two men on board a yacht, dressed in casual shirts with their arms about each other's shoulders, waving champagne glasses at the camera. Petissier was grinning.

And so was *Maître* Laurent Vauquelin.

–

Rocco walked out to the shed with a leaden feeling in his stomach. He found a brick-built firepit behind it, leaking a trail of smoke and fine ash which danced on a breeze from the lake. He leaned over the pit. The bricks of the wall were surprisingly warm, and all that was left of the fire at the bottom was a dry, grey soup, leaving no trace of anything which could have been useful.

A metal container stood on the ground nearby. He sniffed at the open neck but already knew what it would be. Petrol.

He went back to the house and found the phone. There was a notepad alongside it, containing local and useful numbers, including the police station. He dialled the number and identified himself, and asked to be put through to the investigating officer.

'Captain Souchay,' said a voice. 'Can I help you, Inspector? Sorry there's nobody down there to help you but we've had a bastard of a gastric epidemic tear through here like Attila the Hun and it's left us really short-handed. Did you get the keys all right? I left word at your office about where you'd find them.'

'Yes, thanks. Your man Hubert gave them to me.'

'Say that again?'

'Officer Hubert.' Rocco sensed instantly that something was wrong. 'Short, thick-set, fifty-ish? Rides a big motorbike.'

There was a brief silence, then Souchay said, 'Sorry, Inspector, but like I said, there's nobody been assigned from here to hand over the keys because we don't have the manpower. Furthermore, we don't have anyone called Hubert at this station.'

Rocco felt his skin go cold. 'So who did you assign to search the building?'

'We didn't. After the body was removed, we were instructed to seal the place and leave it be. We thought you'd be the one doing the searching.'

Chapter Thirty-six

Rocco headed towards Mers-les-Bains. It was less than twenty minutes away and he needed to check something out. He was cursing himself under his breath. He'd been fooled by an expert. Whoever the man calling himself Hubert really was, he'd been cool and confident, adapting to Rocco's arrival with a convincing explanation and getting out of there as quickly as possible. He'd done a good job of clearing out any paperwork from Petissier's desk and torching it, reducing it to a fine dust just in time.

Who the hell was he? There had been a definite military air about the man, and he'd been well-prepared, even knowing Rocco was due to visit and that there was a sickness epidemic at the Abbeville police station. That took either inside knowledge or thorough and clever preparation. A professional, in other words.

He'd known several former soldiers who had worked for criminal gangs in the past. They had a good work ethic, followed orders to the letter and weren't afraid of facing up to trouble if it came along. But something about Hubert had been different. He'd clearly been sent to obliterate all trace of embarrassing papers that might surface and reveal a criminal connection. But it was a clean-up operation on whose behalf? The state's... or somebody else's?

He realised, with frustration, that he'd probably never know.

He used his radio to contact the Mers-les-Bains station to see if they still had an officer on duty at Gambon's house. They didn't, but the duty officer promised to send someone down there with a key immediately.

When Rocco arrived, a young woman *gardienne* was standing outside the front door. He got her to open up and walked through to the living room where he'd seen the painting and the photographs. He checked the photographs one by one. Nothing. Then he looked through the drawers where he'd found the photo albums, this time paying close attention to each page.

There were no fewer than five photos featuring *Maître* Vauquelin. Three had been taken at what looked like official functions, while two were at more relaxed events, showing that Gambon and Vauquelin were acquainted by more than professional contact.

He closed the books after taking out the two last photographs, which he placed in his pocket along with the one he'd retrieved from Petissier's study.

He thanked the policewoman for her time, left her to lock up and drove back to Amiens. On the way he got through to Dreycourt.

'Hello, Lucas. What's new?'

'I need you to check a couple of things at Bourdelet's house. I don't have time to get there right now.'

'Sure. Is it urgent?'

'Yes.'

'Well, I'll certainly help if I can. But I should tell you that I've just been ordered to step down from this investigation. The call came from the Ministry ten minutes ago. I'm surprised they haven't got to you yet.'

'I've been keeping a low profile.'

'Clever man. Anyway, I'll do what I can. What is it?'

Rocco told him and Dreycourt agreed without question, although he sounded intrigued.

–

By the time Rocco got back to Amiens, Dreycourt had an answer for him. 'You've got a good eye, Lucas,' the expert said. 'To be honest, I'd missed it completely.' Rocco thought he sounded almost disappointed. 'I checked the painting and you were right: there's a flower all right. It's small and almost hidden, but definitely not a feature of the original. I've checked the other copies and the same flower is present on those, too.'

At least he wasn't calling them forgeries any longer, Rocco noted. The change of certainty about Cezard's guilt must have been tough to accept. 'What about the signatures?'

'Deliberately vague – and nothing like the originals. He was clever; he deliberately made sure they could not be classified as fakes – at least, not by anyone who knew what they were doing.'

Rocco placed the photos of all three paintings on his desk side by side. Each one, now he knew where to look, contained a tiny white marguerite daisy in the bottom right-hand corner, a easily-missed detail on the floor, as if the flower had been dropped or cast aside in a moment of boredom by the subject of the paintings.

'What about the photos in his sideboard at home?'

'Got those, too. I took the liberty of acquiring three in all. Who'd have thought, eh? Bourdelet and Vauquelin, like best friends. Do you want them?'

Rocco felt a rush of relief. He might never get to use them if the Ministry closed him down, but it was proof of some kind of connection. 'Thank you. Could you send them to Amiens?'

'Will do. What are you going to do now?'

'Talk to the artist and connect all the links.'

First, he tried calling Caspar. He didn't expect to find him at home and there was no answer.

He called Cezard's number but that, too, rang and rang. He put the phone down and sat back in his chair. He felt exhausted and he knew he had very little time left to work this case before the Ministry pulled the plug and demanded a report. Right now, that report would play into their hands because it would contain nothing but suspicion and speculation, an absence of solid evidence the like of which had sunk many a case over the years.

Dr Rizzotti appeared, clutching a sheaf of papers. Dressed in a white coat, the pathologist stopped by Rocco's desk and peered at him as if studying a piece of evidence in his laboratory. 'I had a corpse come in this morning,' he said casually. 'Drunk as a skunk moped rider in his seventies. He was kicked out of a café in the town centre for calling into question the morals of the owner's wife. He went off the road straight into the canal. Got his foot tangled in the pedal and was dragged down. Hell of a way to go. Still, he probably didn't know much about it. I suppose being that drunk has its benefits.'

Rocco tried a smile. 'Your point being?'

'You look worse than he does.'

'Thanks.'

'In fact, if I put you into a drawer alongside him, the undertaker would probably take the wrong body. Go home, for God's sake. You've been pushing it a bit, haven't you?' He leaned forward. 'It's that Bourdelet thing, isn't it?'

Rocco nodded. 'That and a couple of others.'

Rizzotti shook his head. 'You can't solve them all, you know – especially with the Ministry on your back.' He pointed meaningfully towards the door, then walked away saying, 'Doctor's orders. Rest and recuperation.'

Rizzotti was right, Rocco thought. He needed sleep. In his present state he was worse than useless. Pushing himself to his feet, he left the office and drove home. As he walked into the house, his phone started ringing. He scooped it up. It was Claude.

'Lucas. Glad I got hold of you.'

'Why, what's up?' Rocco drank a glass of water, the cool liquid doing nothing to revitalise him. Bed and sleep, that was what he needed.

'I got a call from Georges Maillard down at the café. He said some feller's been in asking where you live.'

'A feller?'

'He wouldn't give his full name, but said he was a friend of yours. Georges didn't like the look of him so he rang me. Considering he's the most miserable man in the village, he's acting like your biggest fan.'

'It's a long story. So, who was the man asking questions?'

'Do you know anyone called Caspar?'

Rocco put the glass down, the tiredness flushing away in an instant. Caspar was here in Poissons? He must have something important to tell to come all this way. Caspar must have been trying to get hold of him, but he'd been so careful to keep a low profile he'd forgotten to check for calls with the duty operator in Amiens.

'Where is he now?' he asked.

'Waiting down by the café. Georges is keeping an eye on him. Delsaire, too, in case he tries to slip away. I'm on my way to see Georges, anyway, so if this Caspar's a friend of yours I'll show him the way, if that's all right?'

Rocco thanked him and said he'd wait. He smiled at the knowledge that the village telegraph was working on his behalf, instinctively closing ranks against suspicious outsiders. Even more amazing given it was no time at all since he'd been an outsider himself – and here they were treating him as one of their own.

He tidied up and set about gathering the makings of a quick meal. He had eggs, tomatoes, mushrooms and ham, and some wine to wash it down. Rough and ready, but at short notice it was the best he could do.

He heard the sound of cars outside and went to the door. Claude waved and drove away, and Caspar got out of his vehicle and walked up the path.

'I didn't realise I was going to run into a reception committee,' said Caspar, grinning and jerking a thumb in the direction of the departing car. 'Suspicious lot, aren't they? Claude didn't say but I got the feeling he's a cop, or was one.'

Rocco nodded. 'Still is. He's a good man. Maillard runs the café and Delsaire's the local plumber. You were lucky you didn't run into the local priest; he'd probably have put a curse on you, though it wouldn't have been for my benefit.'

'Must be nice having them looking out for you. Doesn't happen in the city.'

Rocco led him inside and was about to close the door when he saw Mme Denis pottering up the path. She was carrying another cloth-covered dish.

'I see you've got company,' she said. 'It's good timing because I've made another pie. Chicken this time.' She thrust it at him. 'I hope you like it. There's easily enough for two.'

'Thank you,' he said. 'Are you trying to fatten me up? Not that I'm complaining. The other one was delicious. I'll let you have the dish back tomorrow.'

'No rush. Anyway, it's a pleasure to cook for someone after all this time.' She gave him a sideways look. 'So, what's the latest on the Bourdelet case, then?'

'You know about that?'

She gave a mock frown. 'I read the newspapers. You're quite the local hero now. Next thing you know they'll be putting up a plaque for you on the wall of the *mairie*. Come on, share.'

'Well, it's getting there, but slow going. There are two other cases as well, not so high-profile, and that's making it more complicated.' He added softly, 'My sources say there's possible gang land involvement – but don't tell anyone.'

Her eyes opened wide. 'Really? My goodness, you work fast, don't you?' She peered past him and whispered, 'Who's the young fella – one of your informants come to give you the latest underworld gossip?'

'Damn,' he said mildly. 'You guessed. Well, that's his cover blown. I'll have to shoot him and bury him in the garden.'

She disappeared down the path, chuckling to herself. When he turned to go back in, he found a grinning Caspar watching him.

'Not just the village heavies looking after your back, then? Little old ladies, too.'

'Don't be misled by appearances,' Rocco said. 'She's tougher than the rest of them put together.'

'Like I said, must be nice. I hope Lucille and I can find somewhere like it when we move out of Paris.'

'I'm sure you will. How is she by the way?'

'Great, thanks. She's at her niece's near Dreux for a couple of days, helping with a new baby.'

Rocco put the pie down on the table and removed the cloth. 'I hope you're hungry because this pie needs eating now.'

'Famished. Show me the cutlery and plates and I'll lay the table.'

'And perhaps you'll tell me what you've turned up.'

'How did you guess?'

'You wouldn't have come all this way otherwise. And you're grinning like a dog with a new bone.' He poured two glasses of wine. 'There's a spare bed next door. If you don't mind the fruit rats in the roof, you're welcome to stay the night.'

Caspar raised his glass and they touched rims. 'To good friends and fruit rats. And down with cop-hating lawyers.'

Thirty minutes later, chicken pie eaten and glasses emptied, Caspar finished telling Rocco what he'd discovered in Serban's backyard. 'I thought I'd blown my chances,' he admitted, 'but the photos and letters make a good case, don't they?'

'They'll certainly help stack up the evidence,' Rocco admitted. 'It would help if we could get Peretz the driver to testify against his boss.'

Caspar pursed his lips. 'He might, if he thinks he'll get away without following Serban to jail. If he goes down as well, he won't last five minutes inside. Serban will see to that.'

'Maybe we can use that.' Rocco related what Fontenal had told him about Serban's circle of friends. Peretz was unlikely to want to face up to that kind of retribution in a general prison. But given a guarantee that charges against him would be dropped for giving evidence, he'd probably opt for a new start a long way from Paris.

Caspar nodded. 'Actually, from what I know of him, I think you'd be better going after Vauquelin. He'd do anything to get a reduced sentence once the others start talking. Jail is the last place he'll want to be, even if he makes the mistake of thinking he's among friends who'll protect him. They'd skin him alive just for the laugh.'

'Good point. Thanks for doing this, Caspar. It's been a big help. I hope Lucille won't hold it against me.'

Caspar grinned. 'No chance. To tell you the truth, I enjoyed it.'

'Seriously?'

'Sure. I had a moment back there when I had a bit of a wobble, but it made me realise that I haven't totally lost my nerve. It made me appreciate what I've got now even more. Maybe I need a spark of electricity once in a while, to get the adrenalin flowing.'

'As long as it's only in a while.' Rocco lifted his glass.

'I'll drink to that. But don't forget to call me next time you need help.'

'Will do.'

They clinked glasses. '*Santé*,' said Caspar.

'*Santé*.'

Chapter Thirty-seven

Early next morning, after Caspar had left for Paris, Rocco called and asked Claude to meet him at Cezard's château. As he was about to leave, his phone rang. It was Dreycourt. He sounded sombre.

'Petissier died last night,' he said, 'without regaining consciousness.'

'Thanks for letting me know,' Rocco replied. He wondered if it was his imagination or whether Dreycourt was depressed about losing a potential finger to point at Cezard.

He thanked the art expert for his help, then gathered the photos and copy letters together and headed for his car. He was tempted to check in with the office first, but he didn't want to hear the news that he suspected was waiting for him: that the Ministry had called off the investigation. For now, he was out of reach and intended to stay that way. To make absolutely certain, he turned off his car radio.

The village was quiet as he drove out, the sun already warm and presaging another hot day. The only sign of anyone working was a heavy truck parked outside Maillard's café, the driver puffing on a cigarette as he climbed into the cab. It reminded Rocco of Maillard's offer to buy him a drink if he put in an appearance at the 14th-July celebration. His first instinct had been to avoid it, but it would be difficult to think of a polite way of doing so. Maybe he didn't want to. There were worse ways of spending a few hours than in the company of friends.

He lowered the car window to let in a breeze, revelling in the cool air. One way or another it promised to be an eventful day. Whether he'd get the result he wanted was open to question, but he was determined to file this investigation as a success if he could.

Claude was waiting on the front steps of the château when he arrived, with Sébastien Cezard wandering around kicking at some weeds on the drive, a drift of cheroot smoke following him like a cloud on a leash. The artist didn't look a happy man.

'Lucas,' Sébastien greeted him when he got out of his car. 'To what do I owe the pleasure? Should I get Laurent here?' He tried a smile to reflect the joke but it was clearly a struggle.

'Can we go inside?' said Rocco. 'I have something to show you.'

'Of course. I'll get Eliane to make coffee. Please go through.' He led the way inside and disappeared down the hallway in search of his daughter.

Claude was eyeing Rocco with a faint frown. 'What's going on?' he asked softly, when they reached the room at the back. 'You're planning to drop something on him?'

'Hopefully, just the weight of the law,' said Rocco. 'I want him to feel under a bit of pressure. His daughter, too.'

'Got it. Not too friendly, in other words.'

Minutes later, Eliane appeared with a loaded tray and invited them to help themselves. The smell of Sébastien's cheroot was soon joined by the welcoming aroma of coffee.

'Perhaps you could stay?' Rocco suggested, as Eliane made to leave. 'This will be of interest to you.'

'That's not necessary, is it?' her father suggested. 'I'm sure she has plenty of other things to be doing. Marking papers and so on.' He scowled and sucked on his smoke as if it were the last drag he'd ever have.

Eliane looked from one to the other with an expression of puzzlement. 'No, I've nothing on that can't wait, Pa.' She stared at Rocco. 'What's this about? Is something wrong?'

Rocco took an envelope out of his pocket and placed the three letters face down on the table between them. He spread out the photos of the paintings provided by Dreycourt for them all to see. He was watching Sébastien's face as he did so, and saw the artist stiffen. He made a faint choking sound as if the smoke had gone down the wrong way.

'You've seen these photos before,' said Rocco. 'They're the subject of an investigation into three deaths. I wanted to ask you again, Sébastien, if you recognise them.'

There was a lengthy silence. Sébastien was staring at the paintings as if they were a trio of snakes. Nobody else said a word.

'Well, I know them, as I told you before,' he said gruffly. 'Any artist worth his salt would.' He pointed to each one in turn. 'There's a Chassériau, a Boucher and a Gérard, although as an aside, I prefer the earlier version of the Récamier by Jacques-Louis David.' He looked apologetic. 'Sorry. Can't resist the temptation to show off a little. Madame Récamier was a famed society beauty and much sought-after as a subject for artists.'

'Thank you.' Rocco was slightly relieved. 'I'm glad you recognise them.' He turned to Eliane and Claude to explain. 'These are copies of paintings, one currently residing in the Louvre, another in the Carnavalet in Paris and one in Cologne. I wonder, Sébastien, if you could show us the canvas you had here before, of a woman sewing. A Morisot, I think it was?'

Sébastien shrugged and looked around vaguely, scattering ash. 'I'm sorry, I think I must have moved it.'

'No, Pa,' said Eliane. 'It's still there on the floor.' She went over to the sideboard and picked up the painting, and laid it against a chair leg so they could all see. 'This one?'

'Ah, yes. Silly me.' Her father pursed his lips and studied the end of his cheroot.

'You mentioned before,' said Rocco, 'that when you produce a copy, you include a small addition to distinguish it from the original.'

'I do, that's correct. One can't be too careful these days. Some people are quick to accuse artists of fraud.'

Like Dreycourt, thought Rocco. 'Can you tell us what that difference is?'

'Well, I'm not sure I can. Artistic confidentiality, you might call it, even mystery, and—'

'It's a marguerite, silly!' Eliane said with a laugh. 'See, here.' She pointed at the bottom right-hand corner, where a small daisy lay on the bench alongside the woman's sewing basket. 'You can just see it if you look carefully.'

'Interesting,' said Rocco. He hesitated before moving on. He hated doing this, especially in front of Eliane, but he had a feeling that nothing else would work. He still wasn't convinced that Sébastien was part of the blackmail scheme, simply because he didn't appear to have the right instinct. But he'd been fooled before by accomplished actors. He reached into his pocket and produced three more photographs and laid them on the table.

'What's this?' said Eliane. 'You've already shown us these.'

Rocco looked at Sébastien. 'Is that correct?'

The older man said nothing for a moment. Then he tossed his cheroot into the fireplace and the air seemed to go out of him like a punctured balloon.

'No. It's not.'

Eliane leaned forward. 'Pa?'

Rocco said softly, 'You should look at the photos more closely. Compare them one by one.'

Eliane and Claude both leaned forward and scanned the photos. The silence in the room was intense. Rocco was looking at Sébastien, and when the artist looked up, he did so with an expression of resignation, but also of puzzlement.

Eliane was first to see the difference. 'These three are of your copies, Pa,' she murmured, and looked at her father, then at Rocco. 'I don't understand – he painted these a long time ago.'

'I'm confused,' muttered Claude. 'You've lost me.'

For a moment nobody spoke. Rocco was hoping Sébastien would do so without his hand being forced further. He waited him out.

'He's right,' Sébastien said at last. 'I painted those three... but as you say, *chérie*, it was a long time ago. I did them for a promising client but he reneged on the deal.' He sighed and brushed some ash off his front. 'Hours and days and weeks of work, all for nothing.'

'How long does it take?' asked Rocco.

'Long enough. You can't rush these things. I can always work on other projects in between, but it's not a quick process if you have any pride in your work. And you have to study the originals with great care.'

'You take photographs?'

'I do. But it's better to see them in the flesh.'

'How did you do that for the Boucher painting? Did you travel to Cologne?'

Cezard shook his head. 'I was lucky: it came to Paris on loan for an exhibition, so I haunted the gallery for days, studying the paint, the brush strokes, the light, the application.' He gave a thin smile. 'The staff got quite used to me in the end, although they probably thought I was an obsessive old goat. The thing is, you have to get in the artist's mind, to understand how he went about it. I do, anyway.'

Rocco detected a fierce pride in Cezard's voice, and understood a little of what drove him. 'It must have been a huge disappointment not to sell them.'

'The gallery owner who commissioned them was an important contact in the art world. He said he had a client who would take all three or, if not, that he could sell them individually at a good price. It was an ideal way of getting my name out there, so I took a chance on him. Then he called me to say the client had changed his mind and he didn't have any other takers for them.' He shrugged. 'He paid me a small fee for my trouble but it wasn't the same. In the end he went bust before we could do anything about it. End of story.'

'We?'

Sébastien's eyes were moist as he looked up, and Rocco saw the pain of the memory written on his face. But there was something else, too: a look of disbelief, as if realising that something completely innocent had caught up with him.

'You said "we",' Rocco repeated.

Eliane had also seen the look on her father's face, and stood up, her face flushed. 'Will someone tell me what's going on? Pa? Lucas?' She looked at Claude but he shook his head.

'Don't ask me,' he said. 'I'm a simple rural cop. This is all well over my head.'

Sébastien shifted in his chair. 'I let Laurent have them,' he said at last, with evident reluctance.

'So what?' Eliane queried. 'I wish he wasn't but he's your agent, isn't he?'

He nodded. 'I told him about the gallery owner backing out of the deal and he offered to go after him in the courts, but I didn't want that. Later on, he said he might be able to find buyers for them. It probably wouldn't bring in what had been originally promised, but it would be better than having them lying around gathering dust.' He looked at Rocco. 'I know what you're going to ask: who did he sell them to? He never told me.'

Eliane was looking at Rocco with dawning realisation and, he thought, a hint of accusation. 'You know, don't you?'

'Yes. There were three high-profile buyers involved: Secretary of State Bourdelet bought the Gérard, assize judge Jules Petissier bought the Chassériau and former head of the *Sûreté Nationale*, Jean-Marie Gambon, bought the Boucher. There was no obvious criminal intent, apart from in one case, but that doesn't involve your father.'

Sébastien swore softly, eyes closing. Eliane's mouth opened but no words came out for several seconds. Rocco could see the names registering in her mind, and one by one the identities of the buyers hit home.

'But… Bourdelet's dead,' she said softly. 'And Gambon, too, isn't that right? I heard it on the news.'

'And Petissier, too,' said Rocco. He didn't want to be unkind, but he needed to explain to Sébastien what had happened, that he wasn't to blame for how the paintings had been used. He turned over the letters. 'Each man bought them purely to show off to their friends and families. There's no crime in doing that, but they did so using stolen or criminal money. Each one received one of these blackmail letters, and shortly afterwards took their own lives. They must have known for certain that had they lived they would have gone to jail in disgrace.'

Eliane was staring down at the letters, flicking through them. She dropped them back on the table. 'But who sent these?' she said. 'It wasn't Pa – he couldn't do something like this. Tell him, Pa!'

Rocco said, 'I know it wasn't your father. The only thing we're certain of is that whoever's behind the letters used a Paris criminal contact to deliver them. It had to be someone who was acquainted with all three men. Someone who knew their backgrounds, their foibles and weaknesses… and who knew how they had got their money. A friend, in other words, or at least an acquaintance who knew how to get close.' He produced two more photographs and laid them on the table. Petissier and Gambon, pictured with their friend, *Maître* Laurent Vauquelin. 'These are two of the men. You'll recognise one of the faces. Bourdelet has similar photographs in his home.'

'*Vauquelin?*' Eliane's voice was a whisper. She looked at her father, then Rocco. 'My God, I knew I didn't like the repulsive man! But why?'

'That's what I'd like to know,' said Rocco.

'I know why.' Sébastien spoke quietly. He was looking at his daughter with an expression of regret. 'Lucas is right: Laurent knew all three men from various meetings and conferences over the years. He cultivated prominent people by instinct, the way some people cultivate flowers. If they were potentially useful, he made a point of getting to know them, to get inside their inner circle. But these three… He told me they'd betrayed him, cutting him off after the allegations that he was involved with criminals and had manufactured evidence against certain police officers to win cases.'

Rocco could believe it. After what he'd heard from Santer, Vauquelin must have been highly resentful of the men who'd failed to leap to his defence, adding to his loss of prestige. It could have been enough for him to decide to get revenge in any way he could. And having found out their secrets he'd plunged the knife in deep.

'So it wasn't just for the money?' Claude asked.

'No,' said Rocco. 'If he couldn't get money, he was happy to settle for their humiliation and ruin.'

'He was drunk when he told me,' Sébastien said softly, as if in a trance. 'He'd arrived in a terrible state and demanded more alcohol.' He shrugged. 'I tried to put him off and said he'd be better off sinking a litre of strong coffee instead because he'd probably kill himself on the local roads if he got any worse. He wouldn't have it; he was very emotional and angry and I was getting worried. Eliane was due back home at any time and I didn't want him in that state when she was here. When it was obvious he wasn't going anywhere willingly, I gave him some brandy, hoping he'd fall asleep.'

'It didn't work?'

'Quite the opposite. He became almost hysterical, raging against all the people who'd abandoned him and swearing he'd get his own back in the end.' He waved a hand. 'I didn't realise he'd do it this way.'

'All the people?' said Rocco. 'There were more?'

'That's the impression I got, but maybe he was just sounding off. He did mention some names but I'd never heard of them and forgot them immediately.'

'Are there other paintings out there?' Claude asked.

'A few, yes. Maybe half a dozen. I sent him a batch to see if he could find buyers.'

'Do you have any receipts for them?'

'I'm afraid not. I was never very good with that kind of thing.' He looked worried. 'Is that a problem?'

'Probably not. Has Vauquelin ever said what he did with the paintings?'

'No. I always trusted him to do the right thing. Clearly I shouldn't have been so gullible.' He paused, then, as if finding a glimmer of hope, said, 'They've all got the marguerite on them, though. That should count for something, shouldn't it?'

Rocco nodded. 'It should kill off any suggestions that you produced them for reasons of fraud.'

He wondered if this was what had got Yuri Serban involved. The promise of a long-term source of income from people in authority who'd got their hands dirty must have appealed to the gang leader on a financial level. More than anything, though, he would have liked the idea of having such powerful people in his pocket and terrified that he could drop the axe on them and expose their little secrets. To a gangster with ambitions it would have seemed like a dream come true.

'What do I say if Laurent calls me?' Sébastien queried. He lit another cheroot, his hand shaking, as the full implications of what he'd got involved it hit home.

'Nothing. For you it's business as usual. Tell him we're nowhere with the investigation and leave it at that.'

Chapter Thirty-eight

Rocco headed off first, leaving Claude to reassure Sébastien and Eliane that everything would work out. He couldn't make any firm promises based solely on Sébastien's word that he hadn't known what had been done with his paintings, no matter what Dreycourt might believe. Only a court case would determine that, although he was certain any report he made would carry enough weight to clear Sébastien's name completely.

A flicker of movement in his mirror showed a large truck coming up fast behind him. He paid it little attention at first, because the narrow road away from the château towards Amiens was twisting and dipping, and even in the Citroën he had to take it easy in case he got too close to the edge.

Moments later the truck loomed larger in the mirror, and he realised it was the vehicle he'd seen parked outside the café in Poissons. World War Two vintage, he guessed, one of many still being used for commercial purposes. It was moving at speed with no regard for the conditions, the driver no doubt eager to get past him and on to his next delivery.

Rocco put his foot down and pulled away. He knew that he would be shortly approaching a series of bends, and even this idiot driver would have to slow right down or risk losing traction.

The truck caught up with him again, charging up to within a couple of metres of his rear bumper, the engine roaring and a cloud of dark exhaust smoke billowing out from the side. The truck had something fitted to its radiator. Trying to look in his mirror, as he navigated the sharp bends, Rocco recognised it as a heavy-duty winch wrapped in chain, with what looked like a railway sleeper fitted across.

Rocco felt a stab of concern. This didn't seem like a mad driver adhering to a tight schedule, more like someone using deliberate scare tactics. Had he followed him from Poissons and waited near Cezard's château for him to come out again? If so, why?

He gripped the wheel as he came to the first bend, and the truck nosed up even closer, following him into the curve without dropping back. Whoever the driver was, he knew how to handle the giant vehicle. Rocco put his foot down hard as he exited the bend, but the truck didn't fall back. Rocco waved a hand out of the window to tell the driver to back off, but all he got in return was a loud blast of the horn.

Two hundred metres ahead a tractor was backing slowly out of a field, a heavy plough on the back already well out onto the road. Rocco leaned on the horn and tapped the brakes, looking to see if he had enough room to squeeze past. It was enough for his speed to drop but the truck's didn't. The tractor driver looked up and saw them coming. He reacted rapidly, changing into forward gear and pulling back into the field as Rocco flashed by just centimetres from the curved blades of the plough.

He felt his teeth snap together as his car was slammed in the rear. The collision sent a shockwave through the Citroën's bodywork, and the rear window blew out in fragments under the stress. He saw his rear bumper spin away into a ditch, the chrome catching the light, and the spare wheel cover flew off and bounced down the road.

With the window gone, the noise was intense. He could see in his side mirror that the driver was grinning like a maniac and mouthing something, his face alive with animosity and evil intent.

A clattering noise started up from the Citroën's rear end, and Rocco felt the car beginning to drift as he went around a long bend. It should have been easy to negotiate but the ramming must have done some damage to the frame. If he couldn't rely on being able to steer through even simple corners, he was in real trouble.

There were more bends ahead, with a three-metre drop into fields on one side and a ditch and high bank on the other. Neither offered a chance of escape. Rocco tried one last time to get away, changing down a gear and pushing his foot to the floor. The engine responded, the nose of the big car drifting slightly to one side. He corrected the drift with a slight nudge of the wheel, then he was into the first corner and hoping that whatever was wrong with the steering would hold good for a few more moments. The tyres shrieked in protest before catching the rough edge of the road. It was hard to keep from drifting across the grass verge towards the drop-off. He managed to get the nose back into line just in time to hit the straight. But it was a mere fifty metres or so to the next bend and he realised that, at this speed, he probably wasn't going to make it.

Then the engine spluttered and lost power. He stamped on the accelerator and the engine picked up with a whine, before spluttering again. It was all the truck behind needed. It rear-ended the Citroën, but this time with less of an impact, and Rocco realised the driver was going to force him off the road at the next bend, where the road was edged on the outside by a long drop-off into trees.

Rocco aimed for the inside of the bend, hoping to get launched up the bank on that side. He might bury the nose into the dirt, but it was better than sailing off into the potentially deadly trees waiting for him on the opposite side.

The driver didn't give him a choice. He rammed the Citroën again, the truck's engine howling in Rocco's ears. Rocco thought he could feel its heat on the back of his neck, like a tiger about to pounce. The Citroën took off, becoming suddenly weightless, a loud clunk echoing from the front as the wheels dropped. But the Citroën was too heavy to be airborne for long, too indelicately balanced for any kind of flight. It began to slew sideways under its own weight, and Rocco let go of the wheel and dived along the seat to get out from behind the rigid steering column. It was too late to try for the doors and, even if he got out, the car might land on top of him. All he could hope for was that the body shell wouldn't collapse around him if the car went into a roll.

His world went crazy, surrounded by breaking glass, violent shaking and battering and a hundred and one punches to the body as he was thrown around the inside of the vehicle. The doors were wrenched open as the car hit the ground, and he punched his hand down the back of the seat cushion, gripping the framework to keep himself from being thrown out. He could taste blood in his mouth and feel stabs of pain from a dozen points of impact all over his body. His chest hurt and he felt one leg being wrenched violently sideways.

Then silence.

Chapter Thirty-nine

It didn't last long. He shook his head and heard a ticking noise from the engine. Or maybe it was one of the wheels spinning. At least he could still hear, surely a good sign. He felt a tickle on his forehead and wiped it away. His hand came away smeared with blood. He struggled against the tilt of the seat cushion and realised that the car had somehow landed on its left side hard against one tree, the other side propped up by a smaller trunk and tilted off the ground. He sniffed the air. Another good sign. He could smell: the warm aroma of pine trees.

And petrol.

Damn it. The fumes were strong and sharp, invading the interior of the car. He fought against panic. He couldn't tell how close it was but any fuel spillage in a car crash was bad news.

He reached for the radio. Dead. Like he'd be if he didn't get out of here. He twisted his body, seeking a way out, his knee and back protesting and his head spinning. The taste of blood filled his mouth and he spat it out. He looked to his left. The tree was a giant, its gnarled trunk invading the compartment as if trying to get at him. The door was gone, ripped away, leaving the hinges like broken teeth. But there was no room to get out past the tree. He looked right and up. That door was still on, but only just, wrenched back and leaving him with a good view up the slope towards the road. The car must have spun in mid-air.

Pity Citroëns weren't made to fly, he thought dreamily, his vision beginning to fade. He could have been out of here without a scratch otherwise, up and over the trees. He felt almost drunk and shook his head. Not drunk. Concussed. Mustn't go to sleep. Keep the head clear and try to find a way out. Get to a hospital. Find the truck driver who ruined his car and kill him, very slowly. Bury the body.

Someone was approaching. A figure was scrambling down the bank. A man in a jacket, a cap on his head pulled low. Rocco didn't recognise him, couldn't see him clearly enough. Just a figure, a stranger. Hopefully a helpful one.

The man leaned over the open doorway and studied Rocco for a moment. He was unshaven, ordinary-looking. Rocco tried to speak but his mouth wouldn't work. Useless being a cop if I can't speak, he thought, and felt a laugh beginning to well up. It stopped in his throat and he thought he was choking. He spat out more blood and took a deep breath, determined not to give in to whatever it was that was taking over his body. The idea of a slow death had never appealed to him. Far better a soldier's passing: quick, painless – or, at least, as painless as possible – followed by a quick drop into nothing. Blackness. Bugles, drums, goodbye.

'You're in a mess, aren't you?' the newcomer said, almost chattily. He sounded amused. He was making no attempt to reach in and help Rocco out, but leaned against the side of the car, looking down with no apparent concern. He even had a smile edging the side of his mouth. 'A bit shaky on the wheel back there, weren't you? You really shouldn't drink in the morning, Rocco. Here, have another one on me.' He produced a bottle of whisky and poured half the contents into the inside of the car, splashing Rocco's face and chest.

Rocco lifted a hand to shield his eyes and coughed against the harsh taste as some of it entered his mouth.

'Nothing better for a pick-me-up, I always think,' the man continued. 'Don't feel bad – you won't be the first drunken cop they find killed himself driving too fast.'

Then he produced a cigarette and a lighter, and lit up, puffing smoke into the air, throwing his head back for a moment to survey the road above.

'*Don't light up here, you maniac – there's petrol everywhere!*' Rocco wanted to shout. But although the thought was there the words wouldn't come. What the hell was wrong with his mouth? Why couldn't he speak? He tried to shift himself, to get his legs underneath him and push upwards. But he had no strength and he couldn't even feel his right leg. Damn, that's bad.

The man noticed him moving and said, 'No, please. Don't stand up. We're all friends here.' He grinned. 'Well, this is a fine way to end a great career for a bastard *flic*, isn't it? But that's the way of the world, right? You do your best, work hard, become a regular pillar of the community – not *my* community, mind you, because there we hate your guts – but there's always a payback waiting just round the corner.' He sniggered. 'Or in this case, right here, *on* the corner.' He waved a hand to indicate the road behind him. 'You have to admit, Rocco, that was a seriously good piece of driving, wasn't it? Not by you – you were rubbish, let's be honest. But what do you expect when you drive around boozed up on whisky in a heap of old junk like this? No, I have to say I couldn't have judged it any finer if I'd tried. Bam – right up the arse and you were off like a rocket. Or should I say a Sputnik? Into orbit… well, for all of three seconds, then you crash-landed like a sack of old scrap metal. Cop down.' He made a trumpet sound, a parody of the *dernière sonnerie*, the last post.

'What the hell do you want?' Rocco finely managed to whisper, his throat sore and his mouth dry in spite of the blood.

The man showed a line of yellow teeth. 'Oh, we're talking now, are we? That's not good. And there was I thinking you were about to breath your last. Seems like I might have misjudged things. Still, lucky I came prepared, eh?' He bent out of sight for a moment, then stood up and showed Rocco a wine bottle with a cork in the top. He gave it a shake. 'Fancy another drink, Rocco? No? Well, I can't say I blame you. This isn't what you'd call a good vintage, let me tell you. A bit young for my tastes, not exactly full-bodied, either.' He took the cork out and tossed it away, then tipped the bottle. A dribble of pale liquid spilled out, splashing over the front seat and running down the fabric towards Rocco. It touched his leg with cold and he recognised the familiar smell.

Petrol.

'Oops, didn't mean to do that,' said the man. 'Doesn't mix well with whisky, I suppose. Still, never mind. You won't be wearing that suit where you're going, will you? Nice cut, by the way. They told me you dressed well. Where did you get that?'

Rocco wanted to say London, but he didn't have the energy. 'Why?'

'Why what?'

'Why are you doing this?'

The man frowned. 'Good question. It's not as if I know you, which I suppose is a little rude of me, us never having been introduced. Let's say I'm being paid a nice lot of money, and you've become a pain in the arse to the person paying me the lot of money. It's called business and, in case you've any doubts… I'm here to kill you.'

'What's… name?'

The frown dropped away. 'I'll save that 'til last, Rocco, if you don't mind. But I can give you a hint. Just think of all the people you've crossed, and somewhere down the list you'll be right.' With that he up-ended the bottle, emptying the contents over the seat and Rocco, the smell choking and overpowering.

Somewhere far away Rocco thought he heard the tinny sound of an engine, but it might have been his imagination, hoping against hope. Traffic along this road was hardly regular and usually limited to slow-moving locals. He tried to move again and felt a sharp pain in his hip. God, don't let it be busted, he thought, desperately. That's all I need.

The man looked at his cigarette, but found it had gone out. 'Damn. I'm always doing that: chatting away about this and that and forgetting to take a regular drag. Never mind, I have more.' He looked down, patting his jacket pocket in a ridiculous mime, drawing out the agony. 'Now where did I put them?'

'*Hey!*'

The voice floated down to them, full of authority. Rocco looked up, his heart leaping. A stocky figure was standing on the road looking down at them, a grey 2CV behind him. It was Claude Lamotte. He was holding his shotgun, the barrel pointed at the man standing outside the car.

Rocco shifted his hip again, gritting his teeth against the sudden eruption of pain in various parts of his body. At .

least his head was no longer fuzzy and he could see more clearly. He also understood what was causing the pain in his hip. It was his gun, jammed between him and the seat.

'Get away from there!' Claude said, and gestured with the barrel. 'Now!'

But the man seemed unfazed by Claude's appearance. 'You'll have to come closer to do any good with that *arquebuse*, old man,' he replied. 'Why don't you go back to your stinking farm and mind your own business?' He turned back towards Rocco. 'Bloody peasant. Christ, how do you stand mixing with these people? Still, it won't be for much longer. In fact, when you think of it, I'm doing you a favour, so you should be grateful.' He thumbed his cigarette lighter a couple of times, but it failed to catch. He did it a third time and a flame grew on the wick.

Rocco was taking a chance, he knew that, but he had no choice. The man was right about Claude not being close enough, but for the wrong reasons: Claude was a crack shot with the shotgun, so in no danger of missing his target. But, standing where he was, he'd be in danger of hitting Rocco as well.

'Safe journey, Rocco – wherever the hell you end up,' the man said. 'Oh, and to answer your question, Yuri Serban sends his regards.' He held up the lighter. '*Adieu.*'

That was when Rocco pulled his MAB semi-automatic pistol free from under his hip and squeezed the trigger. There was no time to aim with any finesse but the target was so close he'd have to be unlucky not to at least scare the man to death. The sound was shockingly loud in the confines of the car. He prayed that the flash of the gun wouldn't ignite the petrol fumes and send him up like a *crêpe Suzette*.

The shot missed by a whisker, but the man reared back with a look of shock tugging at his face. He dropped the lighter and grabbed for it, his eyes drawn automatically downwards. Rocco ducked low into the seat, knowing what was coming next. As he did so, there was a second, much deeper report from outside the car. The man screamed and slammed into the side of the car before falling away with a soft groan.

Rocco looked around. No obvious flames but there was a definite smell of something burning. He concentrated on getting out, twisting his body to ease his legs free from where the seat had shifted forward, against the dashboard section. He kicked back as hard as he dared, and felt the seat move a fraction. Kicked again, pushing his back against the seat, and felt it give a little more. One more kick and he was free and scrabbling towards the open air, seeing Claude skidding down the bank from the road, gun at the ready.

'Lucas — you all right?' the *garde champêtre* yelled. He puffed across to the car, placing his gun on the ground to help Rocco get free. 'Is anything broken? You've got blood on you.'

Rocco nodded. He hadn't fallen on his face, so he figured everything was as sound as could be expected. He was probably going to be one big bruise for a couple of weeks, but he'd got off lightly. Which was more than could be said for the Citroën. He turned towards the front of the car where the man who'd tried to kill him was lying, groaning in agony. Claude's shot had hit him in the lower legs, the buckshot shredding his trousers and revealing a mass of peppered skin beneath, oozing blood.

'He had the cheek to call my gun a blunderbuss!' Claude muttered angrily. He nudged the man with the toe of his boot, raising a squeal. 'I should have aimed higher. And he was going to roast you alive, wasn't he?'

'Glad to see you've got your outrage in the right order,' Rocco finally muttered, wincing at a lancing pain in his back. 'He was sent by a man called Yuri Serban. Check him over for papers, will you.'

'Sure. Can you stand up all right?'

'If I can't, just drag me away by my hair.'

While Claude checked the man for identification, Rocco turned and looked at the Citroën, one hand on the side to hold himself upright. It was a wreck. Damn, but he'd been fond of this car. It had been reliable, comfortable and had got him out of a few scrapes in their time together.

He heard a soft '*whump*' and saw smoke seeping from under the bonnet. Whatever had been smouldering had finally decided to get serious. He limped over to where Claude was examining the man's pockets and summoned enough energy to help drag him away from the burning car, ignoring the screams.

When they were at a safe distance, Claude showed him a cheap leather wallet containing an identity card, a wad of folded notes and a few other bits and pieces including a card for a cheap night club in Paris.

'Pierre-Yves Dinal,' he read out. 'Rue Riblette. I know that area – it's near the Père Lachaise. With his lifestyle I wonder if the maggot has had the foresight to book himself a plot?'

Rocco grunted. The only foresight known to Dinal was probably on the barrel of a gun. Père Lachaise cemetery was one of the largest in Paris, and it reminded him that prior to joining the police, Claude had been a taxi driver and knew the city better than most.

Above them on the road, a car drew up and stopped. Rocco recognised M. Paulais, the stationmaster from Poissons, as he jumped out and made as if to scramble down to meet them. Claude stopped him.

Rocco said, 'Tell him to ring Desmoulins in Amiens to send an ambulance and support officers.'

Claude did so. Paulais nodded without a word, jumped back in his car and was gone with a squeal of tyres.

Rocco had slumped down against the slope, his legs finally giving way with the onset of shock. Claude joined him. 'What now, Lucas? This is serious stuff, sending someone to kill a cop.'

Rocco nodded. It wasn't the first time it had happened, but this attempt had ramifications far beyond the man named Dinal, currently lying nearby and groaning softly. Men like him rarely had their own enemies, operating instead on instructions from others, but proving Serban was his boss might be a problem. He had to get more than just a name muttered by a would-be killer in a moment of high drama.

He stood up with help from Claude and hopped closer to Dinal. The man's eyes opened a fraction as Rocco's shadow fell over him, and he fell silent.

Rocco dropped to his knees alongside him and prodded him in the chest to make sure he had his full attention. 'Serban, you said.'

'Wha—?'

'The man who paid you to do this.'

'I don't remember what I said. Must have been the shock of that old goat shooting me. Go screw yourself, Rocco, I'm not talking.' Dinal's eyes blazed with pain, anger and an in-built need to play the tough guy. It was likely that he wouldn't crack easily.

'Claude,' Rocco called. 'Is there anything else in that wallet?'

That woke Dinal up. '*Hey!*' he yelled. 'What are you doing with that?'

'Shut up,' Rocco told him.

Claude stepped over to join them. 'Not much. Rubbish, mostly. There's a card from a cheap and nasty dive called the *Perroquet Bleu*, which is not somewhere you'd want to take your dear sainted mother, quite a lot of cash for a man in his nasty line of business... and, hellfire!' he paused in surprise. He was holding the money in his hand, and from the middle took a slip of paper. He showed it to Rocco.

It bore Rocco's name and home address, written in elegant script, the ink a distinctive shade of violet.

Rocco held it up in front of Dinal's face. 'Interesting item, this. Do you know who wrote it?'

Dinal said nothing, his eyes flicking sideways.

'Never mind, I think I have an idea.' Rocco turned to Claude. 'Do you know the Blue Parrot?'

'I should do. Had to drop a few clients there in my driving days... and scoop them up afterwards. Not a nice place.'

'Is it what I think it is?'

Claude nodded. 'Yes. It's been a gang hang-out for years. Why?'

'I'm wondering what might happen if we make an anonymous phone call to the club and drop a word in their ear that M. Dinal, here, has been talking to us about his activities... and telling us about a few of his friends in the Blue Parrot. What do you think?'

They both looked at Dinal, who stared up at them in puzzlement, before giving them a sneer. 'Yeah, like they'd believe anything you cops say!' He tried to laugh but it lacked conviction.

'You're right,' Rocco agreed. 'But you know what Chinese whispers are like: by the time it goes through several mouths and gets to the ones who care, it'll be a lot more colourful than we can make it. And more believable.' He leaned forward, seeing the first real signs of doubt in Dinal's face as the thought sank in. 'I'm willing to bet that this isn't your first job like this. Took a bit of planning, I imagine, which means a man with your skills will be in demand.'

'You've got no chance, Rocco. Get lost.'

'No? See, I'm just wondering how many of your previous employers are going to sleep easy at night once we set the whisper running that you've become very… chatty.'

'You won't do that – you can't!' Dinal replied.

'You think? You just tried to – what was it you said he wanted to do to me, Claude?'

'Roast you alive,' Claude replied.

'That's right, roast me alive – and get me written off as a drunk. The thing is,' Rocco continued, 'we'll also let it be known where you're being held. And I have to say, M. Dinal, the cells in Amiens are not what you'd call first class when it comes to security. Especially at night.' He got to his feet with some difficulty and dusted off his trousers. 'What do you reckon? Talk and we'll get you in a secure unit… or stay the big brave boy and face the consequences. It's up to you.'

He turned and began to walk away with help from Claude. He'd taken three paces before Dinal shouted.

'*Wait!*'

Chapter Forty

By the time the ambulance and police vehicle arrived, Dinal had folded like a wet copy of *Le Figaro*, taking Rocco another step nearer to completing the case. All he had to do now was keep the would-be killer safe until he got to court.

'Sounds like the cavalry,' said Claude, cocking his head towards the sound of sirens approaching along the road from Amiens. 'Whatever old Paulais said it must have lit a fire underneath them.'

The ambulance arrived first, pulling to a stop above them on the roadside and disgorging two medics who surveyed the scene in surprise. It was followed by three more vehicles and the slamming of doors and running feet.

Rocco and Claude looked up and saw Desmoulins and Rizzotti, then Captain Canet with two of his officers, followed by Commissaire Massin.

'Looks like a works outing,' Rocco murmured dryly.

Desmoulins slid to a stop beside him and surveyed the scene which now included the nicely burning Citroën. 'What the hell happened?'

'I got bumped off the road,' Rocco said. 'What are the others doing here?' He was worried that Massin might be carrying orders from the Ministry to curtail his investigation and, at this stage, particularly with what had just occurred, it was the last thing he needed.

'Sorry,' Desmoulins said softly, watching as Massin descended the bank in a controlled slide. 'He overheard the call when it came in and insisted on coming. I asked the doc to come in case he was needed.'

'Good call,' Claude muttered, nodding at Rocco. 'He's being all brave and manly but I reckon he needs checking over.'

Massin arrived, straightened his uniform, and stared in turn at Dinal, who'd gone very quiet, then Claude, then Rocco. 'I take it this man pushed you off the road, Lamotte shot him and you're otherwise fit for duty, Inspector. Correct?'

'In a nutshell,' Rocco agreed.

'Is that petrol I smell?' Massin leaned forward towards Rocco and sniffed. 'And... whisky?'

'The *voyou* on the ground was going to make it look like Rocco was pissed and had gone off the road and died in the wreck,' Claude said quickly. 'When he saw Rocco was still alive and kicking, he poured petrol into the car and was going to set it alight with Rocco inside. I know he was unarmed, but I had no choice.' He gestured with the shotgun.

Massin looked at him and nodded slowly. 'Yes, I thought so. Good work, Lamotte. Excellent. Pleased you didn't blow his head off, though.'

'Eh?' Claude looked puzzled by the compliment, then pleased. 'No problem. Sir.'

Massin watched as the medics dealt with Dinal and got him onto a stretcher. Captain Canet's two uniformed officers stood in close attendance with handcuffs ready. Canet turned and stared at Rocco and his car with a look of consternation.

'You get in the wars, don't you? I don't think you'll be driving that old bus again.'

'No,' Rocco agreed. 'I'll need to borrow one from the pool.'

'Help yourself. There's a spare unmarked with a radio. Get the keys from the duty desk.'

Massin butted in. 'Now that we've established you're alive and well, Inspector, do you have enough to close this case to everyone's satisfaction?'

'I have.'

'Good. Care to share it with us – in brief?'

Rocco made a rapid summary of his suspicions, the evidence he had so far, especially with Dinal's agreement to confirm Serban's involvement and of the major part played by *Maître* Vauquelin.

'In that case, you'd better let Rizzotti look you over then get on with bringing these people in as quickly as possible.' He paused. 'I trust whatever evidence you have will hold up?'

'It will. There might be some fallout going after Vauquelin and Serban. What about jurisdiction?'

'Your letter of authority from the Ministry will cover that. But if you let me know where you're going, I'll deal with the local stations.' He smiled thinly. 'Let me know just before you go in, to avoid any potential leaks. I'm sure *Contrôleur Général* Ceyton will add his weight to it if needed. He'll understand perfectly the need for the correct procedure to be followed, now we have adequate reasons to do so. Good luck.'

With that he turned and climbed the slope back to his car, leaving the others looking bemused.

'Did he just give you the go-ahead to break some heads?' said Claude.

'I think he did.' Rocco looked down as Rizzotti lifted his arms away from his side and began patting him down. 'What are you doing?'

'I'm seeing where you hurt most,' Rizzotti explained. 'You might have some bruised ribs. I take it you won't be coming into the office or going to anything like a hospital for a proper check-up anytime soon?'

'Absolutely, Doc. Can you make it quick, though? I've got work to do.'

'All in good time.' Rizzotti felt around his neck and shoulders, then checked his legs 'God, you stink, man. How the hell you got out of that thing in one piece is a miracle.' He gestured at the burning car, which was now sending a black plume of rubber-stoked smoke into the air.

'Are you done?'

Rizzotti smiled. 'All done. But I would advise bed rest for a few days. I know you won't take any notice but professional duty means I have to say it.'

Rocco turned to Desmoulins and Claude. 'Right. Time to finish this. I want you two to get to Ivry and locate Yuri Serban and his driver, Peretz. Serban first, though. Watch him and track him if he moves, but don't let him see you.'

'Got it,' said Desmoulins. 'Where will you be, in case we need to contact you?'

'I'll meet up with Caspar and we'll go and see Vauquelin.' He explained what Caspar had said: that Vauquelin was the one to go after. The lawyer was the weakest link because he had no loyalty to anyone other than himself and would be petrified at the idea of ending up in prison where revenge would be swift and painful. 'Once we get him secured and ready to talk, we can go after Serban. If we don't, he'll probably skip town and disappear.' He took a deep breath, relieved that there seemed to be nothing seriously wrong beyond bad bruising and a few cuts, and flexed his shoulders. 'First, though, I need a lift to the station.'

Chapter Forty-one

Laurent Vauquelin's office was located in a commercial building on the Avenue Victor Hugo in the 16th arrondissement, sharing space with other single-practice lawyers and accountants. When Rocco arrived, he saw Caspar waiting in a doorway just along from the entrance. On the way in he'd used the car radio to call Massin, who promised to have local officers on hand to make the arrests as soon as Rocco signalled. The same arrangement would be in place for Serban's location when confirmed.

'I wasn't expecting you to call again quite so soon,' said Caspar with a happy grin. 'But I'm glad you did. A lot of guys would like to change places with me for a chance to nail Vauquelin's ears to the wall.' He stopped, staring at Rocco's face, where the vivid bruising had been changing colour by the hour. 'Christ, what happened to you?'

'I got hit by a truck. It feels worse than it looks.' He related what he'd learned from Dinal and took the paper bearing his name and home address out of his pocket. 'Vauquelin's the linchpin in this whole business, so we need his testimony to knock Serban over. It was Serban's driver who delivered the letters and one of his thugs who tried to kill me.' He passed the paper to Caspar. 'Knowing we've got this should give Vauquelin a scare.'

Caspar read it and smiled. 'One look at your face will do that.'

Moments later a police van carrying three uniformed officers pulled up to the kerb just along the street, and the driver gave a signal that they were ready. It was time to go. Rocco and Caspar went to meet them, and they all walked into the building together, a show of force that he hoped would unsettle Vauquelin right from the start.

The lawyer was alone in his second-floor office. He looked up with a start as the five men walked in, pushing back the door with a bang. The office was expensively decorated and furnished, Rocco noted, the kind of décor that would reassure nervous clients that they were in the presence of an expert, capable of defending them to the ends of the earth as long as they could pay his fees. The outer room held a small settee and an empty secretary's desk bearing a large Adler typewriter. Rocco led the way straight through to the main office, lined with expensive-looking legal tomes and framed certificates.

'What's the meaning of this?' Vauquelin demanded, rising from his desk and reaching for his telephone. His eyes widened when he recognised Caspar. 'You!'

Rocco took the phone off him and dropped it on the floor. '*Maître* Vauquelin – or is it agent Vauquelin – I'm confused about what it is you do these days. We need to have a talk about your future. Please sit down.'

Vauquelin was staring at Rocco's face and clothing. He sank back into his chair. 'I don't know what you mean,' he protested angrily, but he'd gone very pale. 'Aren't you a little out of your jurisdiction?'

Rocco showed him the letter from the Interior Ministry. 'This gives me authority to investigate wherever I see fit the blackmail attempts on Secretary of State for Finance Jean-Pascal Bourdelet, assize judge Jules Petissier and former head of the *Sûreté Nationale*, Jean-Marie

Gambon. In case you haven't heard, all these men are now deceased, apparently because of letters received accusing them of having bought copies of paintings under questionable circumstances.'

'So what?' Vauquelin blustered. 'That has nothing to do with me! And what right has this man,' he pointed at Caspar, 'to come into my office. He's no longer a serving officer!'

'Maybe not,' Rocco agreed. 'But he's acting as my consultant, so is covered by this letter.' He sat down with a sigh. 'Do you really want to argue the toss? I've had a very rough day and I'm feeling irritable, especially after a man tried to kill me using information provided by you.'

'Rubbish!' The lawyer began to rise. 'I've no idea what you mean—'

'Sit down,' said Rocco, 'or I'll have you handcuffed to your chair.' He made a signal and one of the uniformed officers, a *brigadier*, stepped forward and produced a pair of cuffs. The smile on his face left nobody in any doubt that he would enjoy using them.

Once Vauquelin was seated again, Rocco leaned forward and picked up a fountain pen from his desk set. It was silver, heavy and beautifully embossed, a symbolic tool of this man's trade. He unscrewed the top and took the slip of paper from Dinal's wallet out of his pocket. Immediately beneath his own name and address he wrote a single word. Then he turned the note round so that the lawyer could see it.

'Nice colour ink you use,' he said. It was, as he'd suspected, a distinctive shade of violet.

Vauquelin looked down. He did a double take once he realised what Rocco had written. The single word was 'Serban'. The colour of the inks was identical.

'I don't understand. What game are you playing, Inspector?'

'Are you saying you don't know Yuri Serban?'

'Yes. I mean, no. He's a client. So?'

'Good. Glad we've cleared that up. You see, I know you passed this slip of paper to Yuri Serban, who in turn gave it to one of his men, a lowlife named Pierre-Yves Dinal, of Rue Riblette, here in the city. Dinal's orders, which he's prepared to swear came from Serban, were simple: to dispose of me in an arranged accident. As you can see, he failed. See the line of criminal connection I'm drawing here? You were seen in Serban's company very recently, as witnessed by former officer Casparon here, and now here we are with a note of my name and home address in your handwriting in the pocket of an assassin who's prepared to swear both it and the orders came from Yuri Serban. Pretty damning, I'd say.'

This time Vauquelin propelled himself to his feet without being stopped. 'I know nothing about any of that,' he protested, his face turning a vivid shade of red. 'This is outrageous!'

Rocco looked at the *brigadier*, who stepped forward and quickly cuffed one of Vauquelin's wrists to the arm of his chair, then stood over him until he subsided.

'That's for your own safety,' Rocco informed the lawyer. 'You look as if you're getting too excited. I'd hate you to injure yourself before being charged as an accessory to murder – along with the attempted blackmail of senior members of the establishment, resulting in their deaths.'

Vauquelin scowled. 'How could I – I don't even know them!'

Rocco took out three photos, one each showing Vauquelin in the company of Bourdelet, Petissier and Gambon.

'Seriously? You all look very comfortable to me.'

This time Vauquelin's mouth opened but nothing came out.

'Where did the paintings come from? You can tell me that, surely.'

'You know the answer to that already. I got them from Cezard.' His face was sullen and his tone churlish. 'He agreed to me selling them on his behalf. There's no law against it.'

'I'm not saying there is. But you knew these men well enough to know they'd be interested, didn't you?'

'They called themselves art lovers.' He shrugged, evidently feeling he was on safer ground. 'Not that Gambon would have known the first thing about art. All he wanted was a naked woman on his wall. Cezard needed a market for his work and I knew where to find it. They were show-offs to a man. They all knew what they were buying, so you can't twist that against me.'

'I'm not even trying. What about the fourth painting that Gambon sold to an American buyer?'

For once Vauquelin looked genuinely puzzled. 'I have no idea. I only sold him one, a nude.'

Rocco let it go. They didn't have any evidence, anyway. He decided on a change of tack. 'How long have you been representing Yuri Serban?'

The question caught the lawyer off guard. He looked apprehensive again at the mention of the gangster's name. 'I don't know... maybe five years.'

'Doing what?'

'Property transactions, mostly. He owns a number of small businesses.'

'Did you mention the paintings to him?'

'I might have, in passing. We talk about lots of things.'

'In passing.' Rocco let several seconds go by, studying the other man's face in the silence. 'Whose idea was it to send the letters?'

'What letters? I don't know anything about letters.'

'The ones you wrote using the typewriter on your secretary's desk.' He didn't wait for another denial. 'Did you know we can now identify individual machines by their key strokes and the pressure of the letters on the paper?'

'Nonsense. I'd have heard about that. You take me for a fool?'

'Anything but. If you doubt me, try calling the police labs at Rosny; they'll confirm it. We'll be taking the type-writer in for comparison today. I'll be happy to give you a receipt.'

Vauquelin said nothing for a moment, then sighed. 'What do you want, Rocco?'

Rocco felt a buzz of excitement go through him, and was pretty sure it was shared by the others in the room. They would have recognised the signs. Like hearing of a death in the family. Only instead of shock, grief and despair, criminals went through denial to outrage to justification and, finally, confession. He wasn't certain quite where Vauquelin was, but he was moving along the track.

'I want to save your life.'

'Huh?'

'Once Serban hears you've spoken out against him, he'll do anything he can to make sure your testimony never reaches court. But,' he held up a finger as Vauquelin went to protest, 'help us and we can make sure he doesn't get to you.' He waited another few seconds, then added, 'It's your choice: speak up now and get a lighter sentence away from Serban's thugs, or you can take your chances out on the street. You know what he's capable of.'

It was a bluff, but one he was fairly sure Vauquelin wasn't in a position to call. He must have witnessed Serban's real nature up close on more than one occasion, and would know he'd be immediately vulnerable so that Serban could protect his own back. Whether awaiting trial or in prison afterwards, there would be no protection from the Romanian's vengeful nature.

'I had no idea just how far he was prepared to go.' The admission came after a long silence. Vauquelin's voice was flat, unemotional. He was staring at the piece of paper on his desk.

'With what?'

'With everything… and you. All I proposed for him to do was to get the letters delivered and he'd take a cut of the returns. I mentioned it first in passing because I wasn't sure he'd go along with it. But he liked the scheme… perhaps a little too much, although I didn't see it at first. He wanted to accelerate it to more targets. I was only interested in three.'

'He used Georges Peretz to make the deliveries?'

'Yes.' Vauquelin looked surprised. 'How do you know about him?'

'He wasn't as invisible as he'd hoped. A yellow van trying to be a PTT vehicle only works if it's got the right letters on the doors.'

'I might have known. Serban's not one for fine detail.' He sounded bitter.

'So, the blackmail was your idea? Why? I thought these men were your friends.'

'So did I! They all treated me like dirt. I was useful when it came to protecting their interests, but once Petissier took against me after a couple of court cases he didn't like, and began spreading lies about me, they and a lot of others cut me off without a second thought.' He looked at Rocco as if seeking his understanding. 'Pretty soon I was no more than a pariah. Older clients dropped me, new ones were warned off and... and some invest-ments I'd made went sour because people I trusted pulled out.'

'You lost money?'

'Yes. A great deal.'

'What else about Serban's reaction?'

'When he learned that you were investigating the deaths and getting closer, he said I should manufacture some evidence to discredit you. I said I couldn't and he threatened to torch my office and home. The man's a maniac. He's become dangerously ambitious and wants to be the head of a criminal empire here in the city. I'd already decided to cease all dealings with him.' He shrugged. 'Too late, it seems. But I know everything about him.' He looked around at the men in the room. 'I can provide evidence of fraud, criminality and violence going back over at least four years. I kept notes of all our dealings.'

Rocco got to his feet. 'Well, I'm glad we cleared that up.' He turned to the *brigadier*. 'Your arrest, I think. Get him into protective custody and take a detailed statement. I'll send in a report to your office. Just make sure he doesn't fall down any stairs on the way out.'

The officer smiled and said, 'That's a promise, Inspector. We know what he's like.' He unlocked the handcuff, immediately placing it around Vauquelin's other wrist and nodding at his men to take the prisoner away.

'One down,' said Rocco to Caspar. 'One more to go.'

Chapter Forty-two

Yuri Serban evidently had an abundance of faith in his ability to stay out of trouble, in spite of what he'd sent his man Dinal to do. He was where Caspar had suggested Desmoulins and Claude might find him, holding court in the Bacau restaurant.

'Not very imaginative, is he?' commented Claude, from the passenger seat of Desmoulins' car. After checking his office and finding it empty, they had proceeded to the restaurant where an obvious bodyguard was standing outside, scanning the street.

'Like a lot of his kind, he thinks he's untouchable,' said Desmoulins, and grinned. 'I think he's in for a shock.' He opened the car door. 'Fancy a coffee while we check out the opposition?'

'If you're buying, I'm ready.'

'Good. What's your favourite film?'

'Eh?'

'Your favourite film. What is it?'

Claude thought about it. 'I suppose *Rififi* if I'm pushed. Why?'

'Mine, too. And the best scene?'

They walked along the street, discussing the film by director Jules Dassin and tossing scenes back and forth. They passed the bodyguard and turned into the restaurant, continuing the discussion while checking out the patrons and layout.

Yuri Serban was easily identifiable. Seated at the table described by Caspar, he was talking in low tones to two men. They were nodding without speaking. When they left, they were replaced by another man who had been waiting at the counter. This one handed over some sheets of paper for Serban to study before turning to leave.

'Yesterday's takings,' said Desmoulins softly. 'I bet the tax authorities would love to see those figures before they get doctored.'

They ordered coffee and counted three members of Serban's entourage seated around the room. With the bodyguard outside, that made four.

Serban himself seemed relaxed and oozed confidence, master of all he surveyed – at least in this small corner. He only had to raise his head and one of the waiters was by his side awaiting instructions. The remainder of the clientele seemed to be ordinary locals.

'I'll get Lucas on the radio,' said Desmoulins, finishing his coffee. 'Can you stay here and watch the room?'

'Love to,' said Claude, eyeing the pastry counter. 'I might have a piece of cake while I'm waiting, so don't rush.'

–

Forty minutes later Rocco and Caspar arrived, followed by a plain Renault van holding four uniformed officers and two detectives from the local precinct. Rocco used his radio to issue instructions, then sent Desmoulins back to the restaurant as back-up for Claude.

'So,' he summarised, 'Serban and three possibles, with the bodyguard outside.'

'That one's armed,' said Caspar. 'Left armpit, in a shoulder holster.'

'What about the staff?'

'They looked like ordinary restaurant workers to me.'

'Fine.' Rocco got through on his radio to the van and gave orders for the bodyguard to be taken first with the minimum of fuss. The moment the van pulled up and the uniforms took him, surrounding him before he could resist, Rocco led the way across the street and into the restaurant, the detectives spreading out around the room to cover any possible resistance.

It caught Serban and his men completely by surprise. The moment Rocco stepped inside, Claude and Desmoulins stood up and moved into positions where they could cover the three men suspected of being in Serban's employ. Accompanied by the two detectives from the local precinct, Rocco approached Serban's table where he was enjoying a pastry.

'Hello, Yuri.' Rocco slid into the seat on the other side of the table. 'Pierre-Yves Dinal sends his apologies. He hasn't got back to you on account of giving a long statement to the police about what you hired him to do. He's currently being treated for gunshot wounds and wishing he'd never met you.'

'What?' Serban looked annoyed. He glanced around at his three cronies in the room and saw the police officers standing over them, then looked back at Rocco. 'Who the hell are you?'

'My name's Rocco. Inspector Lucas Rocco. I'm here to detain you for ordering my murder, among other things. Oh, and before you protest your innocence and waste our time, we've also got your legal representative, Laurent Vauquelin, singing like a fat lady at the opera.'

'And Georges Peretz,' said Caspar. He was standing next to one of the three men, holding up a wallet with an identity card.

'Mr Peretz will confirm,' added Rocco, without taking his eyes off Serban, 'that he hired a yellow van from Gregnard Motors in Sarcelles on your instructions. But we can talk about that later. For now, you're under arrest, not least for ruining a perfectly good suit and coat.'

At that, Serban roared in fury and rose from his chair. He was immediately pounced on by the two local detectives, who cuffed him and led him away.

Rocco followed them outside and walked over to his car. He got on the radio to Massin and summarised what they had so far.

'Good work,' said Massin. 'I've spoken to Ceyton and the Ministry and they're waiting on your news.'

'They accepted it?'

'The Ministry? Yes, without question. I think they saw the wisdom in not getting in the way but letting it play out. There will be questions to answer, but only above a certain level.' He smiled thinly but with a hint of satisfaction. 'Ceyton is putting his weight behind us because he has no choice. This thing is going to be big and loud. What are you doing now?'

'I'll finish up here and be in tomorrow morning to make my report.'

'Well done. I'm sure you could do with a good night's sleep.'

–

Sleep. That would be a luxury, Rocco thought. And a chance not to think about what lay ahead. He was on his way back to Poissons, this time with Claude alongside him nursing a large serving of layered *lamaita* – lemon cake – from the Bacau. In between licking buttercream from his fingers, he was eyeing Rocco with concern.

'When are you going to make a decision, then?' he asked, flicking a layer of icing sugar off his chest.

'About what?' Rocco knew what Claude was asking but he was playing for time. It had been torturing him for days now, but the idea of even admitting that he'd been offered the new top job in Paris hadn't been made any easier by everything that had been going on with the Bourdelet case. And, apart from Mme Denis, the one person who deserved better was Claude.

'Leaving us.' Claude rubbed his fingers together.

'I'm sorry—' Rocco began, but he was interrupted by Claude placing a hand on his arm.

'Forget it. You've nothing to apologise for.' He patted the cloth of Lucas's coat. 'Sorry, it's only icing sugar – it'll brush off, although the smell of petrol won't. Like I said, no apologies. I know what the system's like: they expect decisions on demand but you can't talk about them until the paperwork's signed off in case they change their minds. Trouble is, everyone else knows, even though you think they don't. Have you told Mme Denis?'

'Not my final decision, no. But she knows about the job; she got it from a woman in the village with a nephew in Amiens.'

'That'll be Sylvia. Her nephew's a chatterbox like his aunt.' He glanced at Rocco. 'You really had the bit between your teeth back there, didn't you? Serban didn't have a cat's chance and he knew it.'

'Call it cause and effect. I don't like being driven off the road and having petrol and whisky poured all over me.'

'But it gave you a buzz, right?'

'Maybe. A bit.'

'When do you have to tell them?'

'Tomorrow. It was always going to be as soon as this case was done.'

'And now you've run out of time.'

'Yes.'

Chapter Forty-three

The office the following morning was abuzz with speculation and chatter. Rocco found himself walking into a crowd of well-wishers, all wanting to add their congratulations about surviving the murder attempt and bringing the case to a successful conclusion. Victories of such magnitude weren't as common as they would have liked, and, when one did happen along, it was enough to lift the spirits of everyone in the station.

He'd gone round to see Mme Denis as soon as he'd got home. She'd been pleased to see him and bustled around with a bottle of wine, asking for every detail of how he'd solved his latest case.

'Sylvia's nephew again?' he'd asked.

'Yes. She was bursting to tell me how you'd been chosen to arrest some big gangster in Paris, although when I pressed her for details she didn't know who or why.' She chuckled. 'So much for her inside information!'

Rocco smiled. He hadn't taken the problem of the leak any further, simply because the loose-lipped nephew hadn't released anything which could compromise the investigation. But that didn't mean he might not drop a word in his ear next time he saw him.

In the end, though, the talk had stalled and the atmosphere had become slightly awkward. Rocco finally told her of his decision.

Now he was on his way to convey that decision upstairs. He doubted there would be the tears he'd witnessed last night – at least, he hoped not. Emotion over a new job in the police, as in the military, was usually kept to a minimum. The stiff upper lip so beloved of the British was just as evident, he'd found, in the French officer corps.

He knocked on Massin's door and heard the call to enter. Inside he found Massin, Perronnet and Canet, uniformed and stiff, seated around a table. A spare chair was next to Canet, a little distant from the others. The embarrassment gap, he thought, in case things didn't go the right way.

Massin stood and held out his hand. 'Well done, Inspector. I've received congratulations all round, from the precincts involved where the arrests were made, and even the Ministry. A very satisfactory conclusion to a potentially sensitive case. I trust you're not hurting too much after your ordeal.'

It wasn't really a question, more an assumption for the sake of good order, but Rocco nodded and thanked him, shaking his hand, followed by the other two officers. The truth was he felt as if he'd been trampled by a buffalo, a night's restless sleep having awakened pains he hadn't known he had. But he wasn't about to let these men in on it.

'There's still a lot of paperwork to do,' said Perronnet briskly, displaying his love of detail. Then he smiled, too. 'But I'm sure we can all help with that.'

'Damn right,' murmured Captain Canet. 'This has been a shot in the arm to everyone. Pity about your car, though. Won't be the same not seeing that old *bagnole* around the place.'

At that the atmosphere in the room became sombre, and Canet blushed. 'Sorry, Lucas. I didn't mean—' He stopped and looked to Massin for help.

'Nicely put, Captain,' Massin said dryly. 'Subtle, even. I'm also sorry, Inspector, but I'm sure you know what else we have to discuss today.' He reached to one side and produced a neat batch of papers which Rocco recognised as transfer documents.

'I do.'

'I know it's not the best time for decisions of this magnitude, but the Ministry needs to know your decision. They have a great deal to do on this new initiative so I'm afraid we'll have to push you for your answer.' He nodded at the two other officers. 'Naturally they know all about the offer with BRI. They'll both be affected should you decide to move back to the city.'

Rocco nodded. 'I understand.'

Massin pulled a face and pointed to a vacant chair. 'Sit down, Rocco, for heaven's sake. You're not on parade and you look ready to drop.'

Rocco nodded and sat. 'Thank you, sir. That's why I'm here.'

'Good. I'm sure we'd all like to know what you've decided.'

'I know I would,' murmured Captain Canet. 'I've got money riding on it downstairs.' He grinned easily at Rocco and said, 'No pressure, of course.'

Rocco took a deep breath. Leaving here would be a wrench, he'd come to terms with that. Leaving Poissons-les-Marais, where he'd fitted in and made friends since arriving in the region just a year ago, especially with Mme Denis, his neighbour, would be far worse – and much harder than he'd ever imagined. On the other hand, going to the BRI in Paris was an opportunity too good to pass up. Jobs like that did not come along every day. If he didn't take it, somebody else would and, barring unfortunate accidents, that particular door would be closed, perhaps for good.

The silence in the office was palpable. He knew that all of them were thinking about the next step forward, and had probably already begun to make plans about potential replacements, shuffling pieces on a chessboard. It was the professional thing to do and, in their position, he'd have done the same.

He got to his feet, ignoring the pains in his back and legs. This couldn't be announced sitting down; it was too important. It wasn't his style.

'Since coming here to this rural backwater,' he said carefully, 'I've been blown up, shot at, nearly drowned, escaped being skewered in the neck by a madwoman, accused of taking bribes, held hostage on a sinking boat and now run off the road and almost burned to death. Most of it was stuff I never had to put up with in Paris. It's been stressful, dangerous and scary and, unlike when dealing with gangs, I've rarely known where the dangers were coming from.'

He paused to take a breath and Massin jumped in. 'I'm sorry, Rocco. I admit we've thrown a lot of unpleasant tasks your way and it can't have been easy. But that was why you were sent here. It's a pity if you see it as having been too much to deal with—'

'I don't.' Rocco felt the pressure of what he was about to say building in his head. 'It's not that. Sorry – I was trying to—' He stopped, lost for words. He felt a tightness in his chest but it was nothing to do with the battering he'd had.

'Is something wrong, Rocco?' A look of concern edged across Massin's face.

'Ha!' Canet's reaction was one of triumph. He pointed at Rocco and slapped his knee. 'I knew it! Told you!'

'Knew what? Told us what?' said Perronnet, looking at them all in turn. 'What are you saying, Rocco? And what is going on out there? Have they all gone mad?' He was looking towards the door, where the frosted glass panelling showed the shadows of several people gathered in the corridor outside, with Dr Rizzotti and Detective Desmoulins just discernible through the haze. 'Rocco?'

'I'm staying,' Rocco said firmly. If he'd had any doubts until now, the immediate sensation of relief swept them away instantly. 'I'm staying put.' Once said, it was done. No going back. He took another deep breath, noting the delighted grin on Canet's face and a rare play of amusement on Perronnet's as his words sank home.

Nodding to them all, he turned to walk out of the office.

'Where are you going?' asked Canet. 'This calls for a drink.'

'I need a long lie-down first,' Rocco replied, 'and I've got a Bastille Day celebration to prepare for. Also, the most miserable man in Poissons has promised to buy me a drink. It would be rude to refuse.'

Canet grinned. 'Damn right. You can't say no to that. Have fun.'

At a nod of assent from Massin, Rocco stepped out of the office and found a group of fellow officers gathered near the stairs, with Rizzotti and Desmoulins at the fore. They were grinning and waiting expectantly.

As he turned to close the door behind him, he saw Massin reach out for the transfer papers and, with what might have been a faint smile, push them off the edge of his desk into the waste basket.

Acknowledgements

To David Headley, for his continued support. To Rebecca Lloyd, for her usual perceptive and brilliant edit. To Jeff Spedding for his generous sharing of all things to do with the art world, and Sally Spedding, for her continued friendship and keen following of Lucas Rocco. And most of all, to Ann, without whose help getting up in the mornings wouldn't be so much fun.